Through

The

Gates

of

Hell

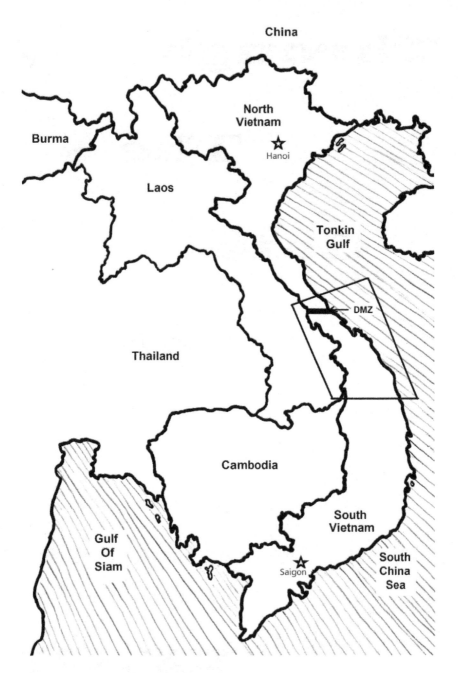

Southeast Asia; Area of Detail

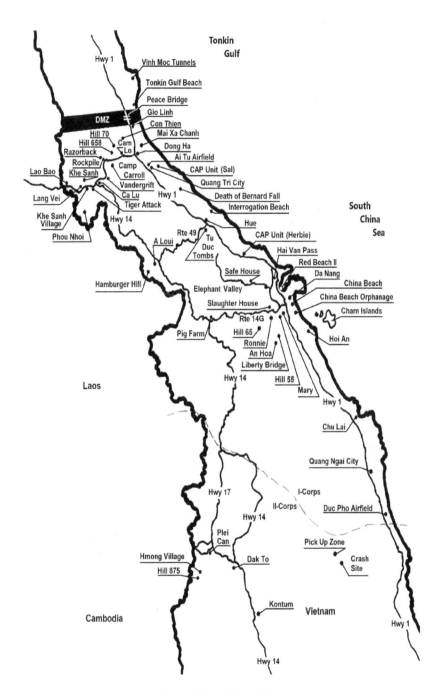

Area of Detail locations

By WILLIAM W. STILWAGEN

And No,
I Did Not See All The Red Flags

VIETNAM War SPEAK:

The Distinctive Language of the Vietnam Era

Through The Gates of Hell

Through The Gates of Hell

A novel by

William W. Stilwagen

Harbor Site Books

First Edition: 2023

Through The Gates of Hell

Cover design by: Jessica Tookey

ISBN: 978-1-7356763-3-3

Library of Congress Control Number: 2022923098

Harbor Site Books
Onancock, VA

Printed in the United States of America

This book is dedicated with respect and admiration to the men of:

Vietnam Battlefield Tours

. . . who work without pay in some of the most remote battlefield areas of Vietnam, Cambodia, and Laos.

They are motivated by a fierce sense of brotherhood with those who were willing to sacrifice their futures for a people threatened by communism and dictatorship.

Through their philanthropic work, they honor those brave Americans who served their country when most of their generation said, *No*.

~~~

Vietnam Battlefield Tours is a non-profit tour company devoted to leading Vietnam veterans, their family members, active-duty military, historians, and film crews to the jungles, mountains, and battlefields of Southeast Asia.

www.VietnamBattlefieldTours.org

Greater love hath no man than this, that he lay down his life for his friends.

~ John 15:13

CHAPTER ONE

As he dove at Steve, Rick Carrofermo felt an AK-47 round smash through his left side, ripping out an egg-shaped chunk of flesh from his back. The next enemy rounds zipped through empty air where Steve had just been walking. Both men hit the ground together. Steve was unscathed, but Rick was bleeding badly. The Corpsman crawled to them and packed Rick's wound with a battle dressing and then injected morphine. Meanwhile, Steve had already retrieved his M-16 rifle and was returning fire at the enemy, protecting the Corpsman and the Marine who had saved his life.

Although the Vietnam war had its share of epic battles, its warfare was essentially a series of quick, nasty unnamed firefights. At the beginning of the war the enemy, quickly realizing it was exceedingly difficult, and deadly, to try to overcome the ferocity and firepower of a Marine combat unit, had changed its tactics to hit-and-run. This battle was no different. Pretty much as soon as it started, the enemy had retreated down the steep hill and into the jungle, which seemed to devour them. This was the norm for Rick's unit, which had for the past two weeks been fighting daily firefights in the remote, rugged jungles of Vietnam at a nondescript area in a remote mountain battlefield called Phou Nhoi.

The Marine patrol then struggled toward a hastily-prepared LZ, a landing zone. A distraught Steve and three other Marines were carrying Rick, where he would be medevac'd by a UH-1E, a Huey helicopter.

Steve looked to the east, "Where the hell is the chopper?"

The radio operator replied, "Checking. It's four minutes out, Corporal."

1

Then Steve heard the familiar whoop-whoop-whoop of the rotor blades, but the helicopter was still unseen. It was flying low and fast, just above the treetops. At the last possible moment, the Huey rose out of the valley to the top of the mountain at Phou Nhoi. The helicopter came in hot, taking fire from enemy guns. Steve covered Rick with his body. As soon as the helicopter touched down, Rick who was barely conscious and feeling no pain due to the morphine, was loaded onto the deck of the loud, vibrating machine that would whisk him to safety.

Moving away from the LZ as the departing helicopter spit sand and debris in their faces at near gale force, the Marines moved on with their mission, to seek out and destroy the enemy. With Rick gone, Steve was now acting squad leader. Steve shouted to the remaining members of his squad, "OK, Marines, let's move out!"

This was more or less a daily scenario. The Marines would patrol in the hot, stinking, and inhospitable terrain waiting to be attacked so they could find and kill the enemy. It was far more agreeable to have a known target location where well-ingrained tactics could be put to effective use. But that was a rarity. Patrols had to be sent out every day, and ambushes and listening posts had to be set out every night. A patrol would likely locate an enemy unit by stumbling upon it, setting off a sudden and chaotic firefight.

Rick awoke aboard the Navy hospital ship USS Sanctuary, which was stationed offshore in the South China Sea. The Sanctuary and her sistership, Repose, would ply the oceanic waters near battle zones to be close to receive the wounded. The first words out of Rick's mouth were, "Is Picante OK?"

Rick was Steve Picante's squad leader, and Rick was utterly serious about looking after his men. Ever since Steve had been assigned to the squad, Rick had taken a special liking to him. After getting to know each other, he discovered that his grandparents and Steve's grandparents had lived near each other in the same *comparimenti,* county, deep in the mountains of southern Italy. Both Rick and Steve grew up as first-generation Italian-Americans. Each had found their parents' struggles coping with the *new world* to be hilarious. In Vietnam, Rick and Steve often shared hysterically funny stories their relatives had recounted in their Calabrian dialect mixed with broken English at various Sunday dinners. Each time told, the stories would become more elaborate and amusing. This intimate connection, coupled with the blood-bond that only warriors share, would make these two Marines friends for the rest of their lives.

After a few days, once Rick was stable, the doctors had him transferred to the 95th Evacuation Hospital at Tien Sha north of Da Nang to recuperate.

Because of the speed with which Rick was given first aid by the Corpsman and then quickly removed from the battlefield, his wounds, although painful, were not life-threatening. The bullet had entered just below a kidney and had passed through soft tissue without damaging any organs and without severing any arteries. He was lucky. Rick just racked it up to doing his job and thought nothing more about it. That was the kind of Marine Rick was, brave, caring, and unselfish.

After a month of recuperation, Rick was back with his squad. Steve was still acting squad leader when Rick returned and was glad to see that his friend, now his savior, was again in fighting shape. "Ah my liege, your faithful servant presents to you the mantle of command. However, we had a meeting, and we all want a raise. We await your wise counsel."

"You guys want my wise counsel, huh? Here it is, don't get shot." Everyone laughed, with handshakes and man-hugs all around.

3

Steve knew that Rick wanted no praise for his heroics. He had tried to thank Rick, but Rick stopped him by asking, "If the situation was reversed, would you have done the same for me?"

Steve replied, "Without hesitation."

"Well then, shut up."

But Steve would never forget the man to whom he owed his life.

CHAPTER TWO

Steve had loved Sharon more than he thought humanly possible. She had helped him through some tough times, suicidal times, when the war came crashing down on him in his nightmares. Sharon had stuck by him when lesser women would have cut and run. She had never felt sorry for him, and she seemed to somehow understand how horrible experiences could affect a sensitive soul like Steve's.

Yes, he was a Marine, tempered by harsh training, and unwavering in the psyche of a warrior, but the suffering of others deeply affected him. Most people held stereotypical views of Marines as bloodthirsty killers who folks would definitely want on their side in times of trouble but would otherwise go out of their way to avoid. With Marines, that was never their true persona. Marines typically fight for those who cannot fight for themselves. It is what drives Marines to be so selfless. Sacrifice of personal freedoms, and many times sacrifice of their own lives for others, defines the essence of Marines.

Sharon always felt safe with Steve, knowing that he would die protecting her and their children. After all, he had been twice wounded and nearly killed fighting for an oppressed people he did not even know.

The first time Steve was wounded, his unit was being inserted into an LZ on top of Hill 658, Dong Ke Soc Mountain, about six kilometers west of the Rockpile. There was a remote Marine OP, an observation post, on 658 that was engaged in a desperate fight with the NVA, the North Vietnamese Army, for control of the hill. The Marines had been fighting since the attack began at four in the morning and were close to being overrun. Steve's unit was pulling duty as a reaction force when they got the call to saddle up and report to the helicopter pad ASAP. Just as dawn broke three helicopters, loaded with Marines, including Steve, lifted off from the Quang Tri airbase. Steve was in 1st squad, 1st platoon, led by Rick Carrofermo. The squad was woefully undermanned. Usually, a Marine squad had 13 men, three fire teams of four men each plus the leader. Attrition and low replacement rates left most Marine squads with seven to ten men. His squad of ten men was in the first helicopter, sitting on the canvas benches that lined the sides of the bird. The second helicopter had the 2nd squad, plus the platoon lieutenant and a Navy Corpsman, a total of 11 men. The third helicopter had 3rd squad, which only had eight Marines.

Steve could see Cobra gunships firing their rockets and miniguns at the enemy hiding below the crest of the hill. Other NVA were atop the hill close to the perimeter wire and Marine bunkers. The Cobras dared not fire at them for fear of hitting the Marines. Those Marines were on their own, outnumbered, and fighting for their lives. The LZ was in the center of the outpost perimeter. On the fast approach, Steve's helicopter started taking hits. One of the enemy rounds punched through the door gunner's nearly worthless flak jacket and into the man's chest. One of the thin Kevlar panels did slow the bullet, but the gunner was badly hurt. He was thrown backward by the impact onto the laps of two Marines who lowered the gunner to the deck and immediately started first aid. Steve jumped up and manned the gunner's .50 caliber machinegun mounted on a pintle and started firing at the enemy, aiming just barely over the tops of the bunkers. From his side of the bird, he could see NVA scattering. He shot most of them as they fled toward the slopes.

The helicopter continued to take hits as it touched down. The ramp was already lowered, and the Marines were charging out. Steve was still providing covering fire and intended to be the last man off. As he turned to exit the bird, an RPG, a rocket-propelled grenade, blew a hole in the helicopter over the crew chief's head, tearing away part of the man's neck and putting a hole in Steve's left arm. The detonation was strong enough to slam Steve to the deck. The pilot engaged the rotors and the helicopter lifted, drifting sideways over the edge of the mountain. That was when the pilot took three rounds in the thigh. The co-pilot took over control of the bird and they rolled out to the southeast. Still taking fire, the helicopter struggled to climb and execute evasive maneuvers. Meanwhile, Steve had pulled himself up and re-loaded the machinegun with a fresh belt of ammo in case they went down in the hostile area. He scanned the terrain looking for movement and muzzle flash, ready for another fight despite his condition, but they were now clear of the mountain. They headed toward the airstrip at Dong Ha Combat Base, the closest base with an aid station.

The other two helicopters disgorged their Marines without incident and Steve's platoon had joined the fight on the ground. Steve was aghast. He yelled, "No!" He should be with his unit helping them to fight off the NVA. He thought of telling the pilot to turn around and take him back to the mountain. But then he looked around the helicopter, saw all the blood and the three wounded crewmen and he knew what he needed to do. He went from man to man stopping the worst of the bleeding. When he had done all he could he took stock of the situation. The pilot was sitting in a pool of his own blood. The crew chief was on the deck in the corner where he had dropped. Steve often recalled in later years, in vivid Technicolor, the blood and bits of flesh sliding down the bulkhead. Steve had a jagged piece of shrapnel protruding from his arm. He didn't dare try to remove it. It appeared that the shrapnel was plugging the hole it made and pulling the thing out would only cause him to hemorrhage. The wounded Marines, stoic as ever, laid on the deck, quietly suffering, staring at the overhead.

Both fuel tanks had been punctured and were trailing gas. There were bullet holes in the transmission cockpit, yoke assembly, and control closet. The co-pilot worked desperately to keep them airborne. The helicopter shuddered and was slow. Steve could feel it straining to stay aloft. By all intents, the bird should have crashed. Everyone prayed. Collectively, privately, they all talked to the helicopter as if it were a living thing, encouraging it, believing in it. Everything seemed to slow down, grow darker, quieter, as they concentrated all their mental energy into the bird.

And then finally, Dong Ha Combat Base came into view. They would make it. "That's a good bird," whispered Steve.

As they were about to set down at the base, the helicopter dropped like a rock from ten feet in the air and crashed. The leaking fuel tanks had run dry, and the turbines shut down without warning. But they were home. And they were all still alive.

A year after Steve returned from the war, he would receive a Silver Star medal for his actions that day and for saving the lives of the wounded Marine aircrewmen. He still bore the scar on his left arm as a permanent reminder of that fight. Steve was a humble man, and he felt a little embarrassed about receiving accolades. But his official citation told the story, so he could not hide the facts.

Steve spent four days at the military hospital in Quang Tri and was returned to his unit. The first thing he did was apologize for not getting off the helicopter with the rest of the guys. None of the Marines were upset with him. As a matter of fact, Steve had scared the NVA silly, and the platoon was able to dispatch the enemy without too much trouble.

The scar on Steve's forehead was another story. No one knew how that had occurred. When Steve was asked about it, he joked that he was sunning himself on China Beach and that Ho Chi Minh had thrown a spear at him. The scar remained a mystery to all who knew him. But it held a dark secret.

CHAPTER THREE

After Rick was sent home from the war, he had wanted to make the Marine Corps his career. But he soon found that a no-war garrison life with all its petty requirements was not for him.

In 1972, after finishing his four-year enlistment in the Marine Corps, Rick stumbled around in various jobs, never finding the societal usefulness for which he craved. He felt comfortable being armed, he was trained and experienced.

He decided the best way to be useful to his fellow man was to join the New York City Police Department. When he graduated the academy, he was assigned to the newly formed Tactical Patrol Force. The TPF was the forerunner to the Special Weapons and Tactics unit, SWAT. In the early days, the TPF responded to violence on the city streets with their own brand of violence. Rick's wife had grown more and more despondent because Rick would more likely than not, come home with blood on his uniform. Not his own blood, but that made no difference to his wife. She insisted that he put in for a transfer to a precinct. To keep the peace at home, he did so. But because of his background in the war and then the TPF, the NYPD assigned him to the 41st Precinct in the South Bronx. The precinct was also known as 'Fort Apache.' The 41st was the most violent in the whole of New York City. More blood compelled his wife to file for divorce.

Rick never married again. It was too painful, and too expensive. The judge had ordered him to pay his ex-wife nearly half his salary. Thankfully, they never had children. The outlays for child support would have been much higher. The payments would only stop when his ex-wife died or if she remarried. Thankfully, after three years, she married some Wall Street guy and the alimony ended.

As in all things he undertook, Rick immersed himself into the job. During his time on the NYPD, he had been shot at seven times, arrested 213 criminals, helped bust 17 drug dens, talked a guy out of jumping off a building, and delivered two babies. He held six commendations and two medals for valor. Although he had drawn his pistol on numerous occasions, he had only once fired his service weapon at another human being. The bullet had struck the fleeing armed felon in the buttocks, stopping his getaway. Rick never lived that one down. Half the police force thought he had shot the guy in the butt on purpose as some kind of joke, rather than making it a head shot. Truth was, it was just a bad shot and Rick was happy that he did not kill the man.

With his full 20-year police career behind him, Rick decided to retire. He then, like so many other NYPD cops, took a job in a private security firm. The job took him across the world, armed, essentially a bodyguard to powerful executives and celebrities. At first it was exciting. He traveled in private aircraft, ate the best foods, and was paid an enormous salary. But little by little, he began to get fed up with the elitist, self-important, wealthy snobs who looked right through him without so much as a thank you nod. He had liked working in the trenches. He missed the Marine Corps. He missed being a cop on the mean streets of New York. He missed what he called 'real people.'

After three years of being a bodyguard, pushing fans out of the way so celebrities could get to their limos, Rick had had enough. He had plenty of money in the bank and had a good pension from the NYPD. He declared his security days over. Rick now pondered what he should do for the rest of his life. He was only 45 years old. He realized his best job ever was being a Marine Corps squad leader. He didn't know what to do next.

He liked attending his Marine Corps unit reunions that met every two years. But he especially enjoyed his yearly reunions with Steve Picante, who he considered his best friend. He felt human with Steve, and he loved Steve's family. Those once-a-year weekends in Oceanside on New York's Long Island grounded Rick. It was the only time he felt truly relaxed and comfortable. Rick was a little jealous that Steve had mastered married life. But he was also so very happy for him. Steve was a fine man, a proven warrior, a great father, a dedicated public servant, and a loyal friend.

Rick often jibbed him, "So Steve, how come every time I lock someone up, you set them free?"

"The question, Rick, is how come every time I set someone free, you come along and lock them up again?"

"That's because you never rehabilitate them, and they go back to a life of crime."

"No, it's because you lock them up again before I can get them rehabilitated."

"Well, at least it gives us job security."

"Amen to that. But let's get serious for a moment."

"Go ahead, Steve."

"Why does your barber keep cutting out the middle? You look like a dang monk."

"I make him do it because my head is pretty. I want everyone to see. Women love it. They think it's sexy."

"Ha! Hey Sharon, do you think Rick's head is sexy?"

"Rick has a very nice head. So do you. Now you two stop your nonsense."

"See? I told you so. Women love it. So, Steve, why is your hair still blonde? To match your intellect? Or haven't you reached puberty yet?"

"My hair is blonde because I was meant to be a surfer. Not my fault I was born in New York. And not a streak of gray like someone I know."

12

"Hey, for your information, it's called salt and pepper. Makes me look distinguished."

"Distinguished? You look like you lost a fingerpaint fight."

These good-natured squabbles, with its multitude of variables, went on at every reunion. Folks listening in would just smile and slowly shake their heads.

CHAPTER FOUR

In 1995, when President Clinton gave Vietnam *Favored-Nation Status*, the doors opened to foreigners to visit the country. Rick jumped at the chance to go back to where the war had been. The tour company he signed on with was exploiting the explosion of tourism to Vietnam. But the company's tour for veterans was a logistical bust. They were woefully inexperienced with Vietnam. The various battle areas and unit locations were essentially a guess on their part and Rick had to correct their many blunders. After a few days, the ill-prepared tour leader acquiesced to Rick's knowledge, and Rick became the ex-post-facto tour director.

After returning home, Rick had outlined the many mistakes made by the company. Never one to complain about something without also suggesting solutions, Rick provided improvements that should be implemented to make the tours more meaningful to veterans and their family members.

Impressed with Rick's professionalism, the owner of the travel company asked Rick to come aboard and be a tour director for their military tours.

Rick took to his new job with gusto. He started leading tours the very next month taking a group of veterans back to the jungles, mountains, and battlefields of Vietnam.

As the company grew, Rick helped develop veteran tours to Korea, as well as to Saipan, Tinian, Iwo Jima, Guam, Peleliu, and other Pacific battlefields. He loved this job, ever the squad leader, and he could clearly see good results. Coming full circle in one's life made positive changes for these former warriors. On tour, they were finally able to free themselves of the self-imposed emotional loads they had carried wherever they went. This was not just the case for Vietnam veterans, but also for veterans of WWII and Korea. Rick saw no difference in the personal burdens and the survivor guilt that most veterans from all wars shared. He was effectively helping them heal. Rick was once again, looking after the troops.

But within a few years, he became disillusioned with the "bottom line" attitude of the tour company owner for which he worked. He was tired of seeing how the owner had slowly diminished the tours to increase profits and to line his own pockets with money from veterans. After making one too many protests to the boss, he was told, "Rick, you've grown away from us. We won't be needing your services anymore."

Rick was crushed. But it turned into a Godsend. The boss's biggest mistake was firing a Marine. Rick went on the counterattack and founded his own company, a non-profit tour company, which would specialize in Vietnam only. He enlisted the aid of a few like-minded veterans in the same capacity, and they vowed to never take salaries when helping their brother warriors. They would pour all profits back into the tours to make them even more rewarding than ever. It would be veterans helping veterans, and veterans helping the families of veterans. Within two years, his non-profit had pulled 90% of the Vietnam business away from his former boss. As the saying goes about Marines, *No better friend, no worse enemy.*

CHAPTER FIVE

For years, Rick had tried to get Steve to come back to Vietnam on a tour. At first, Steve got angry with the idea, never wanting to go back to that dreadful place. But over the yearly reunions with Rick, hearing the inspiring stories, Steve started to give it some serious thought. His kids were grown and out of college, they had married and had families and careers of their own. He had lots more free time, as well as disposable income to spend on Sharon and himself. He started thinking that maybe he should go back, just not right away. Maybe after he retired.

Steve was determined to be the oldest probation officer ever to work in Nassau County. His goal was to be 75 years old when he gave up his career and before he took his first pension check. The best part was that he had accrued almost 40-weeks of paid vacation time and he could take extended holidays away from work. It was either that or lose the benefit.

Steve and Sharon were now empty-nesting. Their son was an amazing biology teacher who taught hormone-crazed, eighth graders, and somehow got them to learn. Their daughter was an athletic trainer, who saved life and limb on high school ballfields. Steve and Sharon had raised their children well, but that part of their life was over.

Even though they were older now, Steve and Sharon never stopped acting like they did when they were first dating. They were always holding hands and acting silly. Whenever one would leave for work or to go shopping or wherever, Steve would always say, "Steve loves Sharon."

Sharon would always respond, "Sharon loves Steve."

Their goodbyes usually solicited a finger down the throat and a fake gag by their children. Secretly, though, their kids loved that their parents loved each other and that they were not afraid to show it so openly.

Sharon wanted to travel the country and to camp in all the national parks. Steve had steadfastly refused to go camping. He had all the camping he needed in his lifetime while serving in Vietnam, and he swore that he would never again sleep on the ground. Throughout their marriage they always found the middle ground instead of argued. Each knew that the other's opposing point of view held some merit, and they respected each other's opinions. Understanding and kindness was the foundation of their relationship. That, and love. They were truly friends and they admired each other.

So, they compromised. He and Sharon had traveled the U.S. for 24-weeks in a motorhome. They had a ball reconnecting emotionally and physically and falling in love all over again. They wandered around the country without a care in the world, like a couple of college kids on perpetual Spring Break. And they "camped" in their motorhome and visited the national parks.

Steve's goal to stop working at age 75 would be one ambition he would not achieve. Sharon got sick. She was diagnosed with pancreatic cancer. Steve immediately retired from the probation department at age 71, so that he could look after his wife in their marital home in Oceanside, NY.

He didn't regret retiring before his self-imposed goal was reached. Besides, it always made him depressed that his success files were woefully thinner than his failure files. It was the nature of the job. He was no bleeding-heart, and he had no reluctance in sending liars and manipulators and parole violators back to jail. He had done so many times. But having turned around the lives of folks on destructive paths was always a reason to rejoice.

However, his wife was way more important than any job. The job didn't make him the man he was. Sharon had made him the man he was. He owed her everything.

Slowly, over the next couple of years, all Steve could do was lovingly care for her, and helplessly watch as her health slowly faded away.

Lying on her deathbed, Sharon was surrounded by family who tearfully bid her goodbye. The last thing Sharon said to him was, "Sharon loves Steve."

He whispered back, "Steve loves Sharon."

On that cold, rainy evening in December, she stepped away from the body that had ceased to serve her and started on her next journey. What those present could not see, however, was Sharon's mother and father who had come to lead the way.

CHAPTER SIX

Now Steve was alone. He took the next few months to grieve, to be angry. He felt an emptiness like he had never felt in his life. There was no one to care for, no one to nurture, no job to go to. No real reason to do much of anything. He finally accepted that maybe he was probably next to die. He determined that this is how life goes. In the beginning, he felt purpose, responsibility, busyness. Something always needed his attention. Then suddenly, he realized that he was indeed 73 years old, and all that activity had come to an abrupt stop. Also suddenly, he had all the time in the world to think, to reflect.

Steve began to survey his life in chronological order. He thought back to when he was a little kid, about the comfort of his mother's loving arms. He thought about his first real girlfriend. He still could feel that abject heartache when she told him she wanted to date somebody else. He supposed everyone remembers, intensely, their first broken heart, probably because they were feeling that pain for the very first time. Other heartbreaks would come, but each time they were less severe than his first. He laughed at that. *Funny how one's experiences can follow you forever.* He thought of his high school days and playing sports and of pompous teachers and of summer vacations. It all made him smile.

Then he thought of the next era of his life when he had joined the military. Instantly his mood turned grim. He became angry. Alone on his living room couch, in the dark empty house, he contemplated his anger for several hours. He slowly came to understand that his pre-war life and his post-war life were filled with fond and happy memories. But that middle part could make him want to take his own life, make him want to strike out, and make him want to crawl into a hole and disappear. He wondered why he felt that way. He had survived the war, but it kept interfering with everything good; it intruded on happy times; it made him feel guilty for having survived when better men than him did not. And it had kept him awake when he was supposed to be sleeping.

He decided to do something new to confront this dismal side of his life. He had, years ago, been through private counselling at outreach clinics, had been in group sessions with other veterans, and had taken the medications. Nothing had helped much.

Steve wanted to start again. He wanted a do-over, to get back to the beginning of this inner turmoil, to understand why the war had such a hold on him. He wanted to do something to bring him back to the beginning of that life-altering experience. The war part of his life was unfinished, and he knew he would never find inner peace until he faced it.

He made the difficult decision to return to the place of his worst nightmares.

CHAPTER SEVEN

It was winter in New York City just after the New Year's celebrations. Rick had just returned home from presenting his seminar entitled, *Traveling In The Company Of Heroes* to the students in the doctoral psychology program at City College in Manhattan. He had developed the seminar to share the healing experiences of traumatized war veterans returning to their battlefields many decades removed. The professors invited him every semester. The emotionally-intense lecture was always well-received by the students.

The phone rang and Rick checked the caller ID. He saw it was his old war buddy Steve. "To what do I owe this most welcomed call, my friend?"

"Rick, I'm coming into the city to see you. I need to talk."

"Everything OK? Are you alright?"

"I'm good. How's tomorrow sound? Lunch time?"

"I'll be here."

Steve showed up at Rick's apartment in the Bay Ridge section of Brooklyn at 11:30 in the morning. As soon as Rick opened the door, Steve said, "Rick, sign me up. I need you to get me back to Phou Nhoi where that two-week campaign took place and where we lost so many guys. I need to stand on the ground where you saved my life. I want to have a memorial service, too. For the guys we lost. Remember that time we went to Washington, DC, to The Wall to see our friends? Their names were there, but they were not. Sure, their bodies came home, but their spirits are still alive. They are still in Vietnam, Rick. Still over there. I feel it, I know it!"

Rick was well aware of the spirits. He had felt them many times on the 68 tours he had already led back to the war zone as a bush guide.

"Steve, calm down. Let's take this slow. Have a seat. You want a beer? Hot coffee? A valium?"

"Yeah, right. I'll take a coffee."

Rick returned from the kitchen with two cups of steaming java made from beans grown on the coffee plantation at Khe Sanh, a repurposing and better use for the old combat base. "What made you change your mind, Marine?"

"OK, listen. I hate Vietnam. Wait, let me rephrase that. I hate the war, not the country, not the people. I don't even hate the enemy anymore. But the war's been with me every damn day. Just thinking about it puts me in a bad mood. But I've been trying to figure it all out. I guess since Sharon passed, I've had all this time on my hands.

"You know, when we were in the fight, we couldn't hold our brothers in our arms while they died. That crap is just in the movies. We had to be aggressive, keep moving forward. For the most part, we only heard the helicopters behind us taking our friends away. We never got a chance to say goodbye. We never got a chance to grieve. There was too much to do. Then there were more casualties. And then more casualties. I'm ashamed I don't remember them all. And then a year had gone by, and we were sent home, one at a time. I don't know about you, but I never got a debriefing, no chance to decompress. Here's your papers, goodbye. I went from being a Marine with a rifle to being a probation officer with a pencil. I left the war, but the war never left me."

Steve took a breath, then a sip of coffee, and continued, "I want to, no, I need to go back to Phou Nhoi. Of all the combat we were in on the DMZ, those two weeks were the worst of it. So many guys were killed there, on both sides. You saved my life there. I got my second wound there. I almost did something . . .

no, never mind that. I want to say a prayer there. Something. Just sign me up."

"It's about time you came to your senses, Steve. Come with me into the office."

Rick had lived in the Brooklyn two-bedroom apartment since he was married. When he separated from his wife, she went off to her mother's house and then later hooked up with that Wall Street guy. Rick saw no reason to move from the rent-controlled apartment on Owl's Head Court. He had converted one of the bedrooms into his office, and from it he operated the tour company. Rick pulled out a couple of old combat maps and spread them out on his desk. Steve's eyes immediately went to Phou Nhoi. He hadn't seen a combat map in 50 years, but the rivers, the contour lines, the roads, and the names were as familiar as if he had seen it an hour ago.

The first tour of the year would be the Northern I-Corps tour in March. However, Rick erred on the side of caution because they might hit the end of the monsoon season. "Instead of the March tour, I think we should go to Phou Nhoi on the April tour. I've been in the western regions before in March and the weather can be iffy. Plus, if it's wet, we'll have to contend with mud, leeches, and poor visibility. We may have a bad go of it."

"Acknowledged, Rick. I can wait another month. The battle was in April anyway. It may not mean much, but I'd like to be there on the anniversary."

"It does matter. We'll plan it for April. Take a look at ingress routes on the map. Where do you suggest for a launch point?" Rick could have easily determined the best way to hike into Phou Nhoi, but he knew that his friend needed to be a part of the planning. Besides, Steve may just surprise him with a better way.

On the large, white, wall-mounted grease board, Rick went over the day-to-day itinerary and explained where and why the other guys needed to get to their special sites. Each day had a dedicated square and he explained, much like a storyboard outline in a TV writer's room, how long it would take to reach each place and do each thing. It included both driving and hiking times, considering the specific terrain challenges and each person's abilities or limitations, as well as naming each location to be visited on each day. Steve was amazed at the attention to detail that Rick put into each person's needs. Rick always went a step further. When the registrations came in, he would research each veteran's unit and study what they had done during the war. That way, he would have a closer connection to every person on the tour and could talk to them with some knowledge of what their unit had experienced. Of course, while on tour, Rick would never try to tell another man's story. He made sure each individual would receive the opportunity to tell their own story personally. It was very healing to do so.

"You're pretty anal about all this, aren't you Rick."

"You bet your ass I'm anal. Get it?"

"Very funny. Har-dee-har-har."

"Keep it up and I'll have you bunking with a toothless, 90-year-old mama-san covered all over with boils and pox."

"You always did know my type."

"Wise ass."

Built into every tour, there were always two days that could be modified to meet the special requests of those going on the tour. Early on, the directors agreed that anyone coming on tour would be able to get to the place most needed by them. They would have their 'boilerplate' tours, but then modify each to make them more rewarding for the veterans. It made the tours more interesting for the guides, too, rather than conducting the same tour time after time, which would tend to prevent the guides from getting burned out.

"OK, this trek to Phou Nhoi will not be easy. Marching in will take about three and a half hours. We should spend at least two hours on the hill. The whole deal should be about ten hours. That means we should be at the Route 9 launch point by six in the morning. Back to the launch point by four in the afternoon."

Steve did some quick calculating in his head, "So we march for three and a half hours to get to the top of the hill, spend two hours on the hill, and then march three and a half hours back. That's nine hours."

"We need to take into account the ages of the group, Steverino. Us old farts are going to be exhausted on the way back. Even though most of it will be downhill, we'll be hurting. We'll need an extra hour to get out."

For the rest of the afternoon, Rick and Steve worked through the logistics. They would dedicate an entire day to the battle of Phou Nhoi. It would be an arduous trek. This area was notorious for its jungle and its rugged and varied terrain. It was also notorious for the misery and grief it inflicts upon those who dare venture into the area. Before this trip was over, Phou Nhoi would live up to its reputation.

Rick made the arrangements. He officially modified the April tour to include the excursion to the Phou Nhoi battle area and locked it into the itinerary.

Steve sat back, happy with the plan and relieved that he had finally made the decision to go. "I'll have that beer now."

CHAPTER EIGHT

Three months later, Rick and Steve boarded a plane at John F. Kennedy International Airport. "Here we go, brother. The beginning of an adventure."

Steve nodded his head but said nothing.

They flew non-stop to LAX, Los Angeles International Airport. That night, they met the 11 other tour participants in the Airport Sheraton Four Points Hotel. After dinner, the group gathered in a small conference room in the hotel where Rick handed out detailed tour books, souvenir hats, and other goodies to the folks with whom they would spend the next 15 days. He answered a few of their questions and explained how the next day, and their flights, would play out. He suggested they all get a good night's sleep. Tomorrow would be the start of a momentous trip for everyone.

The next day after lunch and a late checkout for all, they hopped on the hotel shuttle bus and made their way back to LAX. In the spacious international terminal lounge, the group got to know one other. Two of the veterans had brought their wives, and one had brought his now-adult daughter. Two veterans and the brother of a Marine KIA had come alone. There were also two war widows who met for the first time. They became fast friends, with much sad commonality to share. One of the veterans asked, "Hey Rick, any last-minute advice?"

"Of course. Keep your heads down, and don't volunteer for anything."

Two veterans simultaneously blurted out, "That's what they told us last time." Everyone laughed.

All had come from different areas of the U.S. Seven of them were Vietnam veterans, most of whom were from different units at different times in I-Corps. None of that mattered as they

26

were all intimately connected, having had similar experiences of combat, or having shared their veteran's lives since the war.

Rick had to smile. He had seen the same sense of shared familiarity dozens of times. Each had studied Rick's website itineraries and had signed up for the tour that most interested them. They arrived as strangers, but there was an instant connection between them. It was the warrior bond. Rick sensed that this was going to be another great tour and extremely fulfilling to them all. But he would soon find out how wrong he could be.

They boarded their Boeing 777 for the 15-hour nonstop flight to Taipei. Rick had always pondered how such a large aircraft could stay aloft for so long without refueling. He suspected the tanks were nearly empty upon arrival because they never circled before landing. They always went straight in.

CHAPTER NINE

Their 16-hour flight, although long, was uneventful and they landed in Taipei International Airport at six in the morning. The group had a three-hour layover and would change to a smaller plane for the short flight into Vietnam. Rick used this time to provide a detailed briefing of what to expect once they landed in Da Nang, Vietnam.

Many in the group had arrived in Da Nang over 50 years ago as young, raw, gung-ho soldiers and Marines, and they were starting to get a little anxious. Rick understood this emotion, and over the years he had developed a briefing, part funny and part serious, to ally their fears and to help prevent any cultural faux pas. The lecture was fondly referred to as the Big Speech.

With all feeling a little better after the briefing, Rick cut the group loose to roam the airport, to grab a cup of coffee, or to just sit and chat prior to setting off on the last leg of their journey into the Southeast Asia war zone.

Boarding was announced and the group lined up to enter the British Airbus 321 that would take them directly to Da Nang. Rick joked, "Last chance to back out."

The old veterans chuckled nervously.

When everyone was seated, the cabin door was closed, and the plane was pushed away from the gate. Steve was thinking about a similar scenario pulling away from the gate on Okinawa over a half century before. Sometime during that flight, he was walking in the aisle to stretch his legs. He remembered looking at the faces of his fellow Marines as they flew southwest past Taiwan and across the Philippine and South China Seas. He knew it would be a one-way trip for some of them and he wondered how many of those young Americans would be returning home sightless, or limbless, or burned, or paralyzed, or mentally scarred, or in body bags. Later, he stared at his own reflection in the airplane's lavatory mirror, wondering the same thing about himself.

"Snap out of it, fool." He came out of his reverie when Rick nudged him to take the meal tray from the pretty Taiwanese flight attendant.

After the meal, everyone settled in for the balance of the flight. Most sat quietly, lost in memories. There was no bravado, no cockiness. There was also no turning back.

Next stop, Vietnam.

CHAPTER TEN

Hearts skipped a beat when the pilot announced, "We'll be landing in Da Nang in 15 minutes. Please make sure your seatbelts are fastened and refrain from using the restrooms for the remainder of the flight."

As the airplane neared the airstrip, Steve was amazed at how the town had grown. From his window seat, he could see that Da Nang was now a metropolis with skyscrapers, huge suspension bridges, and brand-name hotel resorts along what he remembered as China Beach. The guy sitting in front of Steve and Rick mentioned to the veteran sitting next to him, "Now that's a target-rich environment." Both men nodded at each other and laughed apprehensively.

With a screech of tires, the plane touched down on Da Nang Airfield. Steve said, quoting Yogi Berra of the New York Yankees, "It's déjà vu all over again."

Rick nodded, "Every time, my brother, every time. Welcome to the war zone."

The veterans were surprised to see that the old reinforced, covered revetments and some of the old hangers were still in use. Only now, they housed MIG fighters. Most of the jets seemed to be wasting away from non-use. Steve caught sight of a few Soviet Mi-8 and Mi-17 helicopters that were in an equal state of disrepair.

"Hey Rick. What's with the commie MIG's and Soviet helicopters? They look like so much garbage."

"They are. There's no money for parts and even less for fuel. So, they just sit there. The Soviets charge them for everything now. During the war, they were free. Plus, there are only a few skilled aircraft mechanics to maintain them. They keep just a handful of military aircraft flyable. Here, Hanoi, Cam

Ranh Bay, and Saigon. For them it's a national embarrassment. It's OK with me, though."

"Me, too, kemo sabe."

"Ya know, Steve, you're becoming a real wise ass in your old age."

"I try my best."

CHAPTER ELEVEN

Passing through immigration and customs went uneventfully, but the AK-47's and the puke-green uniforms of the Vietnamese security guards made the old veterans feel a little uneasy. Walking out of the crowded terminal, the veterans were welcomed by Rick's Vietnamese English-speaking counterpart, Tuan, who would act as translator throughout their tour. Tuan was a slightly-built and middle-aged man, full of fun, a big smile, and a font of information. He seemed to truly like Americans and he even used American slang words and phrases.

Outside, the group was greeted with pastel blue skies and warm, pleasant air. Feeling a bit more at ease, the tour group boarded their waiting motorcoach and exited the airport into the city of Da Nang. The old veterans saw that their wartime recollections of bicycles and hand-pulled carts had been replaced by a massive swarm of motorbikes, cars, and trucks. There seemed to be no order to the traffic; it swirled chaotically. The lines on the roads served only as suggestions. Trucks, and some cars, actually stopped at traffic lights, but most of the motorbikes ignored the signals and moved about feverishly.

Soon the bus was past the inner city and heading south on Highway One, the main coastal thoroughfare that ran the length of the country and which was the main military highway during the conflict. At some point during the war, all Marines were on that road and individual recollections came rushing back to the old warriors. Rick, ever the dutiful tour guide, was on the microphone pointing out various landmarks and describing the many long-ago military installations that had been located along the highway.

As they approached Hoi An, Rick explained, "Hoi An Town, a well-preserved ancient trading port, was a UNESCO World

Heritage Site. Its temples and architecture showed the diverse cultural influences of its time, and its lovely and ancient Japanese covered bridge is unique to this town. Luckily for Hoi An, its importance waned long before the American War, and it was left essentially isolated and relatively untouched. The settlement was formerly known as Faifo, where Dutch, Portuguese, Chinese, and Japanese traders once walked. The town ceased to be an important trade harbor when its inlet shoaled in the late 18th Century, and the port had been moved north to Da Nang.

"Since then, Hoi An had become an inviting and happy tourist town. There were literally hundreds of amazing little shops on its winding, narrow streets. The stores and restaurants stay open late into the evening. Each night near our hotel there is a street festival on roads blocked off to traffic."

An hour after leaving the airport, they pulled up in front of their Hoi An hotel and checked in.

The town reminded the guys of Mardi Gras in New Orleans, only better. After dinner, Rick cut everyone loose on the town. The veterans were loving it.

CHAPTER TWELVE

Early the next morning, the group traveled west to An Hoa Combat Base. Bases were usually named for nearby villages, hills, or obvious formations, and sometimes for heroes. For example: Khe Sanh Combat Base is so named because it is near the village of Khe Sanh; Con Thien Combat Base was named for Nui Con Thien, the Hill of Angels; and Marble Mountain Air Facility, of course, was named for the nearby Marble Mountains. Rick thought with amusement about how some mucky-muck, who must have been unfamiliar with the Vietnamese language, gave An Hoa Combat Base its name. An Hoa means Flower Village. *Flower Village Combat Base* does not exactly strike fear into the hearts of the enemy.

After visiting the base and its airstrip, the group crossed north over the Song Thu Bon, the River Thu Bon, on the new concrete and steel Liberty Bridge. The Liberty Bridge remembered by the veterans had been made mostly of wood and had been built several times and destroyed several times. Once by the Viet Cong, once by massive flooding during one of the yearly monsoon seasons, and once by accident when the freshly creosote-soaked pilings and roadway caught fire.

They then turned west on Route 4, better known as Thunder Road, to a mountain named Hill 65. After climbing the hill, they went down to the rice paddy area between the hill and Charlie Ridge, a massive east-west mountain range just to the north. They walked along the dikes to a stand of trees. One of the veterans, John, explained to the group what had happened there more than a half-century earlier, "I led 23 Marines to a night ambush site just northeast of the hill. We were lying hidden right here along this hillock of trees in this rice paddy. We waited silently in a night eerily illuminated by the moon and stars.

34

"The ambush team had not been set in long before a company of the North Vietnamese Army, the NVA, began passing close by along a dike. My commanding officer on the hill told us to wait and to hold our fire and to report on how many NVA were passing. After another 30 enemy soldiers had walked by, I radioed in the report and told the CO many more were still coming. Certain that we would be compromised at some point, the order was passed for all to open fire when I started shooting. This would be coordinated with heavy support fire from the hill to either side of our ambush team.

"The CO told me to open fire. I unleashed a full magazine of M-16 rounds into the NVA, and every Marine on the paddy hillock immediately joined in the carnage. Support fires in the form of mortars, heavy machineguns, and a 106mm-recoilless rifle opened up from the hill. Pre-registered artillery rounds from An Hoa and Hill 55 impacted in an arc around the NVA, preventing their escape. The artillery batteries began walking rounds closer and closer creating a shrapnel hell for the enemy.

"The battle didn't last more than 20 minutes but firing and killing continued sporadically throughout the night as the NVA tried repeatedly to retrieve the bodies of their comrades.

"As the sun rose early the next morning, we left our fighting holes and swept the area. We collected 68 dead NVA and counted numerous blood trails and body parts. No Marines had been lost."

While joy was expressed among the men at this positive outcome, it had deeply affected John. The abject slaughter he had unleashed on fellow human beings had begun to take its toll on him. Intellectually, he understood that these dead enemy soldiers would have gladly killed his Marines. But this fact gave John little solace. Shortly after he had returned home from the war, he began having nightmares, reliving the slaughter every night for the past 52 years. But here he was, 72-years old, facing his demons head on.

Since John had the chance to tell his story on the very ground where so many people died, an odd thing occurred. The nightmares stopped. That night, John slept straight through to the morning. He has had no bad dreams since. The place in Vietnam that had injured his mind had now healed his mind. The man and the place agreed, 52 years were enough. Now both were at peace.

As John and the group turned to head back to the bus, what could not be seen was the spirits of the dead getting up and walking off, never to return.

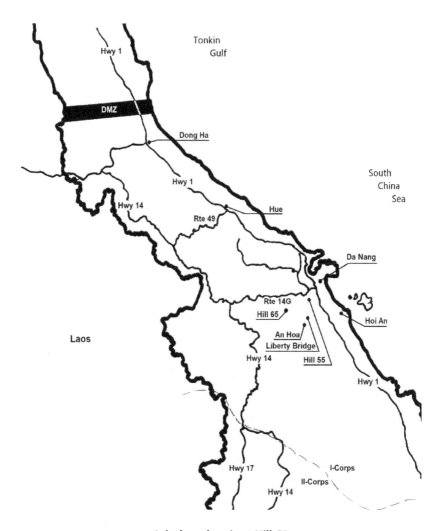

John's catharsis at Hill 65

CHAPTER THIRTEEN

After John's catharsis at the rice paddy near Hill 65, the group drove east on Thunder Road to the next important site on the day's agenda. Ronnie, who as a young Marine in 1966, served as a radio operator with an FO, a Forward Observer. From their lair, the two-man team watched a Marine patrol walk in the distance. They then saw an unarmed Vietnamese woman stealthily trailing the patrol. She may have been just a civilian, but it appeared to the FO that she was gathering intelligence about the patrol. The FO made the decision.

He told Ronnie, "Shoot her."

Ronnie raised his rifle, sighted her in, and slowly squeezed the trigger. The well-placed 7.62mm full-metal jacketed bullet from his M-14 entered her left chest and exited her back in a burst of fine red blood. She dropped to the ground, dead before the sound of the gunshot had reached her.

And for every day since then, Ronnie carried a burden of guilt not knowing whether she was an innocent civilian or an enemy combatant. It had aged him. He had struggled with depression and had refused to speak with his family about any aspect of the war. He would not even say anything war-related to his daughter who had accompanied him on the tour.

Arriving near the location of the killing, the group stayed on the bus while Rick and Tuan went into the nearby village. After interviewing several unconnected sources, they all corroborated the fact that in 1965, all local people were resettled in Da Nang and that anyone who had stayed was a Viet Cong, a Vietnamese Communist. Not only that, but the woman that Ronnie had killed was the first Viet Cong woman to die from that village, and she had been memorialized in a small, one-room museum there. Rick and Tuan re-boarded the tour bus and related the new information. The group cheered. Ronnie began to cry.

They all got off the bus and went to the little museum. It was closed, but the neighbor called someone to open it for the group. About five minutes later, a young woman arrived and unlocked the door. She was the granddaughter of the dead woman. This was an extremely emotional moment for both Ronnie and the granddaughter.

She understood the reason for her grandmother's death and Ronnie was finally able to unload all the emotional baggage he had carried for so many years. By the end of the tour, Ronnie looked ten years younger. He stepped livelier and never stopped talking about his experiences in the war. His daughter was amazed and mentioned she could understand his past silence now, and that she loved and admired her father more than ever.

Moving farther to the east, the last stop was made near Hill 55 for a widow who had come on the tour by herself. Mary had seemed quite hesitant when first speaking to Rick on the phone a few months before. She said she wanted to visit the place where her husband had been killed, but no one would go with her. Rick assured her that she would be with a group of Marines who would watch over her like protective Dads. Plus, there would be another widow on the tour with them. This solidified her decision to go.

Now, here she was next to the Song Yen, the Yen River, beside which her husband had given his last full measure. Mary had never remarried, never had children. Standing at this battlefield site, she asked to be alone, so Rick and the group walked 30 yards away and waited. After about 20 minutes, she returned. When Rick asked if she was OK, she responded, "I just had a long talk with my husband. We talked about so many things that had been on my mind. And when he turned and walked away, I turned and walked away. I think I can finally get on with my life now."

Her husband had waited at that spot for her to arrive, as he knew she would. Mary didn't know it, but the whole time she was talking, she was wrapped in her husband's arms.

Rick recalled a veteran Navy chaplain's testimony about his tour company, *This company provides more healing in 15 days on a tour, than a therapist does in 15 years on a couch.* Rick doubted it was entirely true but without question, the changes were profound.

That night at dinner, Rick noticed that the group had run out of steam. They had left Los Angeles two days ago, arrived in Da Nang, and jumped right into the tour. After a fitful sleep, they were right back to touring again. This was when jet lag hits. *Right on time*, thought Rick. He had built in a free day for tomorrow. He knew a late wakeup call and a day of relaxing by the pool or leisurely exploring Hoi An would do them all good.

Rick made a toast to John, Ronnie, and Mary who had chosen to share their stories with their new friends. Most folks on the tour had not known each other until they had met in Los Angeles, but they would remain close friends for the rest of their lives. They ambled off to their rooms.

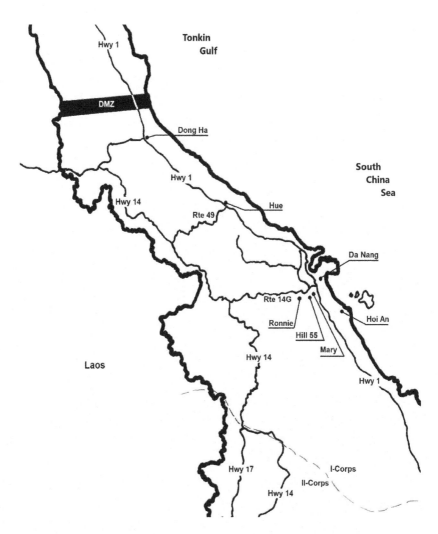

Ronnie is forgiven; Mary's goodbye

CHAPTER FOURTEEN

Two days later, while most of the group stayed in Hoi An to continue relaxing, shopping, and exploring the town, the most able-bodied accompanied the other widow and her sister on a deep-jungle expedition farther south. Janie was a young wife and mother when her Army pilot husband, Howard, was shot down. He had been killed in the jungle crash, along with nine other souls who were aboard his Huey helicopter.

The years went by, and Janie understood her daughter's desire to go to Vietnam. Melanie, after all, had never met her father. She wanted to see where, and to find out how – and perhaps why – her father had to die when she was only 35-days old. Janie had sent Howard a cassette tape of Melanie cooing and fussing so he could hear their baby daughter's voice. Melanie had often thought of how her Dad may have reacted to hearing her voice on the tape. *Did he cry? Did he smile? Did it make him homesick? Did he have his buddies listen?*

Growing up without her Dad was tough. But alas, Melanie died suddenly at the age of 33, just seven years longer than her father's life had been. She had been home visiting her mother and recuperating from a broken ankle. She asked her mom how soon dinner would be ready. "Ten minutes. Go ahead and relax in the living room until it's done."

A minute later Janie heard a thud. When she went to investigate, she found Melanie dead on the floor. A blood clot had broken away from Melanie's ankle and had lodged in her heart. She had died instantly. Melanie never made it to Vietnam, never got the chance to fulfill her goal of going to the war zone.

A few years after Melanie's death, Janie decided to live her daughter's dream and arrived in Vietnam with Rick's little band of intrepid hikers. On their way to the trek launch point,

Rick had the tour bus stop at the field where Howard had landed and picked up the soldiers that fateful day in 1969. None of the soldiers knew as they boarded the helicopter, that they all had just minutes to live. The soldiers were enroute to an outpost named San Juan Hill, which was west of Duc Pho Airfield, Howard's home base. Howard had lifted off from the airfield and had flown the 20 kilometers to pick up the soldiers. His helicopter was the last in a flight of four, all carrying troops to San Juan. About two kilometers from the hilltop, the NVA opened up with a .51-caliber anti-aircraft gun. They concentrated their fire on the last helicopter, not wanting to alert the other aircraft by firing on the first helicopter in the flight. The tail rotor was torn from Howard's helicopter rendering the bird unflyable, and it dropped onto a hillside, rolled, exploded, and burned, killing all aboard.

After a few more miles of driving, the group stopped and geared up. They started their long hike through the hot, merciless jungle. The going was tough and frequent stops were necessary for hydration and rest. The jungle trapped heat and humidity and the elements became oppressive. But the determined little group trudged on, ever deeper into the jungle. Making the trek even more poignant, Janie was wearing Melanie's hiking shoes.

After a three-hour march, the GPS and Rick's old combat map readouts matched up. They had arrived at the crash site. Janie and the group were standing on hallowed ground. Rick used his machete to dig a small hole to accept what was brought. Into it, Janie nested a white cross with the names and dates of birth and death of her husband and her daughter. Janie's neighbor had fashioned the cross and wording as his gift for this occasion. The cross was destined to forever grace that small place in the jungle. A few remembrances were said and two of Melanie's much-loved poems recited.

Janie placed a favorite stone of Melanie's at the base of the cross. They also held a memorial service for all ten Americans who perished that day. Each name was read and a memento for each was left at the site.

Standing at attention, the veterans slowly and reverently saluted their fallen brothers to the trumpet sounds of *Taps*, a heartbreaking, yet healing sound that wafted through the dense jungle in the middle of the mountains.

And then Janie opened a glass vial and poured the ashes of her daughter around the cross. The little girl was finally with the father she had never met.

While the small group shared tears and hugs, Howard walked away holding Melanie's hand as she skipped along. Nine soldierly spirits followed.

The group started their long trek back to the bus. They returned late to the hotel and quietly went to their rooms. Rick was emotionally wrecked. His heart was broken. But he knew this was a healing day and he took comfort knowing that this day would be eternally important to Janie and her family.

Hoi An to the Crash Site

CHAPTER FIFTEEN

After breakfast the next morning, the group bid Hoi An farewell and headed north. The bus traveled on the new beach road past the wartime Marble Mountain Air Facility. The MMAF had been a U.S. helicopter and small fixed-wing airbase during the war. Just north of the base, Steve asked Rick to stop the bus. He had something to say.

Steve pointed to the east and said, "Right over here was the China Beach Orphanage. It was run by Catholic nuns. During the Christmas 1969 cease-fire, my life was changed forever, because of just one visit to that orphanage."

Steve stopped for a moment. "OK wait, let me clarify. Rick, you remember when you and most of the guys were in Phu Bai that Christmas and I was sent to Da Nang on some detail?"

Rick nodded.

Steve got off track again, he had not expected to talk about this, but it seemed so very important at the moment. "Let me begin again. Back around 1990 when my niece, Beth, was in high school, she sent me a lengthy questionnaire concerning my participation in the Vietnam War. It was an interview assignment for her history class. Most of the questions were routine, but one took me by surprise. It was an unusual question, one that required some truly deep reflection. This was the question: *Did you meet anyone of great importance during the war?*

"Of great importance.

"I saw a general once. Big deal. I had a Purple Heart pinned on me by a Colonel. So what. Then there were those important-looking guys. I think they were CIA or something. Now I'm all atingle. Oh yeah, I saw a Bob Hope show once. That was pretty good. All were important, yes, but not people of great importance to me.

"I began to think harder. Just who are people of great importance? I concluded they are people who alter your personal reality to a higher degree. And very often they are not people of renown or even people of learning.

"In every war you will meet individuals who will change your life. And this can take place in a very short period of time. Sometimes you get a glimpse at the fragility of human life and at the extraordinary courage of ordinary people. People who give you these insights are people you remember forever. Far more important to me than any general or any entertainer, were the children at the China Beach Orphanage.

"I went to the MMAF base chapel on Sunday. After the mass, I was last to talk with the Navy chaplain. He asked about my unit and our activities on the DMZ. He was really easy to talk to, like a regular guy, not like the stern priests I knew growing up. He was on his way to the orphanage and asked if I'd like to go with him and help deliver supplies to the Catholic nuns who ran the place. I said 'sure' and hopped in his jeep and off we went. As we entered the compound, the littlest children would run up, hug you, and hold on for dear life. There were so many of them. They were so affection-starved it didn't matter who you were. They just wanted someone to hold them. And so many smiles. Big ones. How they could ever find cheer in the midst of such misery still amazes me.

"After unloading the donated food and supplies, I played tag with the children. It seemed like it was all the kids against me, because I was 'it' most of the time. They laughed when I kept letting them slip by, pretending to not be able to tag them. Later we rested in the shade and made faces at each other, trying unsuccessfully not to giggle.

"But it wasn't all funny."

Steve hesitated and wiped away a tear. "A boy's leg had been torn off by a mine. He hopped around like he never missed it. This was one tough hombre.

"A little girl, she must have been three or four, only cried. She had been brought in from a nearby village. During the night about a week previous, the Viet Cong had entered her village, angry that the villagers had allowed the Americans to help them dig a well. The little girl watched as her pregnant mother was gutted and killed. This was done as a warning to the rest of the village; to not be friendly with the Americans. Her father had disappeared months before. And although the little girl was not harmed physically, she would cry until exhausted, then sleep, only to awake crying. She would not accept food, water, or affection. They did not expect her to live. The medical term they use today to describe this syndrome is 'Failure to Thrive.'

"One little boy stood alone. His face and head were hideously scarred from burns he received in an attack on his village." Now Steve wiped tears from both eyes.

"Anyway, he had never been debrided. He would never receive plastic surgery. One ear was gone. He was very sad because no one liked to be near him. I talked to him for a minute even though he could not understand my language. Then he did something the rest of the children liked to do. He stood on my boot and held onto my thigh with both arms. And this Marine and this little boy took a long tromp around the compound. I think he was smiling.

"Then I had to leave. My job was to cause death and destruction. It was what I was trained to do, and I did it well. I do not apologize for that. Still, for a few fleeting hours, I was able to do something altogether different. It hurt to realize that I just might be better at helping than I was at spoiling. I wanted to stay, but I had no power. I was just a Lance Corporal at the time, two steps up from Private. In the evening, I was back on the helicopter, heading back north to join my unit in Phu Bai. We flew along the coast, and I looked out at the blackness unable to distinguish the sea from the sky. And I knew the war would never be the same for me.

"That was a long time ago. I don't know what's become of the children. I hope somehow I warmed their hearts, at least for that short time. The memory haunts me. It breaks my heart whenever I think of them, and I wonder if they ever think of me. I'll never know.

"Well, thanks for listening."

There was quiet clapping from all on the bus. Most of them were too overwhelmed with Steve's story to speak.

Rick decided to not try to wrap up Steve's talk. He had no comforting words of wisdom. He let it be.

Not much farther ahead Rick called a stop for a Kodak-moment at My Khe on the South China Sea. My Khe was better known as China Beach, which was used as an in-country 'Rest & Recreation' facility by U.S. troops. The old veterans chuckled, remembering their antics here on their three-day respite from the war. But they, of course, could not talk about those experiences in mixed company. Rick pondered that reluctance. *Why,* he wondered, *was it easier to talk about killing than it was to talk about having sex?*

After a few more kilometers, they passed through Dog Patch. Dog Patch was a refugee camp during the war. It was so named after the mountain town in the Lil' Abner comic series. The area had depressed Rick after his discharge from the 95th Evacuation Hospital on his way back north to rejoin his unit. Refugee camps dotted the roads along the entire coastline of South Vietnam. These shanty towns were wretched and infested with rats, disease, and suffering. The refugees lived in shacks they built with scrounged pieces of canvas, tin, wood, and cardboard discarded by the military. These proud, hard-working, gentle people had been driven to the refugee camps by American bombing, or by battles in and near their villages, or by the terrorist activities of the Viet Cong. They could not return to their ancestral homes, and many were forced to beg to survive.

Some stole. Some prostituted themselves. Others would rummage through garbage dumps for scraps of food from military mess halls or for wood for cooking and warmth. Most of the people in the refugee camps were women, girls, children, and old men. The able-bodied teen boys and adult men were drafted into the Army of South Vietnam, the ARVN, to fight against the North Vietnamese communists. Or they were kidnapped by the Viet Cong to be slaves or to be forced to fight against the South. They were literally stuck between the proverbial *rock and a hard place,* and it could be deadly.

Although the U.S., Vietnamese, and other concerned nations did what they could for the refugees, there were just too many of them. It was a miserable and demeaning existence complicated by severe deprivation and sadness. In addition, the refugees were somewhat nomadic. When things simply got too bad to bear, the refugees moved on yearning for something better elsewhere.

Rick wondered if the villagers even cared about politics, about war. He had a sense they just wanted to live their lives, grow their crops, raise their children, practice their religion, and basically be left alone. But then again, don't all people want to be free? Isn't freedom what all people crave? Deserve?

Rick felt uncomfortable and a little embarrassed that he had access to pure water and food, and he was able to get immediate medical care if he needed it. The refugees were horribly impoverished and there was really nothing that Rick, a

50

mere Corporal, could do about it. That was the most difficult thing, to witness suffering and to be unable to help.

Rick still carried that sense of helplessness with him. He was trained for war. He expected the worst during firefights, accepted his role, and did his job well. But he was never trained for, nor was he prepared for, the shock of observing what happens to innocent people who are caught amidst the death and destruction of armed combat. Rick would never shake the images. They were seared into his soul.

Traveling north of Dog Patch, Rick took a moment to stop for photos at Red Beach II, where U.S. Marines made their first amphibious landing in Vietnam in March of 1965. Soon, the motorcoach crossed the Nam O Bridge. Upriver to the west was the notorious Elephant Valley. It occurred to Rick that one of the orders given that distressed him most was this: If he saw any elephants, he was required to kill them. The enemy would use elephants to transport war materials through the jungles and forests. Killing the enemy was quite acceptable to Rick. But to shoot a blameless elephant seemed immoral. He was thankful he never encountered such an animal.

The bus started up the Deo Hai Van, the Pass of the High Clouds, where Highway One becomes a breathtaking, winding, no guardrail, mountain road overlooking Da Nang Bay. Stopping at the top, the veterans hopped off the bus to roam the wartime volatile pass area and to buy some pearl jewelry from the happy, local vendors. Continuing down the north side of the pass, the veterans enjoyed the spectacular scenery high above the South China Sea.

Coming off the pass road, they stopped in the fishing village of Lang Co. They enjoyed a fabulous seafood lunch on the patio of a thatch-covered, open-air restaurant perched over the Dam Lap An lagoon. After lunch and feeling in a great mood, the veterans started cutting up during the next two hours on the road to Hue City, the ancient capital of all Vietnam, home of the emperors and their Forbidden City. Upon their return there for another lunch, less than a week away, the group would pick at their food in silence, not feeling at all hungry. One of their own would be missing.

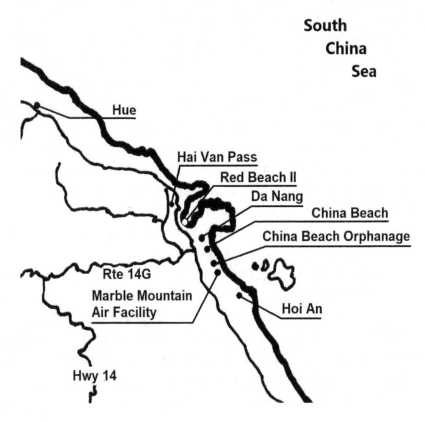

Hoi An to the Hai Van Pass

CHAPTER SIXTEEN

Halfway to Hue, the motorcoach stopped along the road at a small, nondescript village. Above the village was a hill, atop of which had once been an artillery fire support base. As with most bases near populations, curious children would show up at the gates to receive treats and to play with and to laugh with the young Marines. Most Marines in that war, of course, were little more than kids themselves. A veteran, Herbie, who had served on the base told the story of one little boy, about ten-years old, just eight years his junior, that he befriended.

"I used to give money to the child to clean my gear and to do laundry. When the 1968 Tet Offensive broke out, the firebase was quickly moved to a location closer to Hue to support the heavy fighting going on there. I never got back here to the village, but I remember that I still owed the child two dollars. I feel bad that I never got to pay him."

Rick asked, "Do you remember his name?"

"Sure do. It was Trang."

"Hey Mr. Tuan, can you ask one of these villagers if he ever heard of a kid named Trang? If he's still alive, he'd be about 60 years old now."

Tuan asked a local man who replied in Vietnamese, "Yes, I know him. I go get him." And off he went.

The group milled around stretching their legs for about five minutes until the villager returned. He had in tow a man about 60-years-old. Instantly, Herbie and Trang yelled each other's names and embraced in a great bear hug. After more than five decades, they still recognized each other. It was a miraculous reunion.

Before the group left, Herbie gave Trang a hundred-dollar bill, which was a small fortune to a villager, saying, "This is the two dollars I owe you, plus 50-year's interest."

They hugged goodbye.

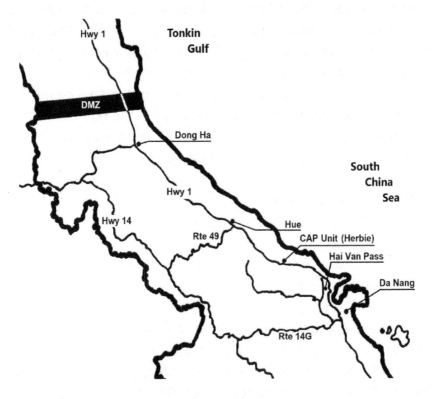

Herbie's CAP Unit location

CHAPTER SEVENTEEN

As the bus crossed the Phu Cam Canal, made chillingly famous by the number of dead NVA floating down it, the veterans became somber. This was a place of urban warfare where two understrength Marine regiments fought a well-entrenched division of NVA for 24 days during the 1968 Tet Offensive. In the end, the communists were driven out of Hue and the nearly destroyed city was liberated. The Marines had suffered nearly 1,000 casualties, the NVA over 5,100. This was also where the North Vietnamese Army had massacred over 3,000 innocent civilians, many bludgeoned to death, or throats cut, or buried alive in mass graves.

The mood changed once again after the veterans had checked into their hotel on the Perfume River, cleaned up, and gathered for dinner. They were attended to by smiling, energetic, and young waitresses, each wearing a beautiful, traditional silk tunic dress called ao dai.

The girls were asking the veterans many questions. English is a required language in Vietnamese schools. After all, it is the language of world finance. This made Rick's job a little easier. Other than a few curse words, Vietnamese was impossible for him to learn. Also, age is held in great esteem, and the girls had much respect for their geriatric American guests.

The old warriors relaxed and allowed these South Vietnamese ladies to treat them like kings. These aged men, after all, were some of the ones who had saved their Citadel and their city from the communist onslaught in 1968. The young women were in awe. They knew how much the Marines had suffered and sacrificed. Their Vietnamese parents had taught them well.

There is something special about young Vietnamese women. They are mystifyingly beautiful. They are perfectly proportioned, and many have a subtle DNA mix of French and Vietnamese left over from 100 years of French domination. Hue had always been a university town, and many young, pretty college girls wear white ao dais and stroll the streets enjoying the little shops in the evenings.

Even though they were old, this delightful revelation was not lost on the veterans.

CHAPTER EIGHTEEN

The following two days were dedicated to remembering the Hue urban battles and visiting the most important sites in the southern city and within the Citadel walls. They would also take a Dragon Boat cruise up the Perfume River to explore the tombs of ancient emperors.

One of the veterans, Roberto, was a U.S. Marine in the vicious battle for the Citadel during the 1968 Tet Offensive. He had returned to Vietnam twice before, but the unprofessional tour company with which he had traveled was unable, or unwilling, to get him to the places that held such powerful and disturbing memories.

All that changed for him when he signed on with Rick's group. Armed with old combat maps and a GPS, Rick and the group located the back courtyard where Roberto, during the battle, had come upon the unit chaplain, Father McCarthy, who had always been out front with the fighters, tending the wounded and administering last rites to dying Marines.

When Roberto found him, the padre had been bound with wire and shot in the back of the head by fleeing NVA. The group stood there with Roberto as he struggled with his emotions. A Vietnamese woman who had been watching the group, came over and shyly asked what they were doing.

Roberto explained, "During the war, I found a slain priest here. Later we used this house as an aid station because it was a doctor's house. The doctor helped with the wounded Marines. He didn't have to help, and he wasn't forced to. He did it because he was a good man and he wanted to help ease the suffering. I'll never forget him."

She said, "The doctor was my father."

Although the doctor had died years before, Roberto was amazed that the doctor's family still lived there. The woman was equally amazed, and honored, that an American would remember her father from over a half century ago and had come all the way to this house from America to pay his respects.

Roberto suddenly realized that this woman and he were interconnected through a common history, and he would never have known it unless he had come full circle in his life. Priest, doctor, and Marine, all linked by war, and now the daughter, too. After exchanging addresses, the woman and Roberto wished each other good luck and promised to write to each other.

As the group was leaving, Father McCarthy's spirit stood in a back corner of the courtyard, made the sign of the Cross, blessed them, and disappeared.

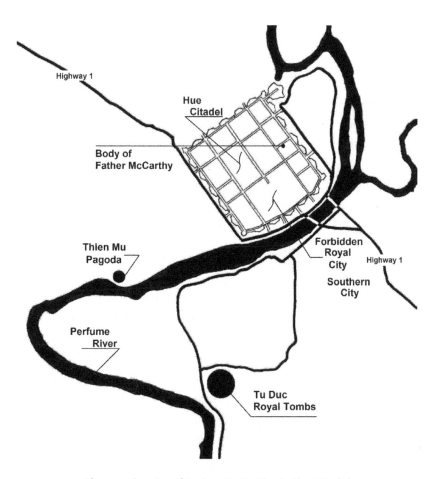

Highway 1

Hue
Citadel

Body of
Father McCarthy

Thien Mu
Pagoda

Forbidden
Royal
City

Highway 1

Southern
City

Perfume
River

Tu Duc
Royal Tombs

The murder site of Father McCarthy in the Citadel

CHAPTER NINETEEN

The next morning, the group started its drive up to the old Demilitarized Zone, the DMZ. The term was an oxymoron to the veterans because they knew better than most that while it was indeed a zone, there was nothing de-militarized about it. It was a very evil place. Rick remembered when he first landed in-country as a newbie. He and the other new guys, after arriving by plane from Okinawa, were trucked to the staging station at Freedom Hill on the west side of Da Nang. They were called individually to the desk to receive their unit assignments and to find out where they would be sent in the war. The clerk looked at Rick's military record and said, "You're going to the Dead Marine Zone."

Not believing his ears, he said, "What? Where?"

The clerk replied, "The DMZ."

When he had first arrived at the Rockpile with a couple of other new guys, the seasoned Marines welcomed them to the 'Grim Reaper's Playhouse.'

The company Gunnery Sergeant had given them their initial briefing, "The entire DMZ is a place of alarm. Other than the coastal end of the DMZ, which is a sandy hellhole in and of itself, the rest of the DMZ consists of steep, unforgiving mountains that, even in bright sunlight, will hide deep, dark forbidding ravines that can bring an instant, grateful death or a lingering, painful death. You don't get to choose which one. Keep your rifle clean, your mouth shut, and your eyes open."

The group was now in Quang Tri Province, the most consistently contested warzone in South Vietnam. It bordered the enemy country of North Vietnam, as well as 'neutral' Laos where the communists had set up its sanctuaries and had built a series of supply-line trails, cumulatively called the Ho Chi Minh

Trail. The mission of the Marines in this northernmost province was to curtail enemy infiltration and communist exploitation of helpless civilians. The Marines had taken to it with gusto.

Steve sat in his bus seat without speaking. Despite the air-conditioning, sweat broke out on his back.

With the memory of the slain priest still reeling in his psyche, Rick remembered back during another tour when a legless Lutheran priest had accompanied the group. Pastor David had crawled down into the crater. He complained, "Are you sure this is the right hole? I can't find them anywhere."

He was referring to his legs. Rick had brought the priest back to the exact spot in Vietnam where a land mine had made the crater and which had also severed David's legs from his body. The good pastor was making light of his trauma to allay the group's collective dread at the realization of what had occurred at that place. But that was the kind of guy he was. David had been a young lieutenant in the Marine Corps leading his rifle platoon when he stepped on the mine. He later became a priest. That's all most folks knew. He kept his horrors to himself.

Rick shook his head and came out of his reverie in time to stop the tour bus at the My Chanh River Bridge. It was here that the ARVN held the line against invading NVA forces during the 1972 Easter Offensive and from which they launched their counterattack to drive communist forces back toward the DMZ.

Rick explained the rarely shared facts, "North of here is the section of Highway One known as the 'Highway of Horror.' During the Easter Offensive, thousands of local refugees – most of which were old people, women, and children trying to flee south – were mercilessly slaughtered by communist NVA troops and their artillery. The north side of the bridge is where the worst of the massacre occurred. Massive numbers of people were trapped because the downed bridge prevented escape. It was an atrocity only over-shadowed by the exterminations at Hue. The bodies had lain in the hot sun for two months and were eaten by hogs, vultures, and insects."

The Marines had left this area two years before, and the U.S Army which had replaced the Marines, had left just a year after that. Rick knew that if either U.S. military branch had been allowed to stay, the Easter Offensive invasion from the North would never have been so costly nor so destructive to the South Vietnamese people and their cities.

Going back to the French Indochina War this coastal area was hotly contested. The bus came upon a desolate area to the east of the road. Rick explained, "Off to the east, about 12 kilometers, is a road that parallels Highway One. It is Route 555, better known as La Rue Sans Joie, The Street Without Joy. The famous Austrian/French writer, Bernard Fall, wrote a book by the same name. It was about the French Indochina War. Curiously, in 1967, Fall was a foreign correspondent in our war and was on patrol with U.S. Marines near the Street Without Joy. He tripped a landmine, and both his legs were blown off, killing him. He's buried in Washington, DC. His legs are buried in an unmarked grave in Vietnam, not far from here."

The group was silent. Riding along, they stared out the windows to the east and to where Bernard Fall had perished.

The group soon arrived at the obliterated city of Quang Tri. It had been literally wiped from the face of the earth during the communist 1972 invasion from the North. The bombed-out skeletons of one church and one school remained. The group walked through the eerie destruction reminiscent of Berlin at the end of WWII. These two buildings provided a shocking and violent reality of the *Battle of 81 Days and Nights* for Quang Tri City and its Citadel. The battle is infamous for the huge amount of ordnance fired by both ARVN and NVA forces in their seesaw attacks to hold and to regain the city. In the end, there was nothing left to fight for.

Moving east through the rebuilt city, Rick directed the bus using his GPS to get to a little village just outside of town. Sal, a Corpsman, needed to return to his CAP village east of Quang Tri Town. Combined Action Platoon unit Marines lived in the hamlets full time and helped the local people defend and improve their villages. These were very successful programs, and the CAP Marines became close friends with the Vietnamese. While wandering though the village, they found a woman in whose family hut Sal had lived with a few other Marines.

She didn't recognize him at first; he had aged quite a bit as they all had, but she started rattling off names of the guys, "'Bac Si,' 'Johnny with black face,' 'Tommy-Boy,'" and so on.

Sal told her that he was Bac Si, which means 'doctor' in Vietnamese, and showed her a photo of herself when she was just 14 years old. She screamed and laughed and said, "I hated you, Bac Si."

"You hated me? Why?"

"Because you wash my hair in front of whole village. You embarrass me."

But she no longer held any anger. She was so happy to see him again and was amazed he returned to her little village after such a long time and from so far away. She still had fond memories of the Americans who helped her family and her village during those terrible war years.

The group was staring at Sal, contemplating the weird hair-washing incident. Sal explained, "As the Corpsman, the medical man, I was responsible for the health care and the health education for the village. I had washed her hair with a special soap to teach the village how to control lice."

Everyone felt better after that. Before leaving the village, Sal promised to return again and to pick up where he left off so many years ago. Friendships bonded in war never die.

The group then spent some time exploring the wartime airfield of Ai Tu, better known as the Quang Tri Airbase, bordering the Song Thach Han. Rick reminded the group of why this airfield was placed here. Pointing north, he said, "It was just out of range from the big guns located across the Demilitarized Zone, in North Vietnam. We're exactly 23 kilometers from the DMZ. As soon as we are north of the airfield, we'll be in range. Put on your flak jackets and helmets."

A few people groaned, "Come on Rick. How many more of these bad jokes are we expected to endure?"

"Heck, I'm just getting started."

Rick was happy with the way the tour was going. The group was now fully engaged and enjoying itself, and other than a few emotional moments, all were amazed with how well the country had recovered. And they were humbled with how the South Vietnamese were openly thanking the Marines for their sacrifices during that merciless war.

It was not just that. The Vietnamese genuinely liked Americans. After the war, the Soviets had arrived and treated the locals brutally. The French and the Europeans have always looked down their noses at the Vietnamese. And the Chinese had warred against them for a thousand years. But they knew the Americans were different. The Americans treated the Vietnamese as friends, joking around with them, buying them drinks, and being otherwise friendly and generous and polite, looking for nothing in return.

No one in the group could imagine that the tour would soon go terribly wrong.

64

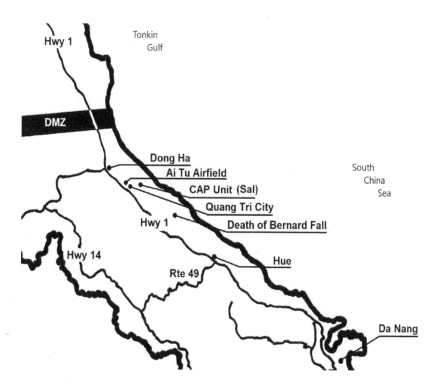

Hue to Dong Ha

CHAPTER TWENTY

That night the group stayed at a beautiful hotel in Dong Ha near the confluence of Route 9 and Highway One. After dinner, some of the folks retired to the rooftop bar and sipped cool drinks on the dimly lit patio. Below, just to the northeast, they could clearly see the old LCU ramp, the Landing Craft Utility ramp. It was still in use, although not for war materiel coming down the Song Cua Viet. To the north was the Dong Ha Bridge. Off to the west was the Dong Ha Combat Base, now overwhelmed by the city itself.

After a while, Rick and Steve were the only two left at the bar. Steve had been drinking a little too much and Rick recognized the anxiety symptoms. Until now, Steve had been having a great time and he had enthusiastically helped Rick on several occasions. But there was a change in Steve that made Rick concerned for his friend.

"Steve, what's going on? You look like you've got something on your mind."

"Dammit Rick, I'm freaking out. This is the start of Route 9. At the other end is Phou Nhoi. It's why I came, but now I don't think I want to go. What are the chances I can stay here for a few days and wait for you guys to get back?"

"Not a chance in hell."

"I'm really nervous, Rick. This is too real. I don't think I can hack it."

"Look, man. You're my best friend and you were a heck of a Marine. Hell, you're still a Marine. Once a Marine, always a Marine. Right? Just what the heck do I tell the Army guys on this tour? What should I tell the ladies? That you put on a diaper, hugged your binkie, stuck your thumb in your mouth, and curled up in the fetal position?"

"Screw you, Rick. I just think it's a bad idea now."

66

Steve's hesitancy was not based in cowardice, it was based in healthy trepidation. Phou Nhoi was a dark, mysterious, and dangerous area. It had been left mostly alone for thousands of years. Locals fear it, and they bypass it in their daily lives. They believe something malignant lurks there.

Phou Nhoi sits in the middle of an oddly shaped area of South Vietnam that is nearly surrounded by Laos, making no logical sense as far as borders go. It is like a ready-to-pop, diseased boil that bulges down into Laos and follows, for a time, the meandering Sepon River. Usually only hapless, unknowing soldiers venture into the place, and they are forever sorry they did. Others who walk into the area stumble out, forever changed. Or they did not come out at all.

"Tell you what. Tomorrow, we go to the Hill of Angels and then up through the DMZ into North Vietnam. Let's see how you survive the NVA tunnels. We come back here for a night before we make the next move all the way west. You can decide then. Fair enough?"

Steve pondered Rick's words, "Fair enough, brother."

Rick knew his friend would snap out of it. He's just had too much to drink. He knew Steve to be fearless in battle. And the NVA had been gone from there for 50 years.

Well, maybe the NVA were gone, but something more sinister awaited them.

CHAPTER TWENTY-ONE

The next day, after crossing the Washout, a bridge just north of Charlie-2 firebase, the group stopped along the *Rough Rider* road from Cam Lo. They geared up for an excursion into the western foothills. Paul, the little brother of a Medal of Honor posthumous recipient, now a grown man, wanted to visit Hill 70 southwest of Con Thien. The site was where his big brother, Jack, had sacrificed his life for his men and had earned the country's highest award.

The group trekked to the hill and arrived at the location where Jack, a Marine lieutenant, after having his leg severed at the knee by an enemy mortar, ordered his men to the rear as the enemy approached through the forest. Refusing medical aid, Jack jammed his stump into the dirt to stem the bleeding, leaned back against a tree, and continued firing fleshettes, dart rounds, at the advancing NVA with his shotgun. This gave his Marines time to regroup into a defensive perimeter to repel the large enemy force. Jack was subsequently killed-in-action at that tree.

As the group stood at the site, Paul related stories about growing up with his big brother. Then, after reading the Medal of Honor citation and respecting a moment of silence, the group members milled about the area, trying to picture how this horrific battle had developed. Scanning the ground, a near-perfect fleshette was found. It was probably from the lieutenant's shotgun. No one could see Jack nodding his head. The group revered the fleshette solemnly, and it was handed to Paul who would return home with a small part of his big brother's life.

Rick saw that Steve was standing alone, in deep contemplation, in a dark area of the trees. He wanted to run to his friend, but he hesitated, figuring that Steve probably needed this time alone.

The group then explored the base at Con Thien (the Hill of Angels). It was named by French troops during their Indochina War in deference to how many men had died there. During the American War, a battalion of Marines ran operations from this base. At that time, it was akin to the trenches of WWI France where everything was underground because of the intense, nearly daily barrages of enemy artillery that punished the base.

Rick was always mystified by this place. Whenever he visited with a group, even during the hottest weather, they could feel cold spots, like icy zephyrs, passing through the skin. He thought it might be the angels this hill was known for. The momentary coldness was never scary or disturbing. It seemed to him a closeness, or a recognition, maybe a *thank you* for coming to remember those who died on this, the Hill of Angels.

Before embarking into the DMZ proper, the group made a quick stop at Forward Marine Base Gio Linh, which perched high over no-mans-land. On bright, sunny days the enemy country could be clearly seen on the other side of the 'demilitarized zone.' This place marked the northeast corner of what had become known as Leatherneck Square. Con Thien in the northwest; Cam Lo in the southwest; and Dong Ha in the southeast corner made up the *Square.*

When they reached the center of the DMZ, the group disembarked and walked over the Peace Bridge, another oxymoron. This original wartime bridge still spans the Song Ben Hai. Rick explained that the Ben Hai River was the only true physical demarcation between the North and the South. They walked over the rickety wood bridge. Rick mused silently to himself, *This was something that had been denied to us by the fools in Washington, DC who had been running the war from the basement of the White House.* The tour bus had crossed the new bridge to meet them on the other side. Now in North Vietnam, the group drove to the tunnel complex in the artillery village of Vinh Moc. Rick explained, "The Vinh Moc Tunnels are an incredible maze of tunnels that were dug by local people to hide from the constant U.S. counter-battery bombing of the area. The tunnels included kitchens, wells, and a 'hospital,' as well as living quarters for roughly sixty families. The tunnels, which are at a depth of 30 meters underground, saved the lives of many villagers and were still in exceptionally good condition."

After visiting the little museum, Rick advised, "Now listen up and take this seriously. If you are even the slightest bit claustrophobic, then you should stay back at the museum and you should not enter the subterranean labyrinth. If you become claustrophobic while we're in these tight confining places, and you decide to make a break for it, you may never find your way out. No shame in not going in."

Most, including Steve, followed Rick down into the network of tunnels and had a great and enlightening time.

Early that afternoon they ate lunch on a peaceful beach of the Tonkin Gulf. The waitress who brought cold drinks looked at them and said, "You been in tunnels."

When she was asked how she knew, she said, "Many shoulders dirty."

They looked at their sleeves. Sure enough, they had dirty shoulders from rubbing up against the narrow, dirt walls of the tunnels. A dead giveaway. Everyone laughed.

After they were finished eating, the group walked on the beach and took photos of the strangely shaped and very colorful fishing boats. Steve sat on the beach by himself in deep contemplation.

Rick walked up and sat down next to his friend, staring out at the ocean, "What's up Marine?"

"Oh, I was just thinking about the tunnel rats. You and me were too big to go down into the tunnels during the war. The ones we just went into were a decent size, but the ones where we served were too tiny to get our fat butts down into. The small guys had big cojones to take a flashlight and a .45 automatic down inside, sometimes for hundreds of yards, alone. Some never came out."

"You ain't lying. Brave souls, no doubt."

"It just kind of gives you a different perspective. Most of us think of our war as just that, our war, what we did. Not what others did. I'm thinking of stuff I never thought of before. This is an amazing trip, Rick. Thanks for talking me into it."

"I'm glad you're here, my brother."

Rick had to coerce folks back on the bus. The eating and relaxing on the beach was feeling surprisingly good to these old codgers. No one wanted to leave the warm, idyllic cove with its beautiful views of the Tonkin Gulf.

The group witnessed another interesting thing there in North Vietnam. The public-service campaign signs, educating villagers about how disease is spread, were a hoot. The government had erected huge billboards which showed very graphic images which emphasised the dangers of doing bad things. For example, there was a billboard of two skeletons fornicating, showing how AIDS can kill. On the other side was a happy, smiling condom with arms waving and no one is dead. There was one with a girl with her pants down defecating by the river, complete with squiggly lines denoting rising odor. In a circular pictorial it also showed the cycle of a fly landing on the poop, the fly landing on food, a person eating the food, the person getting sick, and the sick person pooping by the river

71

again. The group had to stop to take photos of the entertaining, but edifying billboards.

One last event awaited the group.

They recrossed the Song Ben Hai and into South Vietnam on the brand-new beach road. Dozens of new hotels were being built along the white sandy beach. Soon they turned west along the Song Cua Viet toward Dong Ha. At the little village of Mai Xa Chanh, Rick had the bus stop at a colorful pagoda. Here he related a story of a tour some 20 years back. The story still had a profound effect on him, and he always shared it with his brother veterans. Rick told the group, "In 1968 a battalion leader in the battle of Dai Do, also known as the battle of Dong Ha, had commandeered this Buddhist pagoda to serve as his battle headquarters. While there, and during one of his trips back and forth to his warship in the Tonkin Gulf, he took a sacred, wooden turtle from the pagoda as a souvenir. At first the turtle's presence on his Virginia sun porch didn't bother him. But as the long years passed, he began to experience guilt for having taken a pious relic. Yes, even the toughest of Marines can feel pangs of guilt. And this was one of the toughest who ever lived. There is a famous photograph of the commander wounded and lying on his back on the ground, smoking a cigar, and holding up his own IV bottle. When the commander heard that he could travel to Vietnam for a visit, he made up his mind to return the turtle to its rightful place. As the old Marine entered the village, the Buddhist monks were informed as to why the American was there. Word went out and within minutes, the villagers all gathered at the pagoda excited that what once had been missing was being returned after so much time. The monks performed a ritual service with the commander at the head of prayers and at the placing of incense. The turtle was ceremoniously passed to the head monk."

Rick summed up, "The grateful villagers held no animosity toward the Marine commander and were amazed at how far the turtle had traveled. They were forgiving and gracious. They realized that this American was a man of honor. And this was truly good luck for the village. The sacred turtle had returned home."

Late that evening in the deserted hotel rooftop bar, Rick and Steve finished their drinks and got up to head back to their rooms. Steve stopped Rick and said, "If that lieutenant at Hill 70 could jam his bloody stump into the dirt and still fight off the enemy, then I sure as hell can stand on the ground at Phou Nhoi and remember our fellow Marines who gave all they had. Please forget what I said last night."

"Forget what?" replied Rick.

They both pounded their chests and proclaimed together, "Semper Fi, Do or Die!"

Unfortunately, Rick would come to regret talking Steve out of his fears. That macho mindset would soon lead them both through the gates of hell.

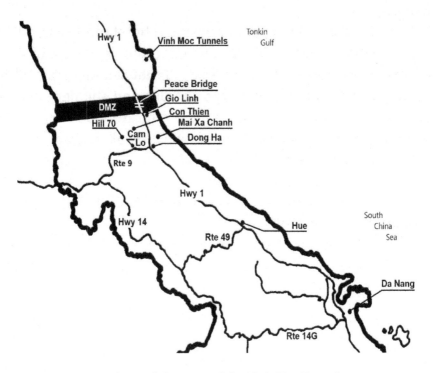

Leatherneck Square and the Vinh Moc Tunnels

CHAPTER TWENTY-TWO

The next day, the group would travel west on Route 9, a major trade route between Vietnam, Laos, and Thailand before the war. But most Marines remembered it as a narrow, extremely dangerous dirt resupply road. Now, Route 9 was paved, and many of the perilous switchbacks had been straightened out. Bridges had been built where previously military trucks would have had to ford streams. Much of Vietnam had new infrastructure, but no new roads had been built in the dark and mysterious Phou Nhoi area. Superstitions based in this ominous area kept people away. Even in bright sunlight, Phou Nhoi seemed gloomier than surrounding areas. There was a palpable, negative aura there which was impossible to put into comprehensible form. Locals had deemed it evil for centuries. They would not talk about it at length for fear it would drive them mad.

When the bus was loaded, they left Dong Ha behind. All were in good spirits and looking forward to the day's events. Their first stop was the artillery plateau of Camp Carroll with its panoramic views. To the west, they could see Dong Ke Soc Mountain (Hill 658), where Steve had earned his Silver Star. Steve stared at the hill. He got chills remembering that day on the helicopter when he had left his unit to fight without him.

Next the group stopped at the Rockpile, where they hiked to the Razorback and located a stash of .51 caliber Soviet-made bullets. A one-legged Vietnamese man using a metal detector had dug up the ammunition crate and had removed all the brass shell casings to sell as scrap. Tuan asked how he had lost his leg. The man replied, "Digging up bombs to sell."

Rick explained to the group that 5% of all American-fired ordinance never detonated, while 15% of all enemy ordinance were also duds. The same was true for the French and Japanese wars in Vietnam. Add to that all the Chinese UXO's, unexploded ordinance, from over 1,000 years of fighting. There is a lot of scrap metal lying atop and just under the surface of the ground. Some of it still deadly. Back on the bus and continuing west, it seemed as if someone had flipped the calendar back to 1969. The modern, vibrant countryside suddenly turned Third World. New, contemporary housing gave way to huts on stilts with thatched roofs. Tribal people walked out of the mountains after a morning of hunting and gathering, their yield in baskets on their backs. Children played barefoot in front of huts. Their toddler siblings wore nothing from the waist down. Pigs and chickens roamed free. Water buffalo grazed on the roadsides and wallowed in muddy drainage ditches. "This is how I remember it," said Steve. The other veterans agreed.

This western DMZ area seemed very remote from the gleaming cities of the coast, and it was. It looked like time had stood still. Several of the veterans sensed the area unsafe and felt their anxiety build. They looked for movement in the hillsides, they scanned ahead for probable ambush sites, and they sank a little lower in their seats.

Rick's voice broke their tension as they stopped at the trailhead leading up to LZ Stud. "Listen up! Covers, cameras, and water!" This meant that those getting off the bus for the hike would need their hats, their photographic equipment, and plenty of hydration.

Rick would bark these orders for as long as they were in these more remote, and dangerous, areas. He was in squad leader mode. "Welcome to LZ Stud. Incidentally, it was named after my friend, Steve here."

"Yeah, in his dreams!" came the retort from somewhere in the back of the bus. Everybody laughed.

"Let's move. Everyone off the bus."

After the visit to LZ Stud, which had later been renamed Vandergrift Combat Base, the group stopped at an unremarkable area to take an excursion to the site where a veteran had requested a visit. As they started out from a tribal village, Rick knew this was going to be a rather unusual trek. One guy's wife, a sweet but short and rotund woman, was attempting to cross a single-log 'bridge.' Under the log was six inches of fast-moving water in a ditch about two feet wide and about two feet deep. Refusing any help, she attempted to balance her way across the log, but slipped and went back first, buttocks upstream, legs in the air, into the ditch. Of course, she was stuck, her arms and legs wagging about like an overturned turtle. The water began to back up immediately, her butt plugging the ditch, acting as a dam, and a small lake started to form very quickly, threatening to overflow its uninvited embolus. It was like watching the formation of a natural reservoir in fast-forward geologic time. Rick and Steve jumped down and pulled her free with a shlur-popping sound. It was all they could do to not pee in their pants from wanting to laugh out loud. She was fine, although a little ego-bruised, but still wanting to make the hike with her husband. What a gal. After spending time at the site, the group returned to the bus, being very careful recrossing the log bridge.

About two kilometers after a critical war site named Ca Lu, Rick called a stop along the Da Krong River. He had met a lot of amazing people on these trips and one of them was Tiger Tom. Rick held the group in awe as he related the tale: "Tiger Tom's mission one night was to walk his squad out of his Ca Lu base, penetrate deep into known enemy territory, and set up an ambush alongside an abandoned road, this road, Route 9, which had been cut off by the NVA during the 77-day siege of Khe Sanh. Moving through the pitch darkness and incessant rain, this young corporal stealthily led his squad to the designated coordinates. He set the men in line just below the edge of the road on a slope that rose from the river. Once everyone was in place, Tom began to reach toward his radioman. When tapped, the radioman would click his handset twice which was the voiceless code to the base to say they were in position and secure. As he extended his arm toward the radioman, a tiger bit down with its massive jaws onto Tom's right arm. Tom screamed, but the Marines couldn't get a clear shot at the big cat as the Marine and the tiger grappled in a death grip. Tom smashed the beast in the snout with his left fist. The tiger wrenched its head to the side, tearing out a huge mass of Tom's flesh with it. That's when the Marines started shooting. The tiger disappeared into the darkness with its hard-earned dinner, meat torn from Tom's elbow up to his shoulder. Their mission compromised, and their leader badly wounded by the tiger, the squad started its long journey back to its base. They made it without further incident and Tom was sent home for surgeries and discharge from his beloved Corps."

Thirty-two years later, Tom had stood at this location of the tiger attack and told the story and showed his tangled scars. He became quite a celebrity to local villagers when they learned how he had fought a tiger and had lived to talk about it. Rick laughed and said, "They thought he was some kind of Zen god."

The group stopped in Khe Sanh Village for a lunch of French baguettes, Vietnamese soup, pineapple, bananas, and watermelon. They were less than 13 kilometers, about eight miles, north of Phou Nhoi.

After lunch, they headed north for three kilometers and visited the old combat base at Khe Sanh. Rick went into his spiel, "Under President John F. Kennedy, the Khe Sanh base was a U.S. jungle outpost just 13 kilometers, about eight miles, from the border with Laos. It's about 64 kilometers, about 40 miles, from the coast. The base was obviously strategic. The area grew into a major military base and airstrip under President Lyndon B. Johnson and was the scene of a 77-day siege in 1968 in which 206 Marines were killed-in-action. The NVA in the surrounding countryside lost 12,000 souls. In addition, the outlying mountains had absorbed many victims in the legendary hill fights of 1967-68. After the NVA were vanquished and the siege lifted, the Marines were ordered to abandon the base for which they had fought so hard and on which they had suffered so long."

The group spent almost two hours exploring the old base and reminiscing.

Back on Route 9 and heading ever farther west, Rick called the last stop at Lang Vei. He explained that Lang Vei was a frontier Special Forces camp that had been overrun in the first-ever NVA tank assault. Co Roc Mountain soared to the heavens just across the border in Laos. Co Roc had housed a *Guns-of-Navarone* type of enemy artillery, which was so well hidden, it was never destroyed by counter-battery fire.

They overnighted in the border town of Lao Bao, which literally means Laotian Border, in spartan accommodations. But it was the best there was on the border.

Tomorrow would prove to be a long and emotional day. The group would head deep into the jungle, on foot, to the battle site at Phou Nhoi. Rick had worked into the itinerary a full day for this expedition. It was for his friend, Steve. And a little bit for himself. In the 68 times he had traveled back to Vietnam as a bush guide, Rick had never been back to Phou Nhoi.

He and Steve believed it would be a momentous day. How right they were. Both of their lives would be changed forever.

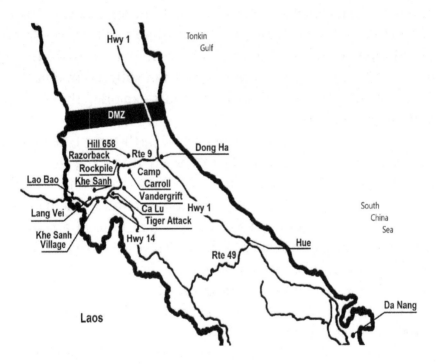

The route from Dong Ha to Lao Bao

CHAPTER TWENTY-THREE

Rising early in Lao Bao, the group met in the hotel restaurant for breakfast. Rick looked at Steve and started laughing, "What the hell kind of shirt is that?"

"Why, what's the matter with it?"

"What's the matter with it? What kind of hard-charging Marine wears a red Hawaiian shirt into the jungle? Who are you, Magnum, P.I.? A Tom Selleck wannabe?"

"I like this shirt. It was either this or a Rambo muscle shirt. I chose Don Ho. Want me to sing *Tiny Bubbles*?"

"Oh, hell no! That would be worse than your shirt."

Immediately after breakfast, the group boarded their bus for the drive to their step-off point on the south side of Route 9 about two and a half kilometers, about a mile and a half, west of Khe Sanh Village. The bus pulled up to the trailhead and the group unloaded their supplies. Each person geared up with food and plenty of water. Rick checked everyone and when he was satisfied, he announced, "OK, let's move out."

The happy group then walked into the brush along a water buffalo trail following Rick who was carrying his trusty machete. Rick was looking forward to this long trek, because although he had been to hundreds of obscure battle sites and had entered them into the extensive list in his GPS, he had yet to record Phou Nhoi. Soon the brush turned into heavy forest. They crossed a couple of small streams balancing on wet rocks, and then slowly entered dark, dense jungle. The trail narrowed here, the jungle trying to reclaim it. Rick stopped the march. "Listen up, I need everyone to close ranks. Do not lose sight of the person in front of you. If you do lose sight of the person you are following, be sure to immediately call out to stop the column. Noise discipline will not be an issue like during the war. We will

81

come back to you. I want no one getting lost. It can be very dangerous to leave the trail.

"Does everyone understand?"

All responded in the positive.

They moved forward. Rick, who was in the lead, was at times hacking away at the restrictive trail with his machete. Wielding a machete was more tiring than it looked. But Rick had conditioned his upper body to take it, and he only hacked as necessary. Steve was second in line, being careful not to get too close to Rick, remembering back to the war when one Marine had gotten too close to a swinging blade. It nearly cost the Marine his head. It was bloody, but the Marine had survived.

After an hour, Rick sensed something odd. He had many times felt the hairs on his neck stand on end during the war and he took those premonitions seriously. And even though the war was long over, Rick occasionally felt the same uncertainty while trekking through the jungle. He would stop, slowly lower himself down, look carefully around, and listen intently. He had once found tiger tracks and had also come across a huge cobra that had fortunately chosen to slither away rather than strike. But this time, he thought he felt a human presence, like eyes watching their every move. Steve, who was the second man in the column, picked up on Rick's hesitation, and asked what was wrong.

"Probably nothing."

After a moment, Rick disregarded the feeling, owing it to the darkness of the jungle and memories of long ago. It was an ignored instinct he would regret for the rest of his life.

CHAPTER TWENTY-FOUR

The group trudged on. Every few hundred meters, Rick would get that feeling again. Like someone, or something, was watching them. He contemplated turning around and heading back to the safety of Route 9, but this pilgrimage was too important to his best friend, and he could not let Steve down.

Rick was getting tense. The group was making too much noise, talking and joking as they progressed. He had to keep reminding himself that noise discipline was no longer an issue since the war. They were not on a combat patrol. Still, something was off. Rick stopped the march and had everyone take a rest and hydrate. He asked if anyone would like to head back to the bus. After all, they were no spring chickens any longer, and the group still had at least an hour's climb up the hill.

Marines called mountains 'hills.' Every hill had a number correlating to how many meters the peak was above sea level. For example, this hill, Hill 600 was 600 meters high, or 1,968 feet above sea level.

Not one person wanted to turn around. They would all keep going. *That's the problem with Marines,* thought Rick. *They call mountains hills, and they do not quit.* He grinned remembering on a past tour how one veteran's wife had reacted when her husband said, "Let's climb up these rocks. It looks like a good trail."

She had shaken her head and said, "Only a Marine would say a pile of rocks was a trail."

Rick told the group to saddle up and move out. The group did so, among groans and creaking joints. Rick had to smile. The guys were still griping, just like back in the day, but they would not back down from a mission.

Two hours into their trek, they started up the gradual incline that was about to turn steep long before they came atop Hill 600 and the Phou Nhoi battlefield. Again, Rick called a rest break. As the group was sharing snacks and drinking water, Rick heard movement about 30 meters into the now receding jungle. He stood and peered in the direction of the noise. He could see nothing; the vegetation was too thick. The noise did not return, and Rick relaxed a little. He wanted this day over. He wanted to be back at the hotel drinking beer with the guys and swapping remembrances of today's brutal hike. Well, there was only one way to get this day over. And that was to get it over with.

They moved up the mountain at a pace slower than Rick had wanted, but with folks this old he did not want anyone having a stroke or a heart attack. And out here there would be no help. There were no helicopters, no ambulances. Even if there were, rescuers could never get to them in time. That is why Rick had them walk, well, like old folks. At 71-years-old, he was still taking care of his squad. Rick was in great shape, having maintained his rigorous training routine ingrained since his Marine Corps and police academy days. His workouts increased as a bodyguard, mostly from boredom, and he had kept up his strenuous workouts ever since.

At last, they were at the top of the mesa-like mountain. Like many mountaintops in the high western wilderness, Hill 600 was covered in low grasses, and many bomb craters. They had climbed up the northeast side to avoid the steepest terrain, but it was still tough. The rewards, though, were certainly worth the effort. The views were fantastic, the air cool, and the battlefield area virtually untouched.

"What's your first impression, Steve?"

"Well, it feels pretty good to stand upright, walk around, and not get shot at."

"Amen to that, brother."

Still distinguishable were fighting holes, trenches, remnants of claymores, and various destroyed pieces of equipment. There were also dozens of spirits milling about that no one could see.

Rick asked Steve to relate to the rest of the group what had happened at this place back in 1969. Rick could have told the story since they both experienced the same battles here, but he knew the telling would be good for Steve. He wanted his friend to shed all that emotional baggage he had been carrying on his shoulders for more than 50 years.

For 20 minutes, Steve had the group mesmerized with the facts of that two-week operation so long ago. He said he wished his wife, Sharon, had lived long enough to be here with him, but he felt that she was, in some way, standing right next to him. The women were crying, Steve was crying. Everyone else was having trouble controlling their own tears.

Steve stared at the ground for a few minutes without saying a word. Folks thought he was praying, and they remained still and silent. But he was not praying, he was deciding whether to tell the story about the scar on his forehead. All eyes were on him. They waited.

Very slowly, Steve raised his head and took a deep breath, "I've never told anyone this, not even my wife. But a half century after it happened, I am still haunted by it. Maybe haunted is the wrong word. It's more a feeling of shame and self-loathing that I could do something so foul, so repugnant, so wrong.

"It was after the NVA's early morning attack that took place right here, right where we are standing. Rick had already saved my life and had been medevac'd out a few days before. I started my two-hour watch at midnight. At two in the morning, I woke PFC Barrett to take the next watch. And then I slid down into my hole and fell asleep instantly. I was so exhausted, we all were. We had been humping these hills for weeks, doing more with less than any unit should ever be asked to do. Anyway, at about three o'clock, all hell breaks loose. We're taking small arms fire from the south. Everyone's awake now and firing back at the NVA. Suddenly, a Chicom grenade comes flying in and detonates in front of Barrett. It tears apart his face. The NVA retreat down the hill followed by our fire and grenades. A piece of the grenade that hit Barrett had hit me in the forehead."

Steve thought rhetorically, *Why is it we never dig our holes deep enough?*

He continued, "The NVA's probing action was over pretty quick. A couple of guys and the Corpsman carried Barrett inside the perimeter about 50 yards to work on him. I went too because I'm bleeding pretty bad. Head wounds usually do, but all I had was a scratch compared to Barrett. The Corpsman sewed me up with a few sutures and covered my head with a battle dressing. No big deal.

"So after Barrett is stabilized, I'm sitting alone with him. The Corpsman wanted us to stay together, for me to watch him, until the first helicopter arrived at sunup to medevac us out. So Barrett's lying on his side, propped that way with a couple of sandbags so he doesn't drown in his own vomit. Most of his face is gone, he's missing most of his upper teeth, part of his tongue, and his entire lower jaw. He's all wrapped up in gauze and bandages. He was a bloody mess."

Steve stops talking and begins trembling. Collecting himself, he continues, "Anyway, Barrett isn't doing too good. He starts making these sounds. Every once in a while, I think I hear Mom or Mommy, but I'm not sure. Most of the noises he's making seem like the sounds a goat makes. It was inhuman sounds. I try to talk to him to calm him down, but when I do he starts making the goat sounds even louder. It's freaking me out. It's scaring me, these sounds. I'm sitting there in the dark, I can make out his form, and he keeps on making those noises. I can't stand it."

Steve puts his hands over his ears and shuts his eyes. No one is moving. Rick is as spellbound as everyone. Each person in the group is deathly still. After a minute Steve says, "I raised my rifle and aimed it at his head. I wanted him to stop making those noises, or I wanted him dead. The muzzle was just inches from his head. No one would know I did it. It was dark. No one would see where the shot had come from. They would accept that it was a stray NVA round. I felt my finger on the trigger."

Rick could not believe what he was hearing. He was horrified. How could he have misread his best friend all these years. He thought, *You bastard!*

"In the end, don't know why I didn't shoot him. Something stopped me, I don't know what. And I am so thankful for that. But I was going to shoot him. That is my greatest shame. I can't believe I was willing to kill a Marine because of the sounds he was making while so pitifully wounded. I can't blame it on combat fatigue, or temporary insanity, or whatever. I have no excuse for what I almost did. For what I was willing to do to him. For what I needed to do to him."

Rick felt relief wash over him. His best friend was still the man he knew and loved. He then recalled that Sharon had confided in him during one of the yearly reunions, that Steve had tried to commit suicide. It happened after a fun family outing when the children were still young. They had been having a wonderful time up in the Catskills during a vacation. They had visited a petting zoo with the kids. When they entered an enclosure to handfeed the goats, the animals started bleating. Steve froze. He just stood there, rigid, staring straight ahead.

After a while, the children got scared. They didn't understand why their father was doing that. After a few minutes, Sharon coaxed him out of the pen, and they had left the zoo and went back to their rented cottage. Steve never uttered a word. The next day Sharon cut the vacation early because she felt something was terribly wrong. Steve usually drove, but this time he got into the front passenger seat and sat silently for the rest of the ride home. That night, Steve went on the back porch with a strong drink. Sharon went looking for him when he didn't come to bed. She had found him unresponsive on the deck. He had swallowed every pill the veteran hospital doctors had given him. She called an ambulance. They saved his life, but Steve would never tell anyone why he wanted to die that night. Rick now saw the entire scenario fall into place.

"When the helicopter arrived at first light, I helped lift Barrett aboard. But I didn't get on. I took the battle dressing off my head and pulled my helmet down over the wound. We were so low on personnel, and I just couldn't listen to Barrett for even one second more. I don't know if he made it. I'm so ashamed of myself. I'm sorry. Thank you for listening to this horrid old fool."

When Steve was done, long unabashed hugs were freely given. Everyone told him he had nothing to be ashamed of; that he was just a teenager thrust into terrible circumstances; that he had done nothing wrong; and that he had somehow found the strength to do the right thing.

Steve started feeling a little better. He wondered why he had been unable to talk about this for so long. He thought maybe he could now think of Barrett without wanting to kill himself. He decided that once he gets home, he will try to find out what happened to PFC Barrett after that terrible day, and to try to find him if he was still alive, or at least to visit the Marine's grave.

Rick was the last one to hug Steve. "Full circle my brother, full circle."

Steve wiped the tears from his face, drew a deep breath, and nodded.

Rick offered a prayer for the fallen and everyone poured a little water on the ground to refresh the souls who had given their last full measure of devotion at this very place. The Vietnamese guide, Tuan, came forward and handed each person a stick of incense. As he went to each person to light the incense, he explained that the smoke provides purification of the soul, displaces negative energy, and helps the spirits find their way to heaven. As the incense smoke curled toward the sky, the group remained silent, lost in their individual visions and thoughts.

CHAPTER TWENTY-FIVE

After Steve's revelation, they spent about two hours on the hill at Phou Nhoi, first eating the boxed lunches prepared that morning by the hotel staff. They milled around, picking up a few artifacts still there after a half century, and tried to contemplate how this horrible battlefield could have taken so many lives. But then it was time to go.

Rick asked Steve to be the last man out and to make sure there were no stragglers. Rick would lead the group back down the mountain, through the jungle, then the forest, across the streams and brushland, and back to Route 9. It would take over four hours. Rick thought he should pick Steve to be their six, the last man in the column, because Steve was in such great shape. "Are you up to being tail-end-Charlie?"

"Of course, I am. And don't call me Charlie. I'm Superman."

"You're super crazy is what you are."

Even at 73, Steve could probably outlast Rick and anyone else in the group. Steve was a lifetime runner who had competed in several marathons every year since his discharge from the Marine Corps. He did less bodybuilding than Rick, and he still looked like a lean, mean, fighting machine. Minus the mean, of course. He was determined to stay fit and to live to 100.

As they started hiking down, Steve felt transformed, younger, lighter. Somehow, the heaviness of the war had left him. He had understood, intellectually, that the war had been over for many decades, but subconsciously it had always felt like the battle took place an hour ago. Upon arriving at the top of the mountain, Steve was startled that Phou Nhoi was no longer a battlefield. There was no screaming, no automatic weapons fire, and there were no tormented cries from the wounded. It was now just a quiet, peaceful plateau atop a mountain. There was a soft, cool breeze and he could hear birds chirping. *How odd,* he thought, *I feel pretty good.*

There was still a long hike ahead of them and all were anxious to get to the hotel. They were sweaty, dirty, blistered, and tired. They were looking forward to showers, clean clothes, a hot dinner, and a few cold beers, followed by a good night's sleep. Rick had purposely planned a late departure so the group could sleep in before heading out on the next day's movement back to Dong Ha. They followed Rick down the hill.

Halfway down, the vegetation grew evermore thick until at the base of the mountain, they were consumed again by the jungle. As they entered, Rick again told the group to not lose sight of the person in front of them. As before, they would march single file along the dark, narrow trail. He reiterated, "If you lose sight of the man in front of you, call out immediately. We'll stop the column. Don't get lost."

After a while, Rick called a rest stop and checked on everyone. Steve said all were in the groove and no one had dropped back. When everyone had water and a snack, they were up and moving again. After another hour's trek, the jungle was searing hot. Folks were getting fatigued, and another rest was called. The last segment would be a little easier. Rick gave the group a pep talk, well, more of a drill instructor speech motivating the troops. Secretly, he decided to make it a slow walk rather than try to keep everyone at a crisp stride. It would probably take an hour and a half at that pace, but that was fine – they were in no rush. The call to move out was once again met with good-natured moaning and groaning, and a creaking and popping of old joints. He checked with Steve, "You still OK with walking tail-end-Charlie?"

"Good to go, El Capitano."

"Wise ass."

CHAPTER TWENTY-SIX

The last rest stop was called after another hour's hike. They had just come out of the jungle and were in the forested area. The group was 30 minutes and an easy walk away from Route 9 where the motorcoach would be waiting to take them to the hotel and to comfort. Rick started checking on everyone, making sure they were in good spirits and had enough water for the final push to the bus. All were good.

But Steve was missing.

Maybe he hung back to take a leak, Rick thought. He asked if anyone had seen him. No one had. Most had been looking down at the ground, putting one foot in front of the other, following the guy in front of them for the past hour. Rick started back up the trail for ten minutes looking for Steve. He called out, louder each time.

Nothing.

He stood there and listened intently. He was always amazed at how the jungle swallowed all sound when it wanted to. Sometimes the jungle was a shrieking loud cacophony of sound, but like now, the silence could hurt your ears. It made you think you were deaf. Sometimes it amplified a man's heartbeat. That was what was happening just then. Rick could not hear a thing, because the pounding of his heart was thunderous.

He called out loudly, "Steve!" and the racket of his heartbeat disappeared.

Nothing but quiet.

Rick ran back to the group and got them up. "Mr. Tuan, I need you to lead the group out to the bus and to take them to the hotel for the evening's dinner, and to get them settled in. I'll call on my cellphone when I find Steve and have you send the bus back to retrieve the two of us."

To put the now alarmed group at ease, Rick joked, "Dang that Steve. He probably found a mama-san and decided to shack up with her."

But the group was not buying it and they wanted to help search for Steve.

He told them he needed them to get back to the hotel, "Look, I can move much faster without you. It will be dark soon and I don't want anyone else getting lost. Then I'd have two, three, or more of you to find."

And that was that. Rick accepted extra water and good wishes from the guys. He turned and headed back up the trail at a near run.

CHAPTER TWENTY-SEVEN

Rick double-timed it for a half hour, stopping every 30 meters or so to call out Steve's name. He realized he was past where he last saw Steve during the second rest stop. He turned and started walking back down the trail, looking for anything dropped, or brush broken at the trail sides. He kept calling out. It was now 4:30, and although the sun would not set until about 6:30, it was already getting darker in the jungle. Rick pulled his old police whistle from his pack, deciding the sound would carry farther than his voice. He also pulled out his flashlight. Every ten steps Rick blew the whistle and then listened. Nothing. He became frantic, saying out loud, "I can't lose my best friend out here, I just can't! God! Help me! Please!"

He kept praying between each sounding of the whistle and each calling of Steve's name. He was becoming unnerved.

He got back to the forest, turned around and headed back up the jungle trail, calling, praying, listening, and blowing the whistle over and over. When Rick got back to the group's second rest stop area, it was nighttime in the jungle. He sat on the ground contemplating what he should do. He pulled out his phone, but there were no bars. A call would not go through. He felt useless, impotent. He had led so many tours through more dangerous terrain than this, yet he could think of nothing. He felt like crying. "Damn!" again, talking out loud, "You're a United States Marine! Do something! Make a plan, execute it, and find your friend."

Rick got up and began yet again his ritual of calling, praying, and sounding the whistle. When he came out of the jungle once more, he had two bars on his phone. He called Tuan. The group was having dinner, the main topic of conversation was Steve's disappearance. Tuan insisted on sending the bus and that

Rick come to the hotel. Rick, of course, would have nothing to do with that idea. He said that he would meet the bus on Route 9 and to have the driver bring him food, water, a flashlight, insect repellent, and a blanket.

"Mr. Rick, jungle is dangerous at daytime, but very dangerous at dark time. Many snakes live in jungle. They hunt at night. You no see them. Also, wild boar out there. They always angry. May attack you. Maybe more than one tiger. Maybe they smell you. Very dangerous, Mr. Rick. I send bus, you come back to hotel."

"Hell, Tuan, we had all that during the war, as well as the NVA and Viet Cong. The way I see it, I'm way ahead staying right here in the jungle. Besides, my friend is out here alone. There's no way I'm spending the night in a comfy hotel bed. Please, just bring me the supplies. I'll be at the trailhead in an hour."

While walking to meet the bus, he started thinking about what Tuan had said about the snakes. Rick hated snakes back in the old days. Hell, he still did. On one of his earliest patrols, his squad had exited a break in the concertina wire and patrolled a 90-degree arc from west to south five or six kilometers, about three or four miles, from the base. The patrol was pretty much uneventful. They found a few enemy fighting holes, but not much else.

They had to ford a river a few hours into the patrol. The water was deep and fast moving. The Marines formed a skirmish line along the bank to protect the point element as they crossed. The point reached the far bank and took up positions as the first fire team started to cross. Rick was in the next group. Halfway across the water was up to their necks. As Rick reached the deepest part, he was having difficulty balancing due to the swiftly running water and the unevenness of the bottom. Plus, he had his M-16, his .45, his bandoleer, and his PRC-25 radio handset and extra battery held over his head, about 35 pounds. He concentrated on the horizontal surface of the water, which was up to his chin, to equilibrate. Off to Rick's right he caught sight of a snake approaching fast. He believed the horrid thing would seek his head as refuge from the current. But the huge black snake swam past, its 12-foot length just in front of his eyes. Although Rick didn't care too much for the NVA, he feared serpents, especially massive ones that come close enough for him to kiss. He froze. In his terrified state, it took what seemed like hours for this creature's full length to pass him. Finally, it was gone. And although Rick figured the snake would not swim back to him against the current, he wasn't going to wait around and find out. And since there is more than one snake in Vietnam, Rick made it to the opposite bank in record time. It was a good thing this event took place in the water. It cleaned his trousers.

He had another incident in a river weeks later. This one was just chest deep. It was a brutally hot day and crossing the cool, murky river was a welcomed task. As Rick reached the deepest area, he felt something big move across his thighs. It felt huge and lethargic, like a manatee, but there are no manatees in Vietnam. It might have been a shark, but there are no sharks in rivers. Or are there? It may have been a python, or it could have just been a piece of canvas. Or perhaps a dead body. Regardless, it was entirely unnerving. Rick didn't much like Vietnam rivers after that.

In the war, he had told his troops: *'There are a hundred species of snakes in Vietnam; 99 are venomous and the other one will crush you to death.'* From his later research, Rick discovered that there are 140 species of snake in Vietnam, 30 of which are venomous. There are several species of cobras, including the King Cobra which can grow over 18'. Then there's the krait which is ill-tempered and aggressive. Its venom kills over 50% of folks it bites, even with anti-venom treatments. But the snakes he feared most were the highly-venomous red-tailed, green tree vipers that hang out in trees and bushes of the same color. They literally *hung out,* and it was nearly impossible to see them until you were eyeball-to-eyeball with them. Hence, bites were usually to a man's face, neck, or arms. Each year, 30,000 Vietnamese are bitten by snakes. Most of the snakes are nocturnal, so you can't see them at all. Then Rick remembered, there is one snake that will crush you to death – the Burmese Python – which can grow to nearly 20-feet long and can weigh up to 350 pounds. They have been known to kill humans in Vietnam. They don't actually crush you. They squeeze you so that each time you breathe out, they tighten around you a little more until you cannot expand your chest to breathe in. Then there's the dreaded *Two-Stepper.* If it bit you, you took two steps and you were dead. It was a black and white banded krait. The quickness of death may not have been true, but it gave Rick and his Marines a healthy respect for this horrid creature.

When the bus pulled up at the trailhead, the driver unloaded all that Rick had asked for, plus a first aid kit and two extra flashlights. He thanked the driver, bid him goodnight, and headed back up the trail, following the same pattern. Still no response of any kind. Rick stopped at the halfway point between the second and third rest stop areas. Every three minutes for an hour he sounded the whistle and listened. Silence. After snacking on three of the spring rolls packed by Tuan, Rick began his all-night ritual of patrols up and down the trail. Calling, blowing the whistle, listening, and praying.

Come on, Steve, prove to me you're really Superman! Hang on until I can get to you. Please, buddy.

CHAPTER TWENTY-EIGHT

By six o'clock, first light started to illuminate the jungle. This was good, because two of the three flashlights were out of power and the third was on its way out. Rick made his way to Route 9 to report in with Tuan, who had already alerted the authorities to form a search party. According to an army headquarters in Cam Lo town, local police would join up with soldiers from a work detail. They should all be at the launch point by ten this morning. Rick was grateful he could trust Tuan. Tuan had proved himself a good man and he could be depended on in stressful situations. That was why Rick hired Tuan to help on nearly every tour he brought from the States.

While waiting for the search team, Rick made another roundtrip hunting for Steve. When he got back to Route 9, Tuan was waiting there with the group.

An officer in a green army jeep and ten Vietnamese soldiers in a large, military truck arrived from an army unit occupying the former Vandergrift Combat Base left over from the American war. They were well armed. Their leader, Lieutenant Minh, told Tuan and Rick that they were happy to be doing something different than the usual drudgery of peacetime work details and army training. Rick was glad they were enthusiastic about the search, but he wondered what the weapons were for. *Tigers?*

A single police officer, Captain Trong, showed up with none of his men. He seemed disinterested in the search. He told Tuan to call him if he needed anything and left almost as soon as he arrived. Tuan disliked Trong. He knew Trong was corrupt beyond all reason, and he terrorized his command area in the Huong Hoa District. If a citizen complained, he wound up missing

98

or in jail on some false charges. Or Trong would devise some way to hurt the person's family.

Rick said, "Mr. Tuan, I need you to watch over the group tonight and to take them back to Highway One and Dong Ha for an overnight."

A few of the guys protested, "Rick, we have all day. Let us help with the search."

"Thanks guys, but we are due to fly home in two days, and we still have to make our way back to Da Nang the next day. Hopefully, Steve and I will catch up with you later tonight in Dong Ha. But if we can't, Tuan will make sure all goes good for your transfer back to the States."

Reluctantly, the group boarded the bus and pulled away.

Rick and Lt. Minh, who spoke broken English, decided that they would move up the trail as Rick had been doing. Minh wasted no more time with chit-chat and started down the trail. When they had passed through the forest and met the jungle, Minh studied the terrain and ordered his soldiers to flank both sides of the trail about 20 to 40 meters out as the jungle allowed, five soldiers per side.

The teams moved to their positions. The going was slow because the flanking soldiers had to cut through thick vegetation in some places. All the searchers were yelling Steve's name, and by doing so, the teams could also stay abreast of each other.

As they neared the original second rest stop area, soldiers on the right flank, about 40 meters out, shouted that they had found something. As the teams gathered to the west of the trail, they found themselves in a muddy area. In the mud there appeared to be two parallel grooves and a set of footprints on either side. The 12 men decided to follow the marks. After 150 meters, about 165 yards, they found one of Steve's hiking shoes. Rick came to the horrifying realization that two people must have been dragging his unconscious friend, and that one of Steve's shoes had fallen off.

CHAPTER TWENTY-NINE

Lt. Minh came to the same conclusion and barked orders at his soldiers. They immediately unslung their rifles. They started following the tracks at a trot. Rick did not understand why the troops were now rifle-ready, but he did not care. They were onto his friend's trail and hopefully, would soon run down the culprits. After all, how far could they get dragging a man. In another half-hour, the terrain headed downhill. Then, after another hour and fifteen minutes of running, they came to a wide river. Rick looked up and down the waterway and saw a shoal where he figured they could get to the other side. He pointed to the place, "Lt. Minh, we can get across the river over there. Let's move."

Minh blocked him, "No. Other side Laos. We stop here. Sepon River. No can go Laos."

"I'm going."

Minh held him back, "No! No go Laos! Bad men kill you. You go embassy Hanoi. You tell all. They help friend."

"The embassy? That will take time. Your men are armed. You are armed. Let's go across and at least try to find them for a few hours."

"No. I am sorry. We not allowed go Laos. It is forbidden. Government say no. I cannot put my men to this duty. I am sad for your friend."

"How about this . . . let me have a rifle and some ammo. Wait here for me. I'll be back in two or three hours. I just want to look around."

"I cannot give you army weapon. It is not allowed. I will be stripped of my rank, and they put me in jail. My family will suffer for it. No. You no go Laos. You go embassy quick."

Rick was torn. His mind was reeling. *Should I enter Laos to search for Steve? I have no contacts, no Laotian money, and I can't speak the language. Should I be the hero, attempting the impossible, and end up dead for it? At that point I would be no good to anyone, especially Steve. I need time to think. I need to work out a plan.*

Rick realized Minh was right. It would be stupid to charge into Laos, alone. Steve may be hurt, but he was alive. After all, there was no sense in abducting a dead man. His friend had been dragged away into Laos for some unknown reason and he is better alive, than dead, to his captors. There was time to plan, to act, to rescue his friend. He would start with the embassy in Hanoi, as the lieutenant had suggested.

CHAPTER THIRTY

Lt. Minh gave Rick a ride to Dong Ha in the jeep. He was upset that they could not help this American find his friend. Minh tried to explain, "Renegades do bad things. We try to kill, but they clever. Sometimes we kill. Sometimes they run back Laos. Never stop. Vietnam seem peace, but not good thing happen always. I fight here three years. People think training. People think peace. But no peace."

"I had no idea, Lt. Minh."

"Please forgive me, Mr. Rick. I have said too much already. I do not mean to burden you with this shame on my country."

"It is no shame, Lt. Minh. I am sure you have heard of the unrest in my country, as well. It is something that makes our police and our armies always alert and diligent. If they were not, our countries would perish. And please know that your words and your honesty are safe with me."

"Thank you, Mr. Rick. It is strange that I talk with you, an American Marine who fought against my grandfather."

"Your grandfather was NVA?"

"No, he was Viet Cong. My grandfather wanted a united Vietnam, North and South together. He wanted self-determination like other countries enjoy. He thought after French go home that Vietnam would be together, happy. But they divide my country. Ho Chi Minh in North was communist and people not happy. Little food. Ngo Dinh Diem in South bad man, but people happier, much food. My grandfather chose communist because they promise to take land from rich and give to poor so everyone same. Sound happy and peace.

"But was not to be. Long war with America. When Americans say goodbye in 1973, South keep fighting. But soon America stop sending supplies to South. In 1975 communists conquer South army, country united. My grandfather very happy. But then Viet Cong pushed aside by NVA. Only few corrupt Viet Cong allowed in government, allowed to help in decisions. When good VC complain, make trouble, they taken away, never see again. Many South people escape communists. Go to sea and drown, some get to freedom. They lucky ones. All South soldiers go to reeducation camps. Many die. All tortured. I think camps make South army people angry, just not say."

"I'm sorry, Lt. Minh, the people of Vietnam deserve much better treatment."

"Sometimes I wish Americans stayed. Help make democracy. Stop communists from taking away freedom. Viet Cong not really commie, more like you say, nationalist. But communist our life now. Commies never go away. We must work around what they do. Most Viets not commies. Most Viets want to go to U.S. or Australia. Have better life than this."

At the hotel Rick thanked Minh and tried to give him $100, but the lieutenant waved it away. "But Lt. Minh, I am grateful for your help today and for the help of your men. Perhaps you can buy them dinner and drinks on me."

"No. We no find friend. We no deserve." Minh bowed, turned, and left. Rick understood that this Vietnamese lieutenant was an honorable, but intellectually troubled man. Rick felt Minh's frustration and he understood the futility of his grandfather's betrayed intentions.

Then he thought of the cop, Captain Trong, who had decided it wasn't worth his time to help in the search. Rick considered him a lazy, corrupt bastard. He had a sixth sense about crooked law enforcement officers.

Rick recalled a couple of corrupt cops on the NYPD. He couldn't do anything directly about them because, at the time, they were his superiors. But a few well-placed, anonymous phone calls to Internal Affairs and to the mayor's office had the corrupt officers investigated, charged, and fired. Rick never felt like a rat for doing it. Those slime balls needed to be exposed for the dirt they were, and for how they made good, clean cops seem bad in the eyes of the public. Rick had gone to bat for many officers who made honest mistakes with no malintent. He took care of his troops, even as a cop.

Rick watched Minh leave. He then entered the hotel and met up with the group. He told them what had transpired during the search for Steve. The loss had placed a dark shadow over the group. They would return home with one man missing. Marines do not do that. Although exceedingly painful, it was out of their hands. The tour, which had started off apprehensive, but had soon changed to a delightful, fun-filled adventure, was now a trip tarnished with sadness and uncertainty.

CHAPTER THIRTY-ONE

Captain Trong had a reason for abandoning the search before it began. As on most days, part of Trong's responsibility was to curtail smuggling coming across the border from Laos. He never really curtailed it, he managed it. Today was a day that had demanded his attention. Through one of his many informants, he heard there was a sizable transfer of illegal cigarettes coming through a Route 9 northside jungle trail. He was determined to stop it. Trong was a chain-smoker and this interdiction excited him. He was determined to steal most of it.

Trong stationed his police along the smuggling trails that run parallel to Route 9. The smugglers were mostly poor, uneducated Laotians who did the legwork, referred to as *buffalos* because they did the heavy carrying, for a more-organized crime syndicate.

Once inside Vietnam, the buffalos would cut through the many jungle trails to Route 9. At predesignated transfer sites, they would meet their Vietnamese counterparts who would pay the smugglers and ride off with the contraband. The buffalos would then return to Laos for another load. This was mostly done at night, even though the jungle at night was disorienting and dangerous. But daytime had its own dangers for smugglers, mostly Trong and his band of thugs. Trong, well aware of the nighttime jungle perils, operated only during sunlight hours. Whatever got through at night held no interest. The daytime belonged to him.

Trong has his goons stop the smugglers wherever they could find them. They would generally take half the contraband, no matter what it was, as Trong's fee for passage without arrest. Trong had a small warehouse full of medicines, toys, rice cookers, cigarettes, and on occasion, drugs. He has his men sell it on the black market.

Usually, Trong's minions do the dirty work for him. But when Trong accompanies them to the smuggling trails, not only does he exact his 'fee,' but he abuses the smugglers physically. He enjoys hurting people. Today was his day to have his fun, and he would not be denied.

Trong had always played both ends to his own benefit. It was Trong who had accepted bribe money for alerting the Laotian renegades that a tour of old Americans would be walking into Phou Nhoi. And that they might be easy pickings to kidnap one or two of them.

Trong could not care less who got hurt.

CHAPTER THIRTY-TWO

The day Steve was abducted, he had stopped to get a stone out of his hiking shoe. He untied it, removed the shoe, and shook out the stone. He slipped the shoe back on but did not get the chance to lace it. He felt something hard bump against the side of his head. He turned and looked directly into the muzzle of an AK-47 assault rifle that was pointed just inches from his face. He slowly stood. At the same time, the Laotian renegade's buddy held a finger to his lips conveying that silence would keep him alive. As Steve showed defiance on his face and clenched his fists, he was hit on the back of his head with something solid.

He woke up the next morning in the back of an old van. He was missing a shoe. His head ached badly, and his vision was blurry. He had one wrist handcuffed to a steel ring on the bulkhead. There was also an ungodly stink in the van. Steve had no idea where he was, but he was terribly thirsty and had to pee something awful.

Pounding on the side of the van caused the side doors to open and the two Laotians shouted what Steve assumed to be *shut up*, because one was again pointing the rifle at his face. Steve pointed to his crotch and held his stomach. The Laotians grasped the meaning and one of them climbed in and removed the handcuff from his wrist. He grabbed Steve's face hard and made a slashing motion across his neck. Steve knew that meant if he tried to escape, they would kill him. Steve nodded and they pulled him from the van. He saw that he was still in the jungle and on a very poor dirt road, but he could not make out any of the surroundings.

After relieving himself, Steve was forced back into the van and his wrist was re-cuffed to the ring. They threw in a bottle of water and closed the doors. Steve drank the water greedily, but quickly realized he had better conserve half just in case no more would come. Lessons from the war do not easily die.

Soon they were on the move. There were no windows in the enclosed cargo area of the van, so Steve had no idea where they were going. *And what the heck was that awful smell?*

CHAPTER THIRTY-THREE

Rick could not sleep. Lying in bed, he stared at the ceiling in his hotel room trying to formulate a plan. First thing in the morning, he would call the American Embassy and file a report about the missing American. And he would not go home with the group. He would see the group off from the Da Nang International Airport, make sure they safely got to their gate, and then he would fly to Hanoi to provide an in-person oral and written account of the abduction and his subsequent actions. After that he had no clue of what to do next.

Rick got up. Trying to sleep was futile. *Was Steve sleeping? How badly was he hurt? He must be frightened and not understanding why this has happened to him. He is alone. Were they torturing him? Damn, I can't stand it. I need a drink.*

He left his room and went to the rooftop bar. The only one there was the bartender. Rick ordered a double whiskey. He sat at a table in the dark and stared out to the west. Somewhere, 40 or 50 miles away, his best friend was suffering.

Before he finished his drink Tuan was standing next to him with two beers. "Here Mr. Rick, have beer. Whiskey make brain stupid. Beer make you smart. Make Bud wiser."

Rick smiled, "That's an old joke, Mr. Tuan."

"Maybe. But funny. It make smart man name of Bud. Like Budweiser. Ha! I get that from American joke book. Some jokes I not understand. But that one I think is good one. That because I smart. I drink lots of beer. Like Bud. Get it?"

"Mr. Tuan, you're in the wrong business. You should have been a stand-up comic."

"I think so, yes."

They sat quietly for the next few minutes. Then Tuan broke the silence, but spoke barely above a whisper, "Mr. Rick, I know why you here alone in bar instead of go to bed. You worry about Steve. Embassy help you maybe. But you no worry if embassy not help. You have me for Viet friend. I know many people. Never mind. You give me many profit for many years work with you. You ask me to help, I help."

"Mr. Tuan, you earned every penny. Besides, it's business. A man works, a man gets paid. I hire you every time because you are really good at your job."

"Thank you for nice words, Mr. Rick. But in my country, very few people make good benefit by work. You help my family live good life. I am bad at planting rice."

CHAPTER THIRTY-FOUR

The large knot on the back of Steve's head throbbed. He could not lie down on the van's floor because the ring his handcuff was attached to was too high. The best he could do was to sit upright on the steel deck. Sometimes he would stand, bent, near the low roof to try to get sensation back into his handcuffed arm. Blood trickled slowly from where the metal cuff had chafed through his skin. It was very hot inside the cargo area. It had no insulation to stop the baking heat of the roof. He wished he could pour water over his head to cool off. But water, he knew, meant survival.

And that dreadful smell persisted. Steve had smelled many horrible odors during the war. Just by recalling, he could smell burned flesh, decomposing bodies, raw diesel fumes, and spent gunpowder. It was like those odors had attached themselves permanently to his nostrils. But this smell was worse. He had no way of knowing, but the stench emanated from an unseen demon, not more than 18-inches tall, that sat in a corner of the van, waiting, watching Steve's every move.

He wondered what had happened to Rick and the other tour group members. *Had they met with a similar fate? If so, would they be reunited at some holding area? Would they be rescued soon?* He knew he could not just wait to be freed, he had to think of a way to save himself, and then he could go to the aid of the others.

Steve listened to his abductors talking on the other side of the thin bulkhead. Although he knew some Vietnamese words and phrases, he could not understand the Laotian language at all. His captors seemed quite pleased with themselves as they talked excitedly.

We are heroes, Analu. And it was so easy. These Americans are weak and care only for their own pitiful lives. I will

112

be surprised if Kelii does not give us promotions and more responsibility. I have dreamed for so long of being recognized as a strong and resourceful leader.

This is true, Pekelo. We shall be remembered on this day forever. I think maybe you should be the leader and Kelii should take orders from you. Now let us move this hostage to headquarters for the others to see.

CHAPTER THIRTY-FIVE

Rick sat in a windowless room at the American Embassy in Hanoi. It contained just a large conference table and twelve chairs. The FBI special agent questioned Rick on the events that had taken place three days ago in Phou Nhoi. Also in the room were the Defense Attaché and two people in suits who never introduced themselves and who said nothing. The group seemed extremely interested in every word Rick had to say and they took copious notes, as well as recorded everything.

After two hours the FBI agent and embassy personnel left to confer with themselves. A Vietnamese aide came in and presented Rick with a lunch of iced tea, spring rolls, fresh salad, Vietnamese soup (better known as pho), grilled mackerel, potatoes, and a hot vegetable medley, followed by ice cream and fresh fruits. The prior interview and this great meal put Rick in a good mood. He believed the embassy was sure to get Steve freed, and Rick would be able to fly home with his friend.

The FBI agent came back into the room as Rick was starting in on his ice cream. "Mr. Carrofermo, we have to assume that it was Laotian renegades who abducted Mr. Picante for a reason. Therefore, the renegades will most likely keep him alive. It is our belief that the renegades will soon surface and make their demands known. They may surface soon, or it may take several weeks before they get the courage to show their hand. . In the meantime, you should return to the States and look after your tour business. I'm sure other veterans are looking forward to visiting Vietnam. The embassy will contact you as soon as something breaks."

"Let me ask this, do you have spies and agents on the ground in Laos who could shed some light on renegade activities? Or could they perhaps rescue Steve before demands are made?"

"I can neither confirm nor deny the presence of operatives anywhere within Laos. I'm sure you understand the sensitive nature of this topic. Just rest assured that the embassy and the United States government will be doing all it can to return your friend to safety."

The agent looked at his watch and got up to go, "Go ahead and finish your ice cream before you leave. Good day, Mr. Carrofermo. We'll be in touch."

That last statement, *'we'll be in touch,'* left Rick with a cold feeling. The delicious food turned sour in his stomach, realizing he had been dismissed. His good mood turned foul.

Rick decided to give them one month. If nothing came from the embassy, Rick would devise and launch his own plan.

CHAPTER THIRTY-SIX

Fools! screamed Kelii, *you will bring destruction to us!*

But chief, the government will give us what we want for the return of the American.

No! If they know we have this hostage, they will hunt us down like dogs. So far they have tolerated us, Pekelo, because we are not making trouble. We are not yet ready to attack, we are not yet strong. Who else knows what you have done?

No one, Kelii. We came straight here, and no one followed. It took us six hours of travel.

You listen to me Pekelo and Analu, you will return this man to where you took him. You will let him go. And after you do, you will not return here. You have acted on your own without orders and have behaved irrationally. You two are no longer with us. Be gone now, before I kill you both myself!

Pekelo and Analu started the van and drove off with their prisoner. Instead of heading northeast back toward the crossing point near Phou Nhoi, they turned south.

Pekelo, where are you going?

We will not release our hostage. We risked our lives to capture him. We can use him for our own purposes. Kelii is a weak leader, and a poor thinker. He is afraid of his own shadow. You and me, Analu. We will start our own army and we will win all. But first we need to get far away from the government authorities, and then we will begin our ascendency to power.

But you heard what Kelii said. We must take the American back to where we captured him.

Damn Kelii to the fire realm! It was not so long ago that the Vietnamese forced their war into our country. Laos was neutral. It wasn't our fight. But they enslaved my father and my brothers and many of our neighbors to build their war roads through the Laotian jungles. Thousands of kilometers of roads through our jungles, Analu! Thousands of kilometers of new roads where none existed before, with constant repairs and rerouting due to bombing, mudslides, and floods. It was never-ending. The Americans destroyed many villages and killed many Lao people with their incessant shelling and bombing of the trails. I was just a baby then. After the war, my father and my brothers never came home. When my mother died of a broken heart, I was only ten-years old. I hate the Viets for bringing their war here, and I hate the Americans for hating the Viets.

But where will we go, Pekelo? I'm afraid.

South, Analu. We go south. Across the Cambodia border where we will set up our base and begin our glorious purpose. Do not be afraid, my friend. With you by my side, we will take our rightful place in Laotian history. I promise you.

CHAPTER THIRTY-SEVEN

Four days later, Rick was back in his home office in New York. He was hopeful the FBI would call and tell him that they got Steve out and he was on his way back to the States. But Rick was not sitting on his hands waiting. He studied his maps and started to develop a contingency plan, a plan to search for and to rescue his best friend.

The tour group, less Rick and Steve, had been home for more than a week and were sorting out their photographs and telling relatives about their adventures. In the back of their minds, they were hoping for a phone call telling them that Steve had been found and all was okay. A few called Rick to inquire, and Rick had told them that the embassy was on top of it and that he expected a resolution at any moment. But Rick had a bitter feeling that his words were nothing more than self-deception. *The embassy isn't going to do a damn thing, except maybe FAX a few inquiries.*

Rick sat at his desk brooding. He kept rolling events over and over in his head. The FBI was right about a couple of things. One, Steve had been abducted for a purpose; and two, the abductors had to keep him alive to achieve that purpose. Rick tried to think like a Laotian renegade, *OK, I abducted an American and dragged him to my sanctuary in Laos where I knew the Vietnamese Army would not follow. I would also know that the heat would soon be on in Laos because of pressure from the American government, which supplies financial aid to my country. If the Laotian authorities were looking for me in Laos, and the Vietnamese were no longer looking for me in Vietnam because I went into Laos, then my safest place would be back in Vietnam. I would recross the border with my hostage into*

Vietnam, into familiar territory at Phou Nhoi, and wait it out. When the time is right, I will make my demands.

Rick thought back to his conversation with Lt. Minh on the ride from Phou Nhoi to Dong Ha. Minh had said, *"Renegades do bad things. We try to kill, but they clever. Sometimes we kill. Sometimes they run back Laos. Never stop. Vietnam seem peace, but not good thing happen always. I fight here three years. People think training. People think peace. But no peace."*

On a few of the tours, Rick's groups had been turned away from various remote areas, because the Vietnamese army was on *'training maneuvers'* using live ammunition. At the time, Rick had no reason to disbelieve them. Now he shivered, realizing the truth of the situation. They were not training. They were hunting Laotian renegades.

Rick began working methodically. He had to figure out a plan to rescue Steve.

CHAPTER THIRTY-EIGHT

Steve's eyes had finally cleared of their blurriness. His head still hurt from where he was knocked unconscious, but at least it was now tolerable. The van kept moving, but every once in a while it would stop, and he was allowed to relieve himself and was given more water and occasionally a few bananas or a dragon fruit. He wondered how many days it had been. Two? Five? A week? He could not tell. He had no idea how long he was unconscious or how long they had been traveling. But his mind was becoming sharper. He was hungry and he knew that his strength would begin to wane if he did not get decent food. If he were to escape it had to be soon, or he would be too weak to do so. He wondered why no one was coming to help him.

He thought back to the E & E, Evasion and Escape training, he received in the Corps. They had taught him that the best time to escape is before his captors reached the prison camp; that he needed to put as much distance between him and his captors as quickly as possible if he did escape. Then he would need to make a plan on how to reach friendly lines. He would have to survive on his own while making his way. The Marine instructors taught him how to evade detection and recapture, how to make simple tools and weapons, how to identify and to catch food, especially easy to catch creatures like grubs, grasshoppers, and snails, and how to make shelter. They also taught him how to make fire with no matches. Steve often wondered why anyone would want to make a fire, with its telltale smoke, while hiding from the enemy. He remembered that the Code of Conduct set down six rules of resisting. Article III was:

'If I am captured, I will continue to resist by all means available. I will make every effort to escape and aid others to escape.'

Steve knew that a prison camp was an extension of the battlefield. He may not be in a war, but he needed to make use of what he had been taught.

Besides escape, hunger and thirst were the first things on his mind. When he escaped, he was ready to eat grubs, worms, and termites just to get some protein in him. Water in the jungle would come easier than food. But he had to remember that in the jungle, he could just as easily become food for the creatures upon whose home he had trespassed.

From microbes to plant life to insects to fish to fowl to mammals to reptiles, everything was something else's food.

CHAPTER THIRTY-NINE

Two weeks of waiting passed. No contact came from the FBI or the embassy despite repeated requests. Rick could not sleep. His anxiety was getting the best of him. He had to keep reminding himself to calm down, that freaking out would do nothing to help his friend.

Finally, in the third week, he received a communication via email. It was not from the embassy or the FBI. It was from the Consulate office in Ho Chi Minh City, the former Saigon:

UNITED STATES OF AMERICA
U.S. CONSULATE
HO CHI MINH CITY, VIETNAM

TO: Mr. Richard Carrofermo
FROM: Department of Defense Attaché'
RE: Disappearance of Mr. Steven Picante, a U.S. citizen

Dear Mr. Carrofermo,

We regret to inform you that we have no further information on the disappearance of Mr. Steven Picante while he was in the jungle environment of Phou Nhoi, Huong Hoa District, Quang Tri Province, Vietnam, on one of your tours.

We have informed Mr. Picante's next of kin, namely his two children, that since there has been no new intelligence proving that Mr. Picante is alive, he has been listed as presumed dead. If any new information develops in this case, we will be in contact with Mr. Picante's children.

Mr. Carrofermo, since you are not a blood relative of Mr. Picante, we must inform you that DOD privacy policies prohibit American authorities in Vietnam from providing any further information to you. Therefore, and in compliance with this policy, you are directed to cease all communication with embassy personnel in reference to the above so-stated matter. If we need any further information from you regarding Mr. Picante, we will make first contact.

Thank you for your interest in the Office of the U.S. Consulate.

Sincerely,
                    . . . for the U.S. Ambassador to Vietnam

Rick felt like killing those sons-a-bitches. *Steve was an American, for God's sake. How the hell could they just write off another countryman, especially a Vietnam veteran? Steve is alive. He has to be.*

•

CHAPTER FORTY

Rick had heard of several American veterans who had returned to Vietnam and had died there. One had jumped off a bridge, committing suicide. One had a stroke and died on the floor of his locked hotel room. One had died from dehydration and improper care by a village doctor. Another had drowned on a local scuba diving expedition out to the Cham Islands. Thankfully, none of those deaths occurred on Rick's watch. And although all were tragic, Rick could not help but feel like the deaths may have been preordained and he felt a little jealous at their passing. He truly believed he should have died in the war over 50 years ago. So many of his friends, better men than him, he believed, had taken his place. For his entire after-war life, he had felt guilt for having survived. He knew the guys who died would not want him to feel bad. They would want him to have a good life, to live the life denied to them, and to do the things they never got to do. Rick tried hard to live up to that ideal, but sometimes it was just so damn hard.

Rick would not accept that his friend Steve was dead. *Steve is freakin' Superman, for God's sake. And he has value to his abductors.*

Rick knew what he had to do next. He would contact Tuan, who he suspected had more important contacts than with just restaurant and hotel owners. Tuan, he believed, had more up his sleeve than just assisting in tours for foreigners. Rick could see it in his eyes. At times, when local authorities would object to Rick's tour group entering certain areas, a hard look and a few choice words from Tuan would change the objector into a smiling, cooperative individual. The man was tough and knew how to run interference.

Rick made the overseas call.

Tuan was receptive to Rick's plan, maybe because he felt some responsibility in the disappearance of Steve on his watch, or because Rick had offered him a small fortune to elicit his help. Or maybe it was a combination of both. Rick did not care which, he knew Tuan was the man for the job.

Rick cashed in his substantial savings along with some stock certificates. He had $60,000 cash in his pockets, and he did not care if he had to spend it all to get his friend back. He could get even more money if he had to.

Rick booked his flights. At the same time, Tuan made the in-country logistical arrangements to get them back to Phou Nhoi. When Rick asked who they would be working with, Tuan merely replied, "You find out soon. Never mind."

Rick realized then that something special, and formidable, was in the works. He believed he could trust Tuan to make the plan succeed.

CHAPTER FORTY-ONE

Rick's big mistake, of course, was that he designed his plans and tactics thinking like the Laotian renegade he himself would be. Unfortunately, the real Laotian renegades were not as smart, nor as savvy in thinking a plan all the way through to its logical conclusion. Instead of returning across the border back into Vietnam, the Laotians fled farther south with their hostage. They evaded detection by venturing deep into the uncharted and dangerous jungles of southern Laos.

* * * *

Pekelo, we are very far from any village. I do not want to get lost in this jungle. Perhaps we should stop and establish our headquarters here?

No Analu, we are not yet out of the reach of the Lao government and its puppet soldiers. When we come to the right place, we will know it. We will grow our own army and take our rightful place, leading Laos into the future.

* * * *

Rick packed a small suitcase. Two pairs of jungle boots, two pairs of rugged cargo pants, several bush shirts, and his Marine Corps boonie hat. He also packed his handheld GPS, his old combat maps, and a bottle of 100% DEET insect repellent. Besides his toiletries, he could get anything else he needed in Vietnam. He always left his bush knife and his machete with Tuan. Tuan would have both resharpened, cleaned, and oiled by Rick's next return. This time, for sure, he would need them more than ever.

Rick had two days before his flight departed. He spent time at the gym, working out harder than he had since his international security job. He also ran his usual route on the pedestrian paths and sidewalks along the Belt Parkway. He would start from the American Veterans Memorial Pier on New York Bay, just down the street from his apartment. He would then run south under the Verrazano Narrows Bridge, and past Fort Hamilton where he had been sworn into the Marine Corps when he first enlisted more than five decades before. He would continue east along Gravesend Bay until the path left the water's edge. From there he ran south on Cropsey Avenue which turned into West 17th Street and through a dicey tenement area of South Brooklyn. West 17th ended at the baseball stadium where he would turn left. Being winded, he would walk the next three blocks to *Nathan's Famous* for a hot dog and an iced tea. He would eat his meal on a boardwalk bench on Coney Island Beach and take a half hour to rest and stare at the water. He would then reverse his route, this time an easy jog, back to the Memorial Pier eight miles away. A little less than a mile north of the Verrazano, the Statue of Liberty would come into view. It was always a motivating sight no matter how tired his run had made him. From there, he always sprinted full-bore to the pier.

He often wondered how his immigrant parents must have felt seeing Miss Liberty's welcoming torch as they steamed into New York Harbor for the first time. But they were gone now, and he felt foolish and impoverished for never having asked them.

CHAPTER FORTY-TWO

During the long flight to Taipei, he kept going over the plan. It was a good, tight blueprint for attack. *Speaking of attack, what will I do when I find Steve's abductors? I may kill them. Or maybe I'll break all their limbs to send a message. Or better yet, drag them to Hanoi and dump them onto the lobby floor at the embassy.* Rick looked around to see if he was talking out loud. *Calm down, Rick. Don't mix fantasy with reality. I'll definitely turn them over to the authorities. Maybe to Lt. Minh. Maybe I should bring them to the hotel and have the FBI fly down and take them into custody. If they want a statement from me, I'll tell them that I can't speak on the issue, because I'm not a blood relative. Mucky-muck schmucks.*

As the wheels touched down at Taipei, Rick shook off his musings and prepared for the transition to a smaller aircraft. Since there was no group with him and therefore no reason to give the Big Speech, he sat and waited the three hours for his final leg to Vietnam. He started brooding again. *If they've hurt my best friend, I will kill them. Screw turning them over to the authorities. If the FBI couldn't find Steve, they'll certainly never find the Laotian renegades, not when I'm done with them. The FBI wouldn't even look. Nor would the Vietnamese, nor would the Laotians. No one would care. Yes, so it's settled. I will kill them and leave them to rot.*

The announcement to board the British Airbus to Vietnam was announced. Again, Rick shook away his daydreaming. He realized this was bad thinking. The mission was to find his friend. He had to maintain focus on the mission. The rest will fall into place on its own.

Rick arrived back in Da Nang almost four weeks to the day that Steve had gone missing. This was an anniversary of sorts and

Rick wanted no more anniversaries to pass without Steve being repatriated. He was frantic to get into Phou Nhoi as quickly as possible. He had to keep reminding himself to calm down. Desperation and inadequate planning before an action could cause mistakes that may destroy his efforts to find his best friend. *Focus*, he kept reminding himself, *focus on the mission like the Marine you are and always will be. Stay strong, stay confident. Focus!*

Through The Gates of Hell

CHAPTER FORTY-THREE

It had been thirty days since Kelii had banished the two hostage takers. The van had run out of gas a few weeks ago. The extra containers of fuel the abductors had the foresight to bring had run dry long before. Steve was glad because it brought an end to shackled travel on the nearly impassable, rutted, and overgrown dirt roads. It also brought a greater opportunity to escape. The bad part was they were now on foot. Walking was only a bit more bearable than riding in the back of the van.

The renegades had given Steve ill-fitting sandals to replace his one hiking shoe. His feet were blistered and bleeding from walking through the hot, wet, god-awful Laotian jungle. His rump was in no better shape. At night they cuffed him around very tall, very thick bamboo stalks. Steve quipped to himself, *Damn, I hate camping. I miss my motorhome.*

The best he could do was to straddle and hug the stalks and try to sleep. His buttocks were raw and bitten by parasitic creatures and was infected by the diseased, rotting muck of the jungle floor. The mosquitoes and insects were unrelenting to the point where Steve no longer felt their bites and their burrowing. He had stopped caring.

The jungle hurts. For all things, especially humans, the jungle forces one to play the ultimate of survival games. It is oppressive. It has a heaviness that sucks the air from one's lungs. It squeezes the life essence from everything. It never allows a creature to relax. Something is always stalking, a mosquito, an earwig, a leech, a tiger, a boar, a giant centipede, a snake, a scorpion, a tarantula, and fire ants. Even diseases are lying in wait. Elephantiasis, encephalitis, filariasis, and all forms of bacterial disease are lurking in the rotting, oozing muck just underneath the crisp, detritus of dead plants. Something is always dying, being eaten, decomposing. Nothing dies from old age. The jungle darkens one's mood. It smells bad. There is no place to rest, to sit, or to lie down without something feasting on or boring into a person. It is a cruel, unsympathetic, painful, and merciless environment.

By day, the one he presumed was subservient, Analu, walked in front. The leader, Pekelo, walked behind with the AK. Steve's hands were freed while walking so he could grab vines and creases in rocks while climbing up and down steep jungle mountains. Considering this, Steve knew the untethered daytime would provide the only chance to escape. It had to be soon. He was weakening quickly.

That night, while Steve was cuffed around a tree, the two Laotians began arguing. He could not understand their language, but he understood the tone.

We have lost our way, Pekelo. And I have lost all reason why we took this man in the first place. Our friends were horrified we had arrived with this hostage. We thought we could use him to get stronger against the government, but we were turned against by our own comrades. We must kill him and be done with it. He has lost all value to us.

No, Analu, we can still take the advantage and make our glorious duty impossible to defeat. He is an asset to our goals, and he will be used to our benefit. If he dies, it is our loss, but why should we purposely destroy an asset and get nothing in return? You must think clearly and deeply.

Look at him. He is sick. He can go on not much longer. He is of no use to us. You must admit we made a mistake. It is better to kill him now, out here where no one comes. We will cut our losses and go on to fight another day. I want to go home, Pekelo.

No, not now. I need time to think. We go on together, you and me and our hostage. I will decide later what to do with him.

131

OK, fine, Pekelo. But I will wait only two days more. Then we kill him if we cannot figure out how to use him to our advantage. Then we go home.

CHAPTER FORTY-FOUR

Always the loyal friend, Tuan was waiting for Rick when he exited the Da Nang airport terminal. He was surprised when they hopped into a derelict Honda taxi. Tuan saw the look on Rick's face and said, "Better to not attract attention. This Chung. He good driver."

"It is a pleasure to meet you, Mr. Chung. Thank you for picking me up."

Tuan translated and Chung smiled and nodded. Rick thought Chung looked like a Chinese, not a Vietnamese.

They were quickly heading north through the new six-kilometer tunnel that had been bored through the Hai Van mountains. A few years earlier the Japanese, as a good-will joint venture, had engineered the massive project. Rick had to admit, it was a much quicker, and safer, route than going over the Pass.

After another two hour's drive they were in Hue, Tuan's hometown. Rick freshened up in his hotel room on the Perfume River, and then settled in. Later that night, he was picked up by Tuan and Chung. Chung dropped them off at a sequestered restaurant on a dark, narrow street in a very poor section in the southern part of the city. There they met with three rough-looking men. Tuan introduced them and explained to Rick that these men would depart in one day, making their way to the western frontier and the town of A Loui. From there, they would head north on Highway 14 toward Khe Sanh Village. Tuan explained further, "You and me go north tomorrow to Dong Ha and meet two more my men. We stay Dong Ha one night. Then we go west Route 9 to Khe Sanh. Two more friends from Lao Bao come, one is Laotian man and other very strong man, his name Tiger. We all meet at Khe Sanh hotel. Laotian man he be translate man when we meet up with Laotian renegades. All spend night in Khe Sanh. They bring much gear. Before dawn, we begin hunting to Phou Nhoi. That seven men good hunters, bring gear for all. You and me make nine men. Each man get $1,000. You bring money?"

"I have enough money for everyone. Plus, more for bribes in case we need it. The rest I want you to take to your home and hide it. I trust only you." Tuan flashed a genuine, appreciative smile and nodded.

As they left the restaurant and stood on the dark sidewalk, waiting for the car to arrive, Rick asked, "Mr. Tuan, is Chung Chinese? He has been very quiet. He says very little."

"Yes, he Chinese. He friend. He shy not talk Vietnamese good. He hate Chinese commies. In China he businessman. Commies take away business, say they own now. They make him work for them. He run away from home in China. Sneak into Vietnam. Now Hue taxi man. He take us Khe Sanh, then come back Hue. You give Chung $50. Him be happy."

In actuality, Chung could speak Vietnamese quite well, but he was too timid to show it. So he kept this skill to himself.

Two days later everyone met, as directed, at a sleezy hotel in Khe Sanh. Over dinner, they laid out their final plans. It was simple enough. Follow the path from the fateful tour's launch point on Route 9 into the jungle. From there they would fan out in groups of three following a search pattern set forth on three identical, war era, combat maps. On one of his tours Rick had purchased the maps, for too much money, on the streets of Saigon. Rick announced that whichever team found Steve first, would receive a $5,000 bonus. They would leave the hotel at four in the morning, drive west to the trailhead and try to be at the jungle by sunup.

CHAPTER FORTY-FIVE

Two vans were waiting in the hotel parking lot when the group exited the building at 3:45am. At that time of the morning, Route 9 was void of traffic. The ride to the launch point was not very far. The vans did two U-turns, one about a half kilometer after the trailhead and again a half kilometer after on the return. Unknown to Rick, they were looking for signs of danger, for undertones of hidden police or army troops. All was clear and they unloaded quickly on the side of the road. There were premade packs for each man containing food, first aid kits, flashlights, extra batteries, a blanket, duct tape, rope, insect repellant, etc. Military web belts and full canteens of water, four to a man, were handed out. In addition, there was a new handheld GPS for each team.

Rick was surprised with the thoroughness of Tuan's supply logistics. Rick was even more surprised when the teams lifted mats from both van floors and began removing weapons from hidden compartments. Grenades, AK-47's, M-16's, a variety of handguns, plenty of extra ammunition and magazines of all sorts, and cleaning kits. There was even a B40 launcher with a bag of three rocket grenades.

"Tuan, what the hell?"

"Lao men have guns. Bad men kill many Viets. We cannot fight back with no guns. We be ready. No want to die. Also, just so you know, we fight commie army and commie police. They call us rebels because we want old ways back. Want commies go back Hanoi, stay there. But for now, these guns use to fight Lao bad men if come."

"Can you trust these men?"

"These men my friends, Mr. Rick. We fight in Cambodia War together. They strong. They loyal. They fight seven years in Cambodia. They help to stop genocide."

The leader of the rebel group, a man they call Tiger, adds, "We save Cambodia people from Khmer Rouge. Vietnam government treat us bad after war. Throw us away. Vietnam police bad. Vietnam army bad. We fight them from hiding places, pretend to be friend. But we want real Vietnam back. Someday we win."

"Tuan, I can't be a part of that. I just want to get Steve and bring him home."

"You need us to get friend back. We need money to help us buy power. We are partners. When we get Steve, you pay, then you go home. We run tours again. Nobody knows."

Rick had no choice, but he refused to carry a weapon, other than his bush knife and his trusty machete.

The vans pulled away and would wait back at the hotel until they were needed to pick up the teams. The group of searchers headed quickly up the trail.

They were able to see in the forest due to the full moon. Reaching the dark jungle edge before dawn they decided to hunker down instead of using the flashlights to keep going. They did not want to risk being detected before blending into the deep, Phou Nhoi jungle where few locals dared tread.

CHAPTER FORTY-SIX

Within 15 minutes, the first rays of light penetrated the forest behind them. There wasn't a cloud in the sky. It would be a very warm day. In another 30 minutes there was enough twilight to enter the jungle gloom without flashlights.

After an hour's hike through the jungle, they reached the abduction point on the trail. They went over the plan once again. All three maps were spread out and each course was reviewed. Each team would take a map and a GPS.

Tuan laid out Rick's plan for all, "OK Mr. Rick, you, me, and Laotian man be one team. We follow path of dragging your friend. Other two teams follow out same direction on the flanks, same as army with you last month. But this time teams be maybe 50 meters away and march to west like us. We move faster than flank teams. Flank teams hike harder terrain. Our team arrive Song Sepon first. We wait for other teams at river."

"Roger that, Mr. Tuan. You got it right." The flanking teams would spread out and search much tougher conditions to the river and then descend on the middle group later. If none of the three-man teams found anything, they would start the next search grid.

They wished each other luck. Rick's team waited for twenty minutes so they would not move too far ahead of the other two teams. While they waited, Rick took out his rosary and started silently to pray. Tuan and the Laotian watched Rick curiously but reverently. They knew he was talking to his God. Twenty minutes passed and Rick's team was on the march.

By now the drag marks had been eroded away by occasional rains, but Rick would never forget the way. He was moving too fast, and Tuan had to slow him down so they could look for possible clues. Rick agreed, realizing he was running toward his friend, the same as last time. But he knew Steve would not be there. They were looking for indications to where he and his abductors may be now. They needed traces of evidence so they could track them down. Their movements became slower and more focused.

CHAPTER FORTY-SEVEN

In the basement of the dingy Khe Sanh hotel, Captain Trong, the police officer who had left the scene of the search party a month ago, stood with a smile on his face. He held the point of his knife to the throat of one of the drivers who had delivered the rebel group to the trailhead. The other driver was tied to a chair. He was bloody and unconscious, his mouth open and his head bent backward. He had one eye missing. Trong has inserted his dirty finger into the socket and popped it out. It was still attached to the optic nerve, but Trong had put the eye into the man's mouth, looking out. Trong thought that was particularly funny. He stepped back to get a better perspective and admired his cleverness for a moment, saying, "Now he can see what he's talking about."

From the wallet of the conscious driver, an army officer, Colonel Khang, removed the terrified man's photo of his wife and daughter. He looked at it and made the driver watch as he rubbed the photo on the crotch of his immaculate military uniform. "Tell us what we want to know, or the next time it will not be your wife's photo. It will be your wife's face. And then I'll pass her around so my men can have their fun, too. After that, we'll enlist the services of your daughter for the enjoyment of my battalion. When my men have had their fill, we will put both of your broken and tortured ladies in prison where they will die very painful and horrible, violent deaths. But if you tell us what we want to know, and if you promise to stop your activities with the rebels, we will set you free."

The man talked. He knew what these northern communists were capable of. He told them everything he knew. He told them how many men were involved, where the trailhead was, about the weapons, and what they were doing there.

"See? Now wasn't that easy? We could have avoided all this unpleasantness."

Khang looked at Trong, "You will gain great favor for telling us about the rebels. Your information will help us destroy the traitors. You are a loyal comrade, Captain Trong. Expect a commendation from Hanoi."

Trong beamed at his good luck. The colonel headed for the stairs, but just before he started to climb out of the basement he stopped, turned, and said to Trong, "Cut the traitors' throats."

The driver who had talked started to protest and Trong backhanded him across the head. Trong turned to the unconscious driver with the eye in his mouth and laughed as he slit the man's throat. Next, he smiled and put the knife to the horrified, remaining driver's neck who was watching his friend's blood pulse in great geysers across the basement floor. Trong giggled as he said, "Looks like you two stuck your necks out too far for your own good." He then slowly, very slowly, pulled the razor-sharp knife blade across the man's carotid artery. A second geyser of blood erupted. Trong watched in gleeful fascination.

Both drivers were dead within two minutes.

Trong snickered, proud of his bloody handiwork. He rifled their pockets for anything of value. And he would confiscate their vans. Trong was a man with no conscience, no integrity, no morality. He was a psychopath who at the end of the day, smiled as he fell asleep. He suspected this night would be no different.

* * * *

Trong spent the late morning and early afternoon drinking in the same hotel where his minions were removing the bodies and cleaning up the bloody mess he had left in the basement. He was quite pleased with himself and with how his life was going.

140

Arriving home early, Trong found his wife, Kim, napping on their bed. This was an unforgivable transgression. His good mood darkened, and he dragged her off the bed. He kicked her hard in the breast. She knew better than to scream. That was one of his rules. "You useless bitch! I work hard all day and you sleep when there is much here to be done? Where's my dinner?"

"My husband, you are home very early. I was just resting before I begin dinner for you. You will be very pleased. I have fish and rice planned, just the way you like it." She winced, holding her aching chest.

"Get to it before I kick your other tit. Go!"

Kim scrambled to her feet and hurried to the kitchen. Trong dominated his wife and subjected her to all kinds of abuse. Any infraction of his many rules and he would batter or molest her. His favorite thing to do was to backhand her across the face. He hated that she had never bore him a child and he accused her of being barren. Of course, Trong would never suspect himself of being impotent in that respect. It would always be her fault.

Kim could not remember him ever making love to her. He always raped her, always belittled her afterwards, always made her feel ashamed. And he regularly came up with new and painful sexual perversions to degrade her, much to his delight. Each time he was done, he made her crawl out of the room like an animal, all the time hurling insults at her. There was never once a show of tenderness.

She despised him more than she thought possible. She hated his dirty mind and was especially repulsed by his equally dirty fingers and what he did with them. His body always had an unpleasant odor, and Kim often wished he was dead. And more often than not, she wished she herself was dead.

After dinner, Trong's continued drinking drove him into a rage. He was never a happy drunk. It made him mean, and unhappy, and unreasonably critical. But this night was like no other. He had turned into a monster. As Kim was clearing the table, the dishes clinked. Trong yelled, "You make too much noise!" He backhanded her across the face, knocking her to the floor and then he beat her into unconsciousness.

After catching his breath, he dragged her into the bedroom. She awoke as he was starting to tear off her clothes. "Trong, my husband of 15 years, please don't hurt me anymore. I'll do whatever you say."

"Undress and lay on the bed."

Kim did as she was told. She disrobed, taking off everything, and laid on the bed as he ordered.

"You ugly bitch." He dropped his pants and climbed on top of her, but he couldn't perform. He was way too drunk. "You don't deserve me. You never have. Don't move or I'll break all your fingers."

He went into the next room and came back with the broom. She was still naked, still lying on her back; afraid to move. "Open your legs."

"Trong, no! I am your wife. I love you so much. Please don't hurt me."

He punched her hard in the face, breaking her nose. The pain shot through her like a bolt of lightning. She coughed blood and curled into the fetal position. She then felt the broom handle penetrate her anus.

"This is what you get for being such a bitch, you whore. Tell me you like it."

Kim felt him ram the stick deep inside her. The pain was excruciating, and she felt a dull snap. Trong had punctured her large intestine. She vomited.

"You're disgusting!" he bellowed, and he shoved the stick in as far as he could. It had missed her bladder and it had pushed between the many folds of her small intestines. In Trong's final violent thrust, the broom punched through her liver. He finally gave up when Kim's diaphragm muscles prevented the stick from further penetration. He then pushed her off the bed with the broom still inside her.

"Fly away on your broomstick, you witch." He started laughing, fell back on the bed, and immediately passed out in a drunken slumber.

Kim crawled out of the bedroom. Lying on the hall floor, she reached behind her and slowly pulled out the broom handle. It was followed by a hot gush of blood. It no longer hurt as bad as Kim thought it should, her nose hurt much more. But she knew then that she was dying. She had felt the ruptures inside her and knew that the broomstick had done irreversible damage, that Trong had done irreversible damage.

She decided that her one last act before going to her ancestors, would be to make sure her pig of a husband could not hurt anyone else. She slowly and carefully stood. Her legs wobbled, but she found strength in the fact that she had little time to live, and much to do. She would make sure that the time she had left would be well lived.

Kim went to the kitchen, opened a drawer, and removed a serrated steak knife.

CHAPTER FORTY-EIGHT

Steve sat in the jungle darkness cuffed around a tree. The Laotians were arguing again. He saw that they were much better off than him physically. Steve had received no food that day and only a small drink of water in the morning. He wondered why. The answer was that Analu had been ordered by Pekelo to feed the hostage each day. Resentful of this lowly duty, Analu was eating most of Steve's rations.

It occurred to Steve that his usefulness as a hostage was wearing off, otherwise they would have to keep him alive long enough to collect a reward. Under these conditions, he didn't think he would last much longer. Either that or they were going to leave him to die alone in the middle of the stinking jungle. He still had no idea where he was, but he knew they had been walking south. He could tell by the arc of the sun. For some reason, he sensed they were somewhere near the border with Vietnam, but he could not be sure. Maybe they were not feeding him because they were near their destination and were eating his rations before they traded him.

The Laotians' arguing grew heated.

Damn it, Pekelo! We must kill him now. We have no choice. We kill him and bury him. No one will be the wiser. Let us be done with it already. I am sick. I think I may have malaria. I want to go home.

Analu, your name means 'Manly', but you are hardly acting that way now. You act more like a woman, caring only about your own comfort.

And Pekelo means 'Stone' and that is what you are! You are inflexible, unable to change direction, to see that we need to kill this man and go home. Use your rifle and kill him!

Stop your complaining, Analu. I grow weary of it. Wait until morning. Things will look better then. I promise to make a decision when the sun comes up. Now feed our prisoner and then get some sleep.

CHAPTER FORTY-NINE

At 6:00 that same evening, two large military trucks pulled out of the main gate of the army base at Vinh on the Tonkin Gulf coast. The camp commander, Major General Pham, saluted the platoon as they passed. In each truck were 20 of his specially trained, elite Vietnamese commandos, fully armed and ready for combat. They were anxious to get into a real fight after these many years of near endless training. They believed they would finally get to put their deadly skills into action. But for now, they settled in for the long ride. The 360-kilometer trip, about 225 miles, would take at least seven hours. If there were no mishaps, they would get to Khe Sanh at about 1:00 in the morning.

There was an army unit stationed at Vandergrift Combat Base situated on Route 9 which was closer, but a commando unit had been requested by Colonel Khang to crush the rebels currently at Phou Nhoi. Khang trusted only the commandos. Army units were conscripted from all over the country, but the elite commandos were recruited only from what used to be North Vietnam. Khang had no use for the descendants of the disloyal South Vietnamese people, even if it had been 50 years since the American War.

At the same time, several towed howitzers were being moved from the Vinh Moc coastal artillery base, just above what had been the DMZ. They were on their way to Lang Vei, halfway between Khe Sanh and the Laotian border town of Lao Bao to provide support fire. *How fitting,* thought Khang. *It was at Lang Vei where our fathers overwhelmed the elite American Special Forces with our tanks. Yes, this is the right location for our artillery. Our ancestors will guide our fight.*

In addition to the heavy artillery, a mortar group would accompany the commandos in their quest for the rebels. MIG fighter-bombers were on standby in Da Nang ready to launch at a moment's notice.

A military mobile surgical hospital was sent to the marketplace in Khe Sanh Village, about three kilometers south of the old Khe Sanh Combat Base. It was close enough to the battle area but not under the trajectories of the artillery at Lang Vei. The marketplace parking area could be used as a landing zone for injured commandos. The head doctor asked Col. Khang, "What about the rebel wounded?"

Khang replied, "There will be no rebel wounded." He planned on killing all of them.

The Vietnamese government was exceptionally serious about mercilessly eliminating rebel pockets wherever they could be found. And Colonel Khang was as vicious and as callous as a Nazi SS officer. He would follow orders from his superiors, right or wrong, without question or hesitation. If Khang could destroy these rebels, he felt sure the communist government would fast-track him for a promotion as a General-grade officer.

CHAPTER FIFTY

It was almost dark by the time all three rebel teams converged. They had found nothing. They decided on a harbor site by the Sepon under a thicket of vines and settled in for the night. They ate their meals distractedly. It had been a hot and physically demanding day, having marched 23 kilometers, about 14 miles, from Route 9 and across terrible terrain. They would begin again at first light. But for now, they needed sleep.

Although no one thought there was any imminent danger, they would post security watches throughout the night. Old habits were hard to break.

Rick volunteered for the first watch. The watch would start at 8:30, and Rick would be the sentry for two hours. At 10:30, Tuan would take over for one hour, then Tiger at 11:30 for an hour. The rest of the men would stand guard duty for one hour each, until dawn broke at 06:30.

Tuan was still awake by his turn at standing watch. Rick hunkered down wrapped in a blanket and quickly fell asleep.

Rick opened his eyes and soon found himself sighting down an M-16 at several shadows walking in the distance. Tuan had his rifle pointing in the same direction. Tuan spoke softly, "No shoot. They not know we here."

Rick eased his finger off the trigger and took a deep breath. He whispered to Tuan, "I'll move off to the north about 50 meters, you send Tiger to the south. We'll be listening posts. Spread the rest of the men out in every direction about 25 meters, quietly. Make a clean, undetected perimeter." Tuan nodded and silently directed his men.

Rick moved slowly and cautiously to the north. He found an indentation in the earth next to a fallen tree. He eased in and looked and listened.

Within minutes he heard footfalls on the mucky jungle floor. The moon cast a human shadow to his right. He peered around the edge of the tree and stared straight into Sharon's face. "Rick? I'm looking for Steve. Have you seen him?"

"Sharon, get down. How did you get here? I thought you were . . ."

"Why are you wearing Steve's ring?"

He looked down at his hand and there was Steve's wedding band.

Rick woke to Tuan shaking him. "Mr. Rick, you make too much noise. Wake up. Be quiet. You have night-scare."

Sweating and confused, Rick replied, "Night-scare? A nightmare? How long have I been asleep?"

"Only ten minute. You OK?"

"Uh, yeah, sure. Man, that was weird. Sorry. I'll stay awake a while with you."

Rick looked down at his hand. The only thing there was his solid gold Marine Corps ring.

CHAPTER FIFTY-ONE

Kim returned to the bedroom with the knife. Trong was lying on his back, naked from the waist down. He was snoring, and his rancid breath fouled the room. She walked up to the bed and whispered. "My husband, I will not kill you. If I kill you, you would follow me into the next life. But instead, I will mutilate you. I will make you stay alive. And you will live in shame. You will never hurt another woman, and your pain will one day drive you to kill yourself. And then you will be damned to the fire realm."

Suddenly, Trong blurted out a few unintelligible words. Kim was startled and shook with fear. She thought Trong would rise and kill her. But he started snoring again, turned on his side, and curled up. Kim stood there rigid, not wanting to make any more sounds, hoping to not wake the monster. To her, each drop of blood dripping from her face onto the floor sounded like a bell clanging and she covered her nose with her forearm.

She finally relaxed enough to make a new plan. His penis was no longer exposed so she would be unable to cut off the offending appendage. If she rolled him onto his back, he might awaken. *Well,* she thought, *an eye for an eye. And an anus for an anus.* She tightened her grip on the knife handle until her knuckles turned white. She raised the knife high over her head, aiming to stab Trong through the rectum. Her arm was a blur of movement as it swung down at its target. The serrated knife sliced effortlessly up into his groin as deep as the blade would go. She pulled it out and readied to gore him again.

Trong screamed as he rolled off the bed and scurried on his hands and knees to the door, not understanding why he was in so much pain. He turned back and saw Kim next to the bed with the knife. She was standing straight, her head held high, with a look of complete satisfaction on her face. Seeing Trong crawl in pain on all fours like he had forced her to do so many times in the past, made Kim feel emboldened.

He had never seen his wife so defiant, and it enraged him to the point where he no longer felt the pain in his groin. The only thing he felt was hatred. With blood running down the back of his legs, he walked to her and backhanded her across the face. She dropped the knife and nearly blacked out. Kim felt loose teeth in her mouth. She spat them at his face.

When Trong was done strangling her, he got up and made his way to the phone and called one of his minions on the local police force to bring him to the hospital.

Early the next morning, his underlings removed Kim from the house. She was quickly brought to a crematory and turned into ash. Her death certificate stated that the cause of death was from internal bleeding due to a 'female' disease.

Trong claimed that his wound was probably from a criminal who stabbed him in revenge for putting the man in jail. He said he did not get a good look at his assailant as it was dark, and it happened so fast.

Once again, Trong got away with murder.

Trong was in the hospital for three weeks. Kim had done a good job. Her knife just missed its intended target and had penetrated Trong's perineum instead. As it continued its course, the knife's serrated blade penetrated deep enough to reach the base of his penis and severed the perineal, upper dorsal, and cavernous nerves, as well as his urethra. Trong would lose not only the use of his manhood, but he would have to be fitted with a urine bag. This would be a constant source of humiliation for him, outweighed only by the constant pain. He cursed that Kim had missed a major artery, and he wished he had bled to death.

151

CHAPTER FIFTY-TWO

Dawn broke and Steve heard the Laotians stir. He wondered what this day would bring. Still cuffed around the tree, he did not think he could go on much longer. The renegades ate bananas and some dried meat, washing it down with water. Steve received nothing. His hunger pangs were dwarfed only by his intense thirst.

Quiet talk between the Laotians quickly escalated into loud, agitated voices.

Speak, Pekelo. What have you decided?

I have decided that the three of us will keep going.

Are you completely mad? This is insane! If you will not kill him, I will!

Analu pushed his mentor to the ground and grabbed Pekelo's rifle. He walked up behind their prisoner and pointed the weapon at the back of Steve's head. He pulled the trigger.

Nothing.

The inexperienced Analu pulled back the bolt to chamber a round. He pulled the trigger again.

Nothing.

The safety! He flipped the safety to the fire position, aimed, and in the next instant Analu's head split wide open. He dropped in a heap, dead. Invisible to Steve and to Pekelo was the dark hand with its cracked, filthy nails and torn, ragged flesh that seized Analu's malformed soul and dragged it down to Hell.

Steve turned and stared at the bloody brain that was bulging from Analu's open skull. He looked up and saw Pekelo standing there with a football-size rock in his hands. Pekelo dropped the rock and picked up his rifle, resetting the safety. He talked to his dead partner. *I am sorry, Analu, my friend. I loved you as if you were my own brother. But nothing can stand in the way of our country's future. Not even you. I will tell everyone that you sacrificed your life for the new and powerful Laos. Now you will sit with Buddha, and I am happy for you. When my work here is finished, I will see you again. But my time is not now. I have much to accomplish.*

Stepping over the body of Analu, Pekelo unlocked the cuffs and motioned Steve to get up and start walking. Steve shook his head and pointed to Analu and made a digging motion. Pekelo hesitated for a moment. He then nodded, turned his back on Steve, and looked around for something with which to dig.

That was when Steve struck. He swung his right hand around Pekelo's neck and smashed him in the throat with a knife fist, dragging him backwards to the ground. Pekelo dropped the rifle when he felt the sudden intense pain of his crushed trachea. He struggled, clawing at the hands that were killing him, but the iron fist would not budge. Steve pulled his fist even deeper into the man's throat with his other hand. With air unable to pass through the larynx, death would come without a sound. Pekelo soon blacked out and his malevolent soul was plucked from his corpse, following Analu's path into the Abyss. A few minutes after the man went limp, Steve finally released him.

Steve had learned this kill technique after graduating Parris Island boot camp while in the Infantry Training Regiment at Camp Lejeune in North Carolina. The skill was perfected as part of his hand-to-hand combat classes. It was one of the ways to silently kill enemy sentries. He never had the occasion to use it during the war, but it came to him quite naturally in this dire life or death situation. His old Marine training had saved the day, and his life. He sat there in a daze, between the two dead renegades, for what must have been an hour.

The loud buzzing from swarms of flies attracted by Analu's blood, snapped Steve out of his stupor. He stood, gathered the remaining food, water, and the AK-47. He studied the AK for a moment, then said out loud to the two dead men, "Disgusting. Any Marine with a rifle this dirty would be court-marshalled."

He searched for a weapon cleaning kit but found none. Even in his sickness, Steve was appalled by the dirty rifle, and he vowed to somehow clean the thing before sunset.

Steve ate some food and drank a bit of water, then turned and started walking. But he had no clue where he was other than in endless jungle. A few things he did know for sure. He knew that refuge and the border with Vietnam, was to the east. He knew how weary he felt. He knew that he was old. And he also knew that if he did not get medical help soon, he would die alone in the middle of nowhere, 10,000 miles from home.

CHAPTER FIFTY-THREE

Colonel Khang was mostly pleased with his progress. The howitzers were in place at Lang Vei and the mobile hospital was ready at the marketplace. The commandos and the mortar team had arrived early in the morning and were rested and were now being fed breakfast. MIG's from Da Nang Airfield had already flown, much to Khang's chagrin, their ridiculous familiarization flights over the target area at first light.

Khang had commandeered the Khe Sanh Combat Base Museum to use as his CP, his command post. Tourists would be turned away at the gate for the duration of the operation.

Khang could taste blood and wanted the killing to begin soon. But he remembered that he needed to be patient. The rebels had evaded him more times than not. This time, he vowed, they would not get away.

At eight in the morning, Khang called the briefing to order. He had a large map of the Phou Nhoi region pinned to the wall. The leader of the commando platoon, Lieutenant Chien, agreed to move his men through the jungle in sweep formation. It would be much more difficult than following each other in a column down a trail, but there was no rush. They needed to be thorough, not fast. Besides, the rebels were good fighters and Lt. Chien did not want to sacrifice too many of his men. Colonel Khang reminded the lieutenant, "This mission is more important than your men, Lt. Chien. This mission will be successful at all costs. Your rank and your future in the army depend on the successful conclusion of this important assignment. Do you understand?"

"Yes, sir!"

At nine-thirty, the trucks were loaded and ready to move the commandos to the trailhead. The commandos would be in place in the forest and ready to move out on their search for the rebels by 10:30am. With them would be the mortar squad. Since mortars would be highly inaccurate firing up through trees, they needed areas with clear sky. They would follow the commandos at a safe distance. The mortar squad would split into two mobile batteries and leapfrog to each new clearing as reported by the commandos. That way, they would always be in ideal range to assist the advancing elite forces. Choung watched the trucks depart, his stomach churning.

The ride to the trailhead took 15 minutes. The troops disembarked and geared up. The commandos, on orders from their commander, Lt. Chien, moved along the now well-worn trail used by Rick and the tour group. Their goal was to get to the south side of the Phou Nhoi Mountain by dark. They would bivouac to the south of the battle area in somewhat friendlier terrain. Despite the hardships, the young commandos, in perfect physical condition and pumped up psychologically by their first real mission, easily made the 14-kilometer trek before the sun went down. They set out their watches and dug their holes. Even though they were tired, few fell asleep for long. They were excited about tomorrow's search for the traitors.

CHAPTER FIFTY-FOUR

Rick and the teams had been awakened by the sound of MIGs screaming low over the Phou Nhoi area. "Probably training missions," said Tuan. "No one know we're here." He spoke the same words in Vietnamese to the teams. The rebels nodded slowly in agreement.

They broke camp after sharing a breakfast of dried beef, cold spring rolls, and hot coffee heated over a small, packable, propane stove.

Their first leg of today's three-leg search would take them south following parallel to the Sepon River for about three kilometers. Right at 7:00am, they started their trek. They would average one kilometer, a little over a half-mile, per hour which was not bad in that terrain. After three hours, they stopped for a quick briefing so they all would be refreshed on the plan. The teams would now spread out and move southeast for about eight kilometers following their GPS readouts. When all three maps were spread out, Rick began, "This second leg of today's search will be the toughest. Leg-two's objective is Hill 556, the Co Van monolith. In another couple of kilometers, we may be able to see its summit. The mountain dwarfs every terrain feature around it. It will seem to grow as we get closer. Once it's in view, it may be easier to navigate using a compass azimuth and your combat maps. But keep the GPS's on in case you need to maneuver around substantial obstacles. It may show you a better route.

"Once we converge on Co Van, we will regroup at the west side of the monolith and then head south on our third leg for a couple more kilometers. There we will find a harbor site on a densely vegetated slope so we can face north overnight. Laos will be to our backs. Any questions?"

157

There were no questions. They wished one another good luck, and then each team moved to its own launch point and started off. This time 71-year-old Rick, city boy Tuan, and the Laotian would have as tough a time as the other teams. Rick did not care how rough it got. All that mattered was finding Steve.

But the rebel teams searching the Phou Nhoi area, once again, found nothing. They were exhausted and as night began to fall, they made camp in a harbor site among dense trees in a dark, thick hillside forest not far from Hill 556. Even though they were two kilometers away, the southwest side of the Co Van monolith, seemed to loom sharply above them.

Sitting in the darkness, Rick felt sick that maybe he was wrong about where Steve might possibly be. He conferred with Tuan who brought in Tiger, the leader of the Cambodian war veterans. Together they decided that tomorrow they will head north one kilometer, then east through the narrow valley on the south side of the Co Van. If they found nothing, they would search northeast through the forest parallel to the Sepon. The day after that, they would head in a northwesterly direction back toward the Phou Nhoi battle area. All agreed it was the best plan.

But something was bothering Tiger. He had a sixth sense that had saved his life many times fighting the Khmer Rouge in Cambodia. He said he felt a strange sensation, a palpable tension in the air. He would advise his men to be extra vigilant tomorrow, not so much for Steve, but for personal dangers.

Before turning in for the night, Tuan told Rick that if they have found nothing in the next two days, they would call off the search and return home. The search teams were getting nervous about staying in one area, exposed, for such a long time. Their usual tactics were hit-and-run. What was keeping them there was not their concern for Steve, but for their desire for a huge payday when they found him.

Rick told everyone to get a good night's rest. They set out their sentries and drifted off to sleep.

CHAPTER FIFTY-FIVE

That night back at Khe Sanh, Colonel Khang was having trouble sleeping. He kept going over his operational plans. The little mobile surgical hospital at the Khe Sanh village marketplace was ready. Being bored, the medical staff had been treating needy villagers who came by with infections and minor illnesses. Khang had told them to turn away all civilians at sunrise and to be ready to receive military casualties at a moment's notice.

Everyone knew their role in the mission. Seek out and kill the rebels at all costs. The howitzers were dug in with plenty of rounds to rain death down upon the traitors. Khang had to hold back from allowing them preparatory fires, because he did not want to alert the rebels. The artillery commander, Major Lam, had argued that without prep fires, he would not be able to properly align and make needed adjustments prior to the attacks. But Khang was adamant, "No prep fires! No showing our hand before it is absolutely necessary. Major Lam, I know you will not fail me. Plan your fires carefully, but do not fire until ordered to do so."

Khang was still livid that the MIGs had scouted the area early this morning, and he hoped the rebels had not been spooked and had already fled the area.

The commandos had reported that they were in their bivouac south of Phou Nhoi but had encountered no enemy. Khang believed his biggest challenge would be the jungle. It gave the rebels immense advantage in terms of cover and concealment, but not escape. It was impossible to move fast through the jungle and if pursued, the rebels would not get far. If he could force them to move east, they would be driven into Montagnard tribal lands which had recently been slashed in preparation for the planting of crops. The rebels would be easy to pick off once they were in the open. Khang planned to maneuver the 40 commandos in a southerly direction to the west side of Co Van and then move them in an arc to the southeast. If they found the rebels, they would force them east into open ground, and to their deaths. If the commandos found nothing, they would continue searching, circumnavigating Co Van and regroup on its north side. They would then split up with 20 commandos sweeping to the west and 20 sweeping to the northwest. Wherever found, the rebels were to be turned and pushed to the east, to open ground.

In addition, Colonel Khang had a Da Nang based Mi-8 Soviet helicopter at the museum standing by at the Khe Sanh Combat Base. At the first sign of trouble, he would quit his CP and be airlifted to observe and to direct, from the air, the ensuing battle, and the destruction of the rebels. The helicopter could be used later to medevac commando wounded, if needed.

Khang hated helicopters, especially the old 1960's Mi-8's the Russians had left for the Vietnamese communists. Only one, other than two in Saigon, now called Ho Chi Minh City, two in Cam Ranh Bay, and five in Hanoi, was capable of flying, and it was assigned to him. He used it as little as possible, though, since repair and maintenance parts were relatively nonexistent. He would prefer to be up front with his troops in the thick of battle, rather than directing it from above. But he believed he was so important, that if he were to be killed in action, it would hurt his country. Besides, he had plans for high office in Hanoi when he retired from the army.

Also, he did not trust the pilots. They looked young enough to be his grandchildren. They appeared competent enough, though, as they oversaw the loading of ammunition belts and a total of 64 rockets into the four 57mm pods mounted on the helicopter's stub-wings. As much as he disliked flying,

Khang looked forward to unleashing all this massive firepower on the unsuspecting rebel traitors.

He could not wait until morning. The anticipation kept him up all night.

CHAPTER FIFTY-SIX

The rebel teams were running low on chow. If they needed the fourth search day, they would have to ration their food, but these men were tough and used to self-depravation. It mattered not if they missed meals.

This morning the men deep-cleaned their weapons on orders from Tiger who also explained to the men what he was sensing. They took him seriously. They respected him and remembered his heroics in Cambodia. He was a very brave man, and a skilled leader.

Today's expedition would start late because of the weapon cleaning and subsequent inspection by Tiger. Once everyone was ready with their maps out, Rick gave the briefing, "Today's first leg of our four-leg search will be over easier terrain than on the previous days. We will hike this forest going north for about one kilometer. The hills are lower than the jungle to the west. On the second leg we turn east for two kilometers through a very narrow valley just south of Co Van. On the third leg we turn north-northeast for three kilometers. Here we will encounter forest and rolling hills. We should make good time going through there but keep looking for clues to our prey. Our final leg will bring us northwest toward Phou Nhoi, eight kilometers away. We will find a harbor site in easy terrain south of the battle site and set in for the evening. The search patterns will be the same, my team in the middle, the other two teams flanking online from 30 to 50 meters out, the men about ten meters apart. Any questions?"

Tiger piped up, "I feel something bad. Look here on map. The valley under Co Van very narrow. It is perfect place for ambush. We all be together. Bad to do. This where I place my men if making ambush. The cover is generous. The kill zone ideal.

I suggest we keep interval of 20 meters between each man, and that we move very fast. We must stay high vigilance."

"I understand, Mr. Tiger. Mr. Tuan, do you have anything to add?"

Tuan shook his head, and then he translated all that was said for the other men.

When everyone was in position and understood their roles, all nine men moved slowly and carefully to the north.

CHAPTER FIFTY-SEVEN

At first light, the 40 commandos ate breakfast and then broke camp. By 6:30am, the well-disciplined platoon was spread out and ready. As Khang had ordered, their mission this day would be to move eight kilometers south to the west side of Co Van, then circle the mountain to the south and east, finally regrouping on the north side. They would then split their forces, half heading west and half heading northwest. Unhampered by stealth-discipline these young, fit commandos would move swiftly and without fatigue. They could easily hike eight kilometers in less than four hours, even across this rough terrain, a rate of about two kilometers per hour.

They stepped off on their mission as if a switch had been flipped starting a motor to hum. They moved quickly and resolutely to the south.

CHAPTER FIFTY-EIGHT

Steve and his captors had traveled over 200 kilometers, about 130 miles, through Laos meandering about 20 miles from the border with Vietnam. When the van had run out of gas, they had continued on foot. Steve did not know it, but when he had killed the remaining Laotian, he was just west of the northeastern tip of Cambodia at its confluence with Vietnam and Laos.

During the next two days, he had slowly and painfully crossed through this narrow section of Cambodia and finally emerged uphill into Vietnam, again not realizing where he was. He just kept heading east-southeast guided by the arc of the sun. Had he gone just five miles north, he would have come to the trade road, Route 11, and someone would have found him. To avoid detection, his captors had dragged Steve across the road at night, but Steve was too sick to remember.

The mountain he faced was Hill 875 southwest of Dak To, scene of a brutal 23-day battle in November 1967. The fight pitted elements of the 173rd Airborne and the 4th Infantry Division against thousands of NVA. In the end, over 2,000 human beings were killed there, with many more wounded on both sides. Steve did not know that and even if he did, in his condition it would not have occurred to him. He only knew he had to keep going east, not west, or north, or south. East was his salvation.

The going was incredibly rough; he thought even a young man would agree. He was climbing ever higher, but he was moving so slow the jungle seemed to be climbing with him. *How is this possible?* he thought. *Is the jungle moving? Is it growing as fast as I'm climbing?*

Twenty meters more to the east he kept thinking. When he had walked twenty meters, he said to himself again, *just twenty meters more*. Over and over, he kept this up. *Just twenty meters more.* He was having trouble remembering why he was walking and where he was going. But something deep inside him, some primal instinct, knew that he had to keep moving ahead.

Eventually he emerged from the jungle, but he was then being scorched by a relentless, red-hot sun. He encountered enormous stretches of thorns and razor grass. It cut through his clothes and lacerated his skin. Trickles of blood slowly oozed from multiple cuts. Steve had run out of water hours ago and he feared the sun was boiling his brain. The rifle slid from his hand. Steve was now too weak to hold it. He did not notice it was gone. He just kept putting one foot in front of the other. *Just twenty meters more.*

Finally, Steve reached the top of this terrible mountain and he dropped to the ground in absolute exhaustion. He was starving and seriously dehydrated and having bouts of delirium. He was sick and completely worn out. He slipped into unconsciousness.

CHAPTER FIFTY-NINE

The rebels stopped as they neared the steep hillsides of the narrow valley south of the Co Van. It would indeed funnel them much closer together than they preferred. But they were searching, not fighting. Still, Tiger was wary. At 10:30 that morning, at the edge of a clearing no bigger than a basketball court, they hesitated, feeling an ominous presence. Hands tightened around their weapons.

That was where the two groups of men met, eye-to-eye across the little field. The commandos stepped out, exposing themselves at the edge of the clearing. Rick and all eight rebels instinctively dropped to the ground and melted into cover behind rocks and fallen trees. They quickly spread out, about ten yards apart, facing the commandos, each determining their own field of fire.

The initial encounter was so unexpected, the commandos momentarily froze. They had never seen an enemy before, let alone an enemy that looked like them. Except for the presence of the American, the commandos thought these Vietnamese may have been foragers. The fact that these people were holding weapons had not yet registered in their brains.

Quickly recovering from their initial shock, the commandos raised their weapons toward the rebels. Their platoon leader, Lt. Chien, stepped forward projecting self-assurance and arrogance. Rick thought he was projecting inexperience and stupidity.

Lt. Chien yelled out for the rebels to drop their weapons and to come out with their hands raised. A quick chuckle erupted from Tuan's throat, and he thought, *Yeah right, that'll work.*

Rick looked at Tuan, "They have us out-manned and out-gunned. What do you say? Do we obey or do we run?"

168

"Neither one, yet. I not trust them, and don't know if we be surrounded. Only see about 25 soldiers. Should be more." Tuan signaled the rebel lying next to Rick and told him to stand up as if to surrender.

The rebel laid down his M-16, stood with his hands up, and yelled, "I give up." He was met with a flurry of commando bullets that nearly tore him in half.

Tuan shouted, "They want no prisoners! Only want to kill," and he let loose a burst toward the commandos, killing the platoon leader, Chien. Rick reached for the dead rebel's M-16, but quickly recoiled without touching it. He knew he would spend the rest of his life rotting in prison, or more likely be executed, for killing a Vietnamese soldier.

The other rebels joined in the firing as they, instinctively, moved quickly to the east trying to get to better terrain from which to fight. To their east were forested rolling hills where maneuvering would be more advantageous. The rebels knew that they would be slowed down, possibly entangled in the jungle if they fled west. Three more commandos were killed in the initial running gun battle.

Although the commandos were highly trained, they had no combat awareness, and they were no match for the battle-experienced rebel warriors. Plus, they were now leaderless. The commandos' only advantage was numbers. They still had 36 soldiers to the rebel's eight. Running parallel to each other, two more commandos dropped, either dead or dying.

Rick was moving with the rebels, and he still did not have a weapon, nor did he want one. He hoped that by not fighting, he would be able to reason with the authorities that he was only there trying to find his friend, not to hurt anyone.

But he knew he was lying to himself. Tuan was right. They want to kill everyone. He had just witnessed the commandos murder a defenseless, unarmed rebel who was surrendering.

Somehow, Rick found himself comfortable in this current chaotic predicament. Subconsciously, he began asking himself, *Could this be who I am? Was I born for this? Is this a dream? Or were the past 50 years the dream? Have I ever left the war? Certainly, the war has never left me. I have to fight! If I don't fight, my friends will die! I will die! And I'd rather die fighting than be assassinated by these North Vietnamese thugs.*

Rick, Tuan, and four of the rebels were now running at full speed. Another rebel was struggling after them carrying the B40 launcher and its rockets, as well as his own M-16. Tiger was last, moving at a slower pace, firing random bursts behind him to keep the commandos from rushing after them.

CHAPTER SIXTY

Colonel Khang had launched in the helicopter as soon as the commandos reported that they were under fire and that their leader was dead. From the air, Khang began to synchronize the platoon's movements. He barked orders at them to push the rebels to the east and into an open field he had spotted. He would be waiting there to greet the rebels with rockets and machinegun fire. That decision was Khang's first mistake. The rebels had outmaneuvered the leaderless commandos, and instead of moving into Khang's killing field from the west side, as expected, the rebels had moved to the north side.

Rick, Tuan, and four of the rebels had come to the middle edge on the north side of a large, dry overgrown field that sloped south downhill to the Sepon River. The field was about 100 meters square. On the other side was Laos. The field had recently been slashed of tall grasses and which was now lying flat on the ground, drying in the hot sun. They pulled back into the forest about 20 meters, into the shadows, and watched as a Russian helicopter over the field searched for them. Rick knew the commandos must have radioed the chopper with intel on the rebel's movements. With the heavily-armed helicopter hunting for them, it would be suicide to enter the field.

Tuan heard them first, then Rick picked up the undeniable flanking movements of the commandos, making him feel sick in his stomach. Rick and the rebels were being enveloped on three sides by the remaining 34 well-trained, well-disciplined, but combat-inexperienced enemy. To move deeper into the forest would lead them into the commando guns. To move into the open, gently sloping field and being stalked by the deadly Soviet helicopter meant almost certain death. Rick and Tuan and the remaining rebels were outnumbered, outgunned, and trapped.

Tuan threw an M-16 to Rick who caught it in one hand, instantly recalling the familiar heft and balance of the assault rifle. Rick checked to make sure the magazine was full, that a round was chambered, and that the safety was off. He had no mind to use it, but the sequence was too intimate to not go through his Marine Corps-ingrained, battle checklist.

Just then, Tiger approached dragging the slowest rebel who had been wounded by a pursuing commando who had been John Wayne-ing it on his own. While Tiger dragged the wounded man, the wounded man was dragging the B40 rocket launcher with its bag of High Explosive Anti-Tank grenades, as well as dragging his intestines which were stretched along the path behind him. Tiger gave Tuan an imploring look. As he started to speak, Tiger was suddenly flung to the ground by a short burst from the pursuing commando's AK. Rick spun in the direction of the shots and fired the M-16, stitching the commando from crotch to forehead. His reaction was primal, conditioned by his war experience, an instant response to Tiger being killed. Once he had pulled the trigger and the rounds started down the barrel, he could not bring them back. He knew then that his fate was sealed. A sudden, cold chill up his spine told Rick that he was in it now. There would be no turning back.

He looked at Tuan who smiled, and nodded as if to say, *Let's do this!*

Unexpectedly, the helicopter moved away. *How odd*, thought Rick, *they would have killed us all inside of 20 minutes.* He quickly understood, as artillery rounds impacted somewhere to the northwest. Rick screamed, "Incoming!" and everyone dropped to the ground and hugged the earth.

Maj. Lam had been denied his artillery preparatory firings under Khang's orders. The initial trajectories were too low to reach the field, and the first two rounds hit the north face of the

Co Van monolith. Khang radioed Lam and made the corrections. Lam, under his breath, cursed Khang for his reckless, prep-fire denials yesterday.

Lam added a powder charge and raised his barrel's azimuth. Now, with the shells arcing much higher, they cleared the monolith. The artillery rounds impacted along the river at the south end of the open field. Khang called a fire-for-effect, and three more rounds hit the south end of the field. The high explosive impacts shook the earth with each successive volley, starting several small fires.

As the little fires began to spread, they interlinked in a V-formation, driven by a soft breeze rising up the hill from the south. The slashed, semi-dry grasses soon started burning in earnest, creating a large amount of smoke which was quickly moving ahead of the flames. Behind the smoke was a slow-moving arrow-shaped wall of fire. It was heading straight for the rebels, hidden just inside in the forest's edge on the north side of the field.

Then a coordinated series of mortar rounds started impacting closer and closer, inching nearer to the rebels. Rick was sure the commandos had moved back to be out of shrapnel range of the shells, but he was just as sure that in doing so, they had maintained their enveloping arc blocking a safe rebel retreat. Hot, jagged chunks of metal zipped through the air just above the rebel's heads, intent on piercing human flesh.

CHAPTER SIXTY-ONE

When the commandos reported that they were enveloping the rebels, Khang had told the pilot to move away from the field. He then radioed his second-in-command, Lt. Col Diem back at Khe Sanh, to coordinate the Lang Vei artillery battery's barrages with the commandos. Diem told Major Lam to start firing the big guns. After the first rounds had hit Co Van, and he had adjusted his fire, Lam laid down a hell-storm of heavy rounds near the river to prevent the rebels from escaping into Laos. From high in the air, Khang could see in the distance the artillery impacts. He then radioed his expert mortar teams to start firing. He watched as the mortar rounds began walking ever closer to the rebels. He smiled at the sheer beauty of the well-coordinated attack, designed off-the-cuff to an ever-changing engagement on the ground. He felt it was like herding cattle into a pen, preparing for their slaughter.

The artillery and mortars would have bracketed and destroyed the rebel clan, but that was something the egotistical and overconfident Khang wanted to be part of himself. He disregarded combat rule number one: *Never underestimate your enemy. When the enemy is at their most desperate, they become very dangerous.* He called off the shelling.

The world was abruptly silent. Rick and the remaining rebels looked at one another, trying to understand why they were spared certain death. They were still lying on the ground trying to make themselves as small a target as possible when they heard the return of the helicopter. The commandos radioed Khang with an updated approximate location of the rebels. Suddenly, hundreds of bullets strafed the edge of the forest, missing the rebels by only a few meters.

Tuan understood. The commandos wanted their first taste of blood. They wanted to kill the rebels themselves, up close and personal. Rick then grasped the situation, as well. Their only hope was to shoot down the helicopter. They could then charge across the field despite the brushfire and ford the river before the commandos could catch up. They would be safe in Laos where the commandos would not follow. Maybe. He would rather face the fire than the gunfire.

The rebels had to act fast. With no more white-hot shrapnel to keep them away, the commandos were again on the move, tightening their envelopment, trying to flush the rebels from the forest and into the open field. Tuan grabbed the B40 launcher and locked in a 70mm HEAT missile. It was essentially a very large armor-piercing, rocket-propelled grenade with an extremely powerful warhead. Tuan cocked the external hammer with his thumb, put the simple iron sight to his eye, and waited. As the helicopter made a second strafing pass, Tuan bided his time, unafraid and unflinching, as another volley of dozens of machinegun rounds zipped through the trees searching for rebel flesh to tear into.

The egotistical and smirking Khang then had the pilot fly at barely more than a hover near the edge of the forest so he could get a better look at what he may have hit.

The old Mi-8 may have been fast and nimble when it was manufactured, but as with all things Russian, it had been deteriorating since the 1960's and should not have been able to fly at all. But it was all Khang had. The young pilot was having trouble maneuvering the helicopter and was struggling to maintain such a slow, sliding speed. The bird was a sitting duck. It was low and wavering slightly from side to side, barely 50 meters away.

Khang saw something odd just inside the dark tree line. He told the pilot to hover, and he leaned forward, squinting his eyes for a better look. It appeared to be a local man kneeling on the ground holding a large bamboo pole on his shoulder, or perhaps it was a pipe. Tuan squeezed the trigger. The rocket, traveling at 84 meters per second, impacted the belly of the helicopter before its launch had crossed Khang's mind. The warhead could penetrate seven inches of armor, so the thin skin of the helicopter only served to prime the grenade's nearly instant fuse. In turn, the fuse ignited the high explosive in the warhead. At that velocity the rocket had already passed through the passenger compartment and entered the base of the overhead twin engine platform. The full effect of the explosion ripped the huge turbines from the fuselage and blew them out sideways. The rotors spun off erratically, high into the air. The rest of the helicopter dropped like a stone into the field, spreading jet fuel in the dry grasses around the crashed aircraft.

"Run!" cried Rick. This was their only chance to make it down the hill to the river. The commandos were still in the forest and moving quickly, closing in on the field. Rick, Tuan, and the remaining four rebels ran past the downed helicopter, trying to keep it between them and the pursuing enemy.

As the commandos burst from the forest, they hesitated for a moment upon seeing the destroyed helicopter lying on its side in the field. They did not register right away that the rebels were almost halfway down the slope and nearing the river. But they quickly gathered their wits and opened fire trying to stop the fleeing rebels who ran toward the now out-of-control wildfire caused earlier by the artillery. Some of the commandos stopped to observe the wreckage and discovered their commander was still alive. Others continued to charge downhill in pursuit of their quarry, firing on the run. By then though, heavy smoke from the burning field had obscured the escaping rebels who disappeared from view.

All those aboard the helicopter, except Khang, were dead before the helicopter carcass crashed into the ground. The Colonel was trapped within the wreckage, and leaking jet fuel slowly soaked his pristine uniform. The fire was slowly being pushed uphill by the wind, closer to the wreckage.

Smoke had now reached the helicopter. The Commandos were not yet fearing the flames which were still more than halfway down the hill. Unfortunately for them, due to the smoke they could not see the red-hot embers drifting toward them on the gentle breeze. They tried desperately to free Khang from the twisted metal, but their leader was held fast by warped aluminum bars, some of which had grotesquely pierced Khang's limbs. Khang screamed at them to stop trying, the pain was too much. The commandos, realizing there was nothing more they could do to rescue their commander, milled around the aircraft looking despondent at their leader, feeling impotent.

With all the commandos looking at the helicopter, the only one who saw the embers wafting gently down on them was Khang, who was on his back and looking up. All he could manage to say was, "No!" before the fuel-soaked grasses around the helicopter ignited.

Seconds later, as the flames touched the aircraft, the helicopter erupted into a ball of flame. The initial woosh of noise, as the fireball lifted skyward, drowned out Khang's terrified screams. But as the fire stabilized itself, Khang could be heard shrieking and cursing as he was slowly incinerated. At one point, it appeared that the flames consuming Khang were drawn momentarily into the earth. Onlookers dismissed it as an illusion, but Khang's burning soul knew better.

Just as the last of Khang's pathetic rants died out, the helicopter's 64 rockets detonated from the heat. Khang and the aircraft were vaporized in a massive explosion. Sixteen commandos were killed in the blast and 12 others were wounded and badly burned.

CHAPTER SIXTY-TWO

Steve was lying unconscious on top of Hill 875. After an hour or so, he awoke. He stood uneasily and scanned the horizon. There, to the southeast, in the far distance, he saw a town. His hope returned. He laughed out loud. He had made it! He tried to run but found he could only stagger like a drunken man. He stopped and collected himself. Bent at the waist with his hands on his knees, he giggled. He looked again to see if it was true. Yes, it was still there. There was a town, and a road, and a river flowing past houses and buildings. He wanted water desperately. He started to move down the steep mountain. As he rushed forward, he slipped off the edge of the precarious, rocky trail and fell back-first into a deep ravine, impaling himself on a dead, bamboo stalk. The thick stalk suspended him off the ground. Steve tried to free himself, but every time he moved, he screamed in unbearable pain. The stalk, holding him tight, had passed through his spine and was protruding up through his gut. He felt like he was floating in air. He looked up at the darkening sky. His arms and legs were spread and hanging down.

As night began to fall, the jungle came alive with insects that began feasting on Steve's flesh and open wounds. His lips were cracked dry, his tongue swollen. It felt like his mouth and throat were coated in acid. He never thought thirst could be so excruciating. The dark night brought out the stars. The cooling temperature gave way to a chilling condensation. The cold dampness made Steve shiver violently. He was in agony.

Then the leeches came. Dozens of them. They inched their way up the bamboo stalk and slimed over him searching for the best places to extract their bloodmeal. As his body was slowly drained of blood from his wounds and from the leeches, Steve thought about his children and he smiled. *What great kids they are.* He was so proud of them.

His thoughts turned to his wife, Sharon, remembering her warm lips and the softness of her body which she had so unselfishly shared with him. A single tear slipped from the corner of his eye. As Steve took his last breath, he died peacefully and gratefully.

But soon Steve heard voices and felt hands freeing him. They sat him up. He looked down and saw no wounds. Nothing ached. The liver spots on his hands were gone. He felt strong. He looked up and there were his long dead buddies, 18, 19, 20 years-old, grinning at him. They pulled him into a standing position.

Steve and the Renegade's route from Phou Nhoi through Laos to Hill 875

CHAPTER SIXTY-THREE

The brushfire and its smoke caused by Lam's artillery was an unplanned, but well-appreciated opportunity that had made possible the rebel's daring escape into Laos. Or was it a miracle?

Rick, Tuan, and the remaining four rebels, had run into the choking smoke expecting the slashed and drying vegetation to burn low and slow. But in fact, the flames were waist high and roaring. The wind was pushing the fire in a ten-foot-wide band of flames uphill, and spreading in a V-shape, encompassing the width of the field as it climbed. After running through 20 yards of thick smoke, the team had burst into the crackling flames at full speed, being propelled ever-faster downhill by gravity and adrenalin. There was no time to think, just to run. As their clothes started to burn, they broke through the flames onto scorched earth. After a few more frantic strides, they leapt into the river. They half swam, half galloped across the Sepon into the dense Laotian jungle.

Just as they crossed the river, there was an enormous explosion behind them. Several rockets from the helicopter pierced the air just to their west, spinning wildly and without purpose. They detonated harmlessly somewhere in the distance. Rick and the rebels kept moving as fast as they could until they found an adequate harbor site.

They sat in the darkness under a tangle of mangrove roots, licking their wounds. They were only slightly singed thanks to the river water that had doused their flaming clothes. One rebel had been killed by the commandos who had been shooting wildly into the fire and smoke. The hapless rebel had fallen into the burning field when an errant commando round had slammed into the base of his skull.

And a lucky shot had torn off a little meat from Rick's left side. He didn't even realize it until Tuan pointed and said, "You got blood there."

Rick pulled up his shirt, "Just a flesh wound really. Nothing to worry about."

Then he muttered to himself, "I bet they won't give me another Purple Heart."

The wound was near the deep, oblong indentation in his back where he was wounded saving Steve's life back in the war. *Damn!* thought Rick. *This is why I'm here. I still have to find my friend. I'm not here to kill Vietnamese soldiers or fight alongside rebels. Steve is all that matters.*

Tuan was dozing. Rick studied his loyal Vietnamese friend. In the 24 years of working with him on tours, Rick had always known Tuan to be a meek, friendly, and gentle soul. He realized now that Tuan was a 'sleeper,' a warrior of advanced capabilities. If it wasn't for Tuan's foresight to bring weaponry, to recruit willing fighters, and to display a total lack of fear, they might all be dead now.

That may be true, but the events of this day had compounded their problems exponentially. A lot of good men were dead. Steve was still out there, the army would not let this pass without resolution, and now they had nowhere to turn. Rick felt a sudden rush of fatigue. Safe for now, he fell asleep.

Through The Gates of Hell

Phou Nhoi search and battle areas

183

CHAPTER SIXTY-FOUR

Back at Khe Sanh, second-in-command, Lt. Col. Diem, swore to Buddha, Confucious, God, Allah, and to anyone else listening, that he will not rest until his colonel is avenged. He made the call to the commando base in Vinh, letting them know that out of the 40 commandos, the rebels had killed 23 and had wounded another 12.

After a long series of curses, the commando leader, Maj. Gen. Pham, offered his entire elite battalion, all 600 men, to hunt down and kill the rebels responsible.

Diem responded, "You need to know that an American is with the rebels. He is an ex-Marine who has been to our country many times since the end of the American War. He knows how to use the terrain, and he knows how to fight."

Pham explodes, "An American Marine? He's an old man by now! I want him! I want to strangle him with my bare hands! Marines killed my father and two of my uncles in 1968. You keep the rebels from escaping. I will bring my battalion to bear and make the lives of those traitor rebels a living hell before I kill them all."

With that the line went dead.

Keep the rebels from escaping? pondered Diem. *They have already escaped!*

He knew the rebels were gone and were now maneuvering through Laos. How he wished he could send the commandos in pursuit, but international agreements did not allow such a foray into neighboring countries. No, he would catch them some other way. He knew the rebels had to return to Vietnam. They would quickly wear out their welcome in Laos. Diem knew the rebels would return to Hue to regroup. It was where most of this rebel cell was from. The van driver had divulged this before he was killed. *Hue was where these traitors were most comfortable.*

Lt. Col. Diem, now in charge of the failed mission, decided to pull all the troops back. Without helicopters, it took an entire day to carry out the wounded. It took two more days to remove the dead commandos, some of which were just random body parts. He left all the dead rebels where they had fallen.

Diem vowed to hunt down the rebels to thank them for making possible his rise in rank and power, and for removing Khang, which made Diem the new commander. And then to slowly, and painfully, kill each one of them, especially the American. *But then again, didn't Maj. Gen. Pham say he personally wanted to kill them? Or did he want most to kill the American to avenge his father and uncles? I think the best plan is for me to destroy all the rebels except for the American. I'll keep him alive and offer him to Pham as a gift to kill him. That will bring great favor on me and will advance my career. Yes, this is working out quite nicely for me.*

CHAPTER SIXTY-FIVE

Later that evening, still in their harbor site, Rick and Tuan considered their options. Rick said, "Look Mr. Tuan, if you want to leave with your men, I will understand. None of us put in for this. It's been a disaster."

"I have spoken with my men. They cannot to go to their homes. And it is too dangerous at this time to return to Phou Nhoi. Many Viet Army will be there for long time. My men say we go south from here. We cut back into Vietnam on road just north of Dong Ap Bia, the place you call hill of hamburgers."

"Whoa there!" said Rick. "You mean Hamburger Hill. Many Americans died there in a vicious 11-day battle. And many, many more NVA were killed there, too. They were ground up like hamburger meat. That's how the mountain got its name."

"OK, OK. Hamburger Hill. Killing many, many NVA soldiers good. We call it Mountain of the Crouching Beast. Now, after we take road north of Hamburger Hill, we cross through mountains to Hue. Many trails. It take maybe three weeks. We find food along way. Jungle give food if know where to look. We know. Also, plenty water in mountains."

"But Mr. Tuan, by now the army knows who we are. Or they are close to figuring it out. If we go to your homes, we will be arrested and executed."

"No go to homes. Wife gone already when I no call. She smart and brave. She have your money. Keep safe. She tough. No worry. Have many friends hate army. Hate police. They help."

"I won't be able to fly out of Vietnam. My passport is at the hotel in Khe Sanh, and I'm sure the police have it now."

Tuan had a dour look on his face, "My friend. You never go home. You one of us now."

Rick recoiled at Tuan's matter-of-fact statement, then felt crushed as he realized Tuan was right. His life was over.

Or was it just beginning?

"And because you one of us now, your money buy new guns, new supplies. We go back Phou Nhoi later to find friend."

Rick was overwhelmed by Tuan's loyalty. It didn't matter that Tuan had never met Steve before the tour. Tuan knew that Rick needed his help. It was all that mattered to Tuan. *How ironic*, thought Rick, *the only one I can trust is a Vietnamese.*

CHAPTER SIXTY-SIX

The next morning, the little team assessed their equipment. They had only four rifles, three bandoliers of ammo, three handguns, one grenade, and no packs, no medical gear. The rest was lost in the chaos of battle and in their mad-dash escape. But at least they had their lives. They could resupply after reaching a safe area. Securing their equipment, they stood readying to leave.

They all froze at the sound of a snapped twig. They slowly lowered themselves to the ground and silently eased their safeties to the fire position. Another snap. Then another. No one breathed. No one moved.

"Hallo! Crazy Viets! I come see you." Then laughter from the hidden voice. "Where you?"

Branches shifted. All weapons quickly pointed at the movement; all fingers half squeezed the triggers. A smiling face appeared. "Hallo crazy Viets!"

Tuan signaled the others to hold their fire. "Don't move! Who are you?"

"Me Hmong. Me come across to see you. Help you."

"Tuan, what's going on?"

"It OK, he Hmong tribal man. Hmong hate army, hate police. Hate commies. I go talk with him. You stay here. Relax."

Rick recalled working with the Bru tribes during the war. They did not consider themselves Vietnamese, nor Laotian, nor Cambodian. The French called them 'Montagnard,' mountain people. They were smaller and darker than the Vietnamese. And they did not understand borders. They always asked, *Why this Vietnam, why this Laos? Same mountain, same place.* The tribesmen seemed stuck in the bronze age and were mostly hunters and gatherers. The Vietnamese had tried to assimilate them into modern society, but the Montagnards resisted.

188

Apparently, thought Rick, *they still resist.* He remembered talking with Army veterans who served in II- and III-Corps, farther south. They said the Hmong were great fighters and they loved killing North Vietnamese and Viet Cong. The tribesmen had readily joined forces with the American soldiers to fight against the communists. Rick remembered the Bru being the same way, loyal and vicious fighters.

Tuan returned with the smiling tribesman. "His name Yang Dua. You can call him Dua. He watch our fighting from hiding spot on top of Co Van, tall mountain to north of us. First he stay in cave. He say he very scared, one artillery bomb land on mountain. Make him fall down. Then another bomb hit, make him bounce up. Then he hear bomb's terrible sound flying through air. He crawl out of cave and see us below, he see helicopter, he see burning fire, he see everything. He pray very hard Buddha help us. He say praying worked.

"Last night he sneak by army soldiers, come to Laos side to see if we OK. He say he always deeply moved by many stories his grandfather had told before his death few years ago. His grandfather fought against Viet Cong, kill many commies. He was saved by U.S. soldiers two times. He said he will now honor his grandfather by helping us."

Rick looked into the Hmong's eyes, "I am saddened by your grandfather's death, Mr. Dua. We welcome your help."

This put an even bigger smile on Dua's face and Dua brought his hands to a prayer position, fingertips touching his lips, and bowed to Rick. Rick did the same in return.

They sat in a tight circle and discussed the next plan of action. With Dua as their guide through the rugged Laotian mountains and jungles, they would move southeast, making sure they stayed in Laos. Hamburger Hill was 65 kilometers away, about 40 miles, in a straight line on the map, but it was probably closer to 160 kilometers, about 100 miles, up and over all the mountains and down into numerous valleys, as well as detours to steer clear of the meandering Vietnam border.

Dua knew the area well. He had grown up in these mountains and had many times roamed for weeks at a time. As with others in his tribe he knew the borders because he had been told, but it was impossible to understand their meaning. Mountains were mountains. How could one be owned? And what was the meaning of 'country?' These alien concepts were too difficult to grasp, so the Montagnard tribe people simply dismissed those notions as nonsense.

CHAPTER SIXTY-SEVEN

At the end of each day's march, the team stayed in tiny tribal villages. The huts had thatched roofs and were built on stilts to protect the inhabitants from floods and tigers. The Montagnard women were topless, and the children naked.

Rick was somewhat a celebrity. Most of the villagers had never seen a White man. The children would touch the hair on his arms and run away giggling. Everyone smiled at him. At night the men would sit around the campfire and smoke from long pipes and pass around some kind of high-proof moonshine. The women and children would sit in the huts looking out at the men from windows and open doorways. Rick felt like he was living in a National Geographic documentary.

Each evening a feast, as it were, was held in the little tribal settlements. Food was plentiful in the mornings, as well. A cheery Dua made their burdens seem light by selecting the best trails to follow. They stayed close to the border with Vietnam, but far enough away to not be detected.

During the day, Dua found wild fruits and coconuts, and water was clean and plentiful in the numerous waterfalls they came upon. Rick thought to himself, *This would be paradise if it weren't for the insects, and the leeches, and the monsoon rains, and the hundred-degree heat, and the snakes, and the lack of Walmart's and 7-11's.*

The little group trudged on through the jungles staying about ten miles west of the Da Krong River which runs through the valley by the same name. This was the closest they had come to the border. Their entry point into Vietnam was close. It would be a small road and border crossing near the border town of Tam Boi at the southern end of the Da Krong Valley and the northern beginning of the A Shau Valley.

It had taken the team 13 days to get to what the Vietnamese called *The Frontier*, the untamed border area. Dua told the team to wait for a few hours while he went ahead to scout the border crossing. When he returned, he said there were many soldiers there and the team would be unable to cross.

Rick asked, "Mr. Dua, what do you think is the most difficult way into Vietnam?"

"Toughest way would be to go maybe ten kilometers around to the south and then east and climb Dong Ap Bia, Hamburger Hill."

Rick was dubious, "That 'hill' is 937-meters high, 3,074 feet above sea level."

Dua replied, "Yes. That why it best way. Safe way. Police and soldiers too lazy to patrol there. Big stupid."

Rick could see how it made sense.

CHAPTER SIXTY-EIGHT

That night, the team stayed in Laos in a hamlet with an old Hmong warrior chief. The old man talked of the American War. He did not understand how one day, all the Americans were gone, and the communists had come. He asked Rick why the Americans had abandoned them. Rick had no answer other than bad politicians made bad decisions. The old man said, "Chiefs should take care of their warriors, of their people, but sometimes chiefs are no good."

Rick slowly nodded and felt an overwhelming sadness deep in his heart.

The old man continued talking with Dua translating, "The communists have made everything worse. Many of my friends were taken away and killed right away. A few returned after many years in reeducation camps. In front of authorities, they claimed to be reeducated, but in reality, they emerged hating the communists more than ever. Since that time, we have slowly picked away at the police and at the army whenever, usually under cover of darkness, the opportunity presents itself."

Rick was impressed with this tough old bird. The old man lived in the harshest of realities that most protected people in the States could never comprehend. *In a way,* thought Rick, *that is very sad.*

While they were talking, two Hmong tribesmen arrived at the little village and were surprised to see a White man sitting with the elders. Tuan explained to the newcomers what they had gone through during the past two months. One of the two men said, "I have heard of a White man being found near a place the American soldiers call Hill 875. It is southwest of Dak To. But he is dead. No one understood how he got there. The local villagers have buried him near the bottom of the hill. That is all I heard. I have not seen this myself."

Rick looked at Tuan, "Could that be Steve?"

"Dak To is 250 kilometers from Phou Nhoi. How could your friend get there? It is probably some other American, or a European. Maybe on a tour or maybe volunteer medical person? There are many those all over Vietnam."

Rick did a quick kilometers-to-miles calculation in his head. He figured it was about 155 miles from the Phou Nhoi battle site to the Hill 875 area near Dak To. "Mr. Tuan, we have to go and make sure."

Tuan nodded.

CHAPTER SIXTY-NINE

Early the next morning, the team started along the jungle trail and climbed the near sheer wall of a mountain that was the border with Vietnam. It took three hours of slow and careful climbing to reach the top the 700-meter-high cliff. Next, they hiked almost two kilometers on rough and descending terrain before they began climbing Hamburger Hill from the southwest. The terrain quickly changed to an almost vertical climb.

Rick wondered how thousands of NVA, with all their equipment, had managed it during the war. The battle had pitted the 101st Airborne's 3rd Brigade against the well-entrenched NVA. Attacking up the hill ten times during the ten-day battle, the Airborne troops finally drove the enemy from the mountaintop on the eleventh try. Over 700 men had died gruesome deaths attacking or defending the hill, which was why they called it 'hamburger.'

About halfway up, they came upon a crashed Huey helicopter from the war. It had vines growing all through it and if it hadn't been for the yellow and white Screaming Eagle logo of the 101st Airborne on the green tail section, they would have missed it.

Just out of curiosity, they stopped to inspect the aircraft. Obviously, it had been shot down. It was resting on its side on a gentle slope under an eroded cliff. Looking inside, they found a skull. Thoughts of it being an American MIA were quickly dismissed because of the NVA helmet lying next to the skull. "Not American?" asked Tuan.

"No Mr. Tuan. When a helicopter crashed, we did all we could to extract the crew alive or dead. Soon the NVA would come along and try to retrieve guns, ammo, and radios. If we considered the aircraft a loss or if it was in a too-hostile area, we'd send in the fast-movers to blow it up. This poor guy was probably trying to scavenge something when it was bombed."

"Fast-movers?"

"Yeah, fighter-bombers."

"Ha, that funny. Fighter-bombers fly fast. So you say fast-movers. Why not say fast-flyers?"

"I guess that sounds more logical. We Americans use catchy slang words for a lot of common military things. It makes it more fun. It also confuses the enemy, which we sometimes called Indians. For example, we might say 'Ma Deuce' for a .50 caliber machinegun. Or we may say 'Going over-the-fence,' meaning crossing into Laos or Cambodia from Vietnam. To announce a supply helicopter, we sometimes called it a 'Slick.' Asking for 'Dump Trucks' would be a call for a B-52 carpet-bombing strike. We also say, 'blow away' or 'grease' or 'nail' or 'waste' or 'zap' or 'hose,' instead of saying 'kill.' I could write a book about the hundreds, if not thousands, of slang words and lingo expressions we used during the war."

"You Americans mighty strange, Mr. Rick."

"No argument there, my friend." Rick turned to their Hmong guide, "Mr. Dua, we better get going."

Dua had been right, no cops, no army. After another three-hour climb, they were at the top of the 937-meter-high Hamburger Hill. Drenched in sweat, bruised, and scraped, they sat on the edge of an old NVA trench line and rested silently for a half hour.

Then Dua said, "My friends, you in Vietnam now and I must leave you. I must return to Laos to Hmong village before dark, or tigers will have me for dinner."

Rick stood, "My friend, Mr. Dua, I will never forget you. And I will never forget your grandfather. You and he are blessed with the same fighting spirit. I am forever in your debt."

Rick knew better than to insult the man with an offer of money. Dua had provided his services from his heart, to honor his grandfather. Besides, what would a tribesman do with money? For thousands of years, their clans have lived off the land in these mountains, sharing and trading. With that, Rick brought his hands in a prayer position, touching the tips of his fingers to his lips, and bowed.

"Mr. Rick, I never forget you, too." He gave Rick a prayerful bow in return. Dua, with his unseen grandfather beside him, turned and started down the mountain.

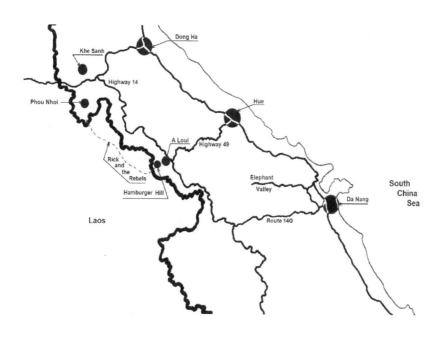

Rick and the Rebel's route through Laos to Hamburger Hill

CHAPTER SEVENTY

Rick, Tuan, and the three rebels lingered at the top of the mountain. On the western horizon, a blood-red sun dipped lower near the peaks of distant, dark blue mountains. Although gorgeous in its grandeur, Rick saw no beauty.

To Rick, these mountains represented nothing but death and suffering. The whole of the DMZ was an endless range of ragged and dangerous battlefields. Phou Nhoi was a mountain that had provided nothing but death and anguish, now, as well as 50 years ago. The hill they were currently standing atop, Hamburger Hill, was given its name because of the many mangled deaths of so many young men in both armies. Rick wouldn't care if he never saw another mountain for the rest of his life. He longed for the flat streets of New York City.

But before he left the hated mountains behind, he would have to find Steve.

"What now, Mr. Tuan?

"We go to safe house I know. Easier climb down mountain from here. Maybe two hours walk. Stay near bottom until very dark. Then go safe house. It in town of A Loui. We stay tonight and talk of our journey to Dak To."

Rick nodded, tears forming in his eyes. Tuan was an amazing friend.

CHAPTER SEVENTY-ONE

They arrived at the safe house in a miserable rainstorm, which had served to cover their movements from prying eyes in this busy town. They entered through the back entrance, greeted by another rebel who posed as a store owner specializing in soaps and cleaning supplies.

Like most shops in Vietnam, the store was in the front of the house, streetside, and the living area in back. Bedrooms were one or two stories above. The house smelled sweet and clean. The men took showers, ate a hastily prepared meal, and fell asleep on futons. They were exhausted from the day's climb and from the unrelenting anxieties of possibly being detected by the hostile authorities.

Very early the next morning, Tuan and Rick said goodbye to the three remaining rebels who had fought so valiantly at Phou Nhoi. The three men departed before dawn and slinked across Highway 14, under the cover of darkness, and into the mountains. The trio would make their way back to Hue and begin planning their next subversive activities. Tuan and Rick would find them later after visiting the Dak To area.

As the sun came up, Rick looked through the front curtains on the second floor and was shocked at what he saw. "Tuan! The district police headquarters is across the street!"

"It is, my friend. We hide in plain sight. They never think to look for us here."

Rick considered the logic and calmed down after the adrenaline rush. Once again, Tuan was right.

The rebel storeowner made calls to arrange for safe transportation. It would take until the next day for a vehicle to pick them up for the drive to the Dak To area. Tuan had spoken with someone who knows the area well, and was told they should go to Plei Can, a village west of Dak To. The hike to Hill 875 would be easier from there, but still a many-hours trek.

In the meantime, Rick and Tuan rested and tried to decompress from the chaos and the horrors of the past few weeks. They took several more showers, trying to scrub off almost a month's worth of grime and stink.

That evening, Tuan said, "Brand new Land Rover come tomorrow. Pick us up at five in the afternoon."

"Another hide in plain sight diversion?"

"Yes. Police think we go back Hue or to Khe Sanh in ox cart, hiding under straw. As Mr. Dua say, 'big stupid.' No one look new expensive car for lowly, frightened rebel."

"Tell me something, Mr. Tuan. How do you stay so cheerful? You lost some very good men back at Phou Nhoi, especially Tiger. I still grieve for the men I lost in the war before you were born."

"Ah, Mr. Rick. You see things wrong. You fight for short time. I fight for all time. Lost many friends so far, but if believe in Cause, if belief right, you fight forever. Sacrifices are certain. Death certain. Never mind. One day I get killed, but OK. Cause for freedom go on. It mean little I die. But while here do best. Try to have life, but ready to be martyr. Must die for important, not stupid. Maybe die sooner, maybe die later. Everybody die sometime. Never mind."

Rick let Tuan's words sink in for a few minutes. *Tuan has total commitment. 100% commitment. He does nothing half-assed. He's more a man than I am.*

"Do you expect to be killed, Mr. Tuan?"

"Oh, yes. One day police or army find me. But they not find me for stupid mistake. They find me for betrayal."

"What? No. I have only seen loyalty given to you by your friends. They would never betray you."

"Ah, Mr. Rick. You still see things wrong. You think this America. You think Vietnam have laws protect people. You think I ask government and government give me freedom. No. I ask, I go to jail. Never come out."

"OK, I understand that. But why would your friends want to betray you?"

"Not want betray. Must betray. Your eyes stay closed, my friend. If I found, it because of betray. Police and commando know torture be messy, take time, not always work. Best way is scare to make talk, tell secrets. They promise torture and death to rebel's family, to hurt rebel's little boy or little girl. Rebel talk. Can not help it. Work every time. Then I found. But OK, I understand. Never mind. Fight still go on. More rebels always."

Rick nodded and did not ask any more questions.

CHAPTER SEVENTY-TWO

At the safe house in A Loui, Rick was able to charge his long dead cell phone and call the States. Early that afternoon, he spoke with Oki, the tour company's Executive Vice President. It was two in the morning in Oklahoma, but Oki was awake. "Rick! Where are you? All hell is breaking loose here."

"As I might imagine. You won't believe what's going on here either."

"Steve Picante's kids called. They said he was declared dead by the embassy. They are terribly upset. The embassy said his body was not found. The kids want their father back. They want to give him a military funeral. If they can't find a body, he could still be alive. I don't know what to tell them."

"He may be dead, but I'm not so sure. The details are sketchy. Listen, I can never return to the States. Long, long story, my friend. I need you to take me off the company roster. You're the president now."

"Yeah, well, there ain't no company anymore. We've been informed by the State Department and by the Vietnamese embassy in Washington that there will be no more visas issued to any of us, for any reason. We are personas non grata in Vietnam. We are effectively shut down. Then the FBI showed up and said you were in deep trouble with the Vietnamese authorities. They ordered us to report any contact with you. They may even have tapped this phone. What am I supposed to do? What the hell did you do?"

"Easy, Oki. Me and some rebels, I didn't know they were rebels at first, were searching for Steve in Phou Nhoi. Vietnamese commandos tracked us down and murdered one of the rebels right in front of us. That started a firefight and a running gun battle. I got caught up in it. I didn't mean for it to happen. Like I said, it's a long story. You need to know that I will never see you guys and my home again. Tell the guys I love them and that it's been an honor serving with them all these years."

Rick was choking up. He could really use their help right now. All the tour guides in his organization had been exceptional fighters during the war. But he cared more about them than he did for himself. There was no way he would put his partners in harm's way for his mistakes.

"Oki, after you hang up, call the FBI and tell them you spoke with me. Don't hold anything back, you'll get into trouble with the Feds if you do. That's the last thing you guys need.

"I'm hiding out in Phnom Penh, Cambodia right now. I'm trying to make arrangements to get to Thailand. Who knows where to after that. Maybe I'll open a bar in Malaysia or Indonesia. I love you my brother, take good care of yourself. I am truly sorry for all this."

"Rick! Wait!"

The line went dead. Rick hated himself for the little lie he told at the end of his conversation with Oki.

"You heard, Mr. Tuan?"

"Yes. Must be my government tell your government you bad man and they need help. Governments work together to catch you. They no care for truth. They want only to kill good Viets and to keep sneaker factories open. Give me phone."

Rick handed his phone to Tuan. Much to Rick's horror, Tuan smashed it on the tile floor, breaking the glass screen. He pulled out the SIM card and ground it under his heel. Then he bent the phone in half. "Later tonight, we throw in river when drive to Dak To."

"Tuan, what the hell."

"Police track phone at cell towers. I watch NCIS reruns. Learn many things. When Land Rover come driver bring burner phones and extra SIM burner cards. I learn that too. No find us by phone. NCIS very good I think."

"I've been out of the police business for a long time, Mr. Tuan. You know more about this stuff than me."

"Yes, it true. Now listen. We only make phone call when must use. Never use for fun. No Myface, no Spacebook."

"You mean Myspace and Facebook."

"Whatever. OK, no fun calls. Never use message unless code. No names, no places, no dates, no times we do something. If use phone to call States for emergency, we break phone after. Never mind."

Rick was impressed with Tuan's strategies. *He is one smart rebel. It must be what has kept him alive all these years.*

CHAPTER SEVENTY-THREE

At 5:00pm, as if on cue, the Land Rover pulled up at the back of the soap store. Rick and Tuan stole quickly into the car, Tuan in the front next to the driver, Rick on the back seat. Rick's Whiteness made him an obvious suspect. So, he would have to endure the 100-mile drive, lying cramped on the seat hidden under a sheet, itself hidden by 30 bundles of new cleaning rags. But at least he wasn't climbing mountains.

The cargo area behind the back seat was lined with open cardboard boxes filled with various cleaning supplies. Rick accepted his plight figuring, *It may be hot and cramped down here, but it does smell nice.* Tuan gave him a couple of bottles of water and started piling on the bundles.

They were soon off, heading down Highway 14. The new road was well-paved and held little traffic. The mountainous scenery was spectacular as the road wound through the wilderness, but Rick could see nothing from his little car cave.

Within a half hour, Tuan announced, "Hey Mr. Rick. Your flip phone just land in river."

From under the cleaning rag bundles Rick replied, "It's not a flip phone. It's an iPhone."

"No. It become flip phone when I bend in half." Tuan broke out in hysterical laughter.

"You're a real wise ass, Mr. Tuan."

They veered off Highway 14 onto Route 17. It was the more direct way to Plei Can. Arriving at 10:00pm, the Land Rover parked in front of a tiny store and the driver and Tuan started unloading the boxes stuffed with cleaning supplies. They opened the car's back door and removed a few bundles of rags. Rick did a low crawl into the building.

After the unloading was complete, the Land Rover departed. The driver would return with the vehicle when beckoned by Tuan.

"Whose house is this, Mr. Tuan?"

"It is home of my mother's brother. My uncle. He was Captain in SVN army. Commies send him to reeducation camp eight years. Hard labor, many lectures, much punishment. He come home broken. Never same. He die young. Now my cousin runs store. That why I have key. He gone to mountain village to get Hmong man. Come back tonight. We leave for village early morning. We sleep now. Long walk later to village."

As Rick laid back on a futon in the darkness, he was drawn back to Christmas of 1969. He was in Phu Bai for the holiday 'cease fire.' Christmas Eve was a quiet night — calm and warm — pretty good for the monsoon season. Some of the South Vietnamese allies, the ARVN, Army of the Republic of Vietnam, were in camp, too. Rick's unit was in a stand-down role, and they got to relax a little.

There were steaks, beer, and a lot of laughs. The USO had provided a scantily clad, all-girl band from the Philippines which sang such songs as *Proud Mary*. But the lyrics: 'Rollin', rollin', rollin' on the river,' in their Philippine accent sounded like, 'Lowlin', lowlin', lowlin' on da libbah.' It was great. He remembered how these USO shows were a short reprieve from war, but they made a great impact on morale. When the show ended, Rick and his squad returned to their SEAhut and continued the festivities.

The rear area SEAhuts, the plywood and tin one-story buildings, seemed like paradise to Marines accustomed to living in the mud.

As the squad of young Marines wandered back in the darkness toward the hut, each of them was filled with their own private Christmas memories.

Usually at night, firing from somewhere nearby, there was outgoing artillery. With every blast from the big guns, there was the knowledge someone on the receiving end was being torn apart, their lives abruptly ending. Their sudden deaths were brought to Rick in dull, distant thuds. It was the music of the night in Vietnam. But that night, was silent. Rick could actually hear the silence, and it was unnerving. It felt like *the calm before the storm*. It felt like something bad was about to happen.

Later that evening, a South Vietnamese Captain named Loc showed up with rice wine and pastries. In turn, the Marines shared with him their booze and the treats that had been sent from their families. Loc and the Marines, weary of death and destruction, took the time to know one another. They talked about their families, and Captain Loc told them about how things had changed in Vietnam since the communists had tried to take his country. He said he was the last of his family. He had lost everyone and everything, his mother and father, and his wife, and his children. Loc told them about each of them. Loc said his life was over. He was crying. He hated the communists and everything they stood for and for everything they had done to his family, to him, and to South Vietnam. It occurred to him that Loc indeed had nothing to live for, except his revenge. Rick felt helpless that he couldn't do anything to make Loc's life better. They all stood and vowed to kill as many goddamn communists as possible. They drank to it and shook hands.

Rick was not sure how the conversation changed, but it did. They began to talk of more pleasant things that teenagers liked to talk about: girls, cars, home. They sang songs in English and Vietnamese, even though they could not understand the words. They even had a miniature plastic Christmas tree and some small presents that had been sent from the States. Nearby the meager decorations celebrating the birth of Christ, were their weapons. They didn't expect to use them, but they were ready just the same. For some reason, Rick recalled the irony of the juxtaposition. It was a quiet night combat-wise. Calm. Nice for Vietnam.

As the night wore on, they were relaxing and talking quietly in the dim light. One of the guys started singing 'Silent Night.' They all joined in, singing softly. There was a long quiet after the song. Each of them was lost somewhere in long ago Christmas's. The mood turned melancholy. There was little talk after that. Rick thought about his family and his hometown. They were safe and there was no war there. They had finished the hustle and bustle of Christmas shopping, had decorated the tree, and were together and happy in the sharing of the gifts and the love and the hope that Christmas renews each year. Rick had wished he was there.

One-by-one, they fell off to sleep.

Early the next morning just before the sun rose, Loc collected his weapons and silently disappeared into the half-light of dawn. Rick did not know why he feigned sleep as he watched Loc go. He should have wished him well. Perhaps he was afraid of Loc's pain, or his own. Or perhaps Rick figured that Loc had enough goodbyes in his life. That was the last Rick ever saw of Loc. He did not know if Loc made it.

From that night on, Rick had been haunted by the hymn 'Silent Night.' It tears him up and overwhelming memories flood into his soul. It always brings him back to the Christmas of 1969, because a silent night in Vietnam was a good night. And he always thinks of Loc.

Now, with the talk of those brutal reeducation camps, Rick thought about Loc. *God, please let him have made it. Let him be happy. Let his heart be at peace.*

That Christmas was tough for Steve as well. He had been sent down to Da Nang by helicopter to the Marble Mountain Air Facility to do some logistical work with a few other guys. He had visited the China Beach Orphanage and Steve was never the same again. Rick had sensed it back then. *Heck, Steve talked about it on the bus. It has stayed with him.*

Rick's mind kept wandering. The night before returning to the field after the ceasefire, both Rick and Steve fought an unexpected battle that would be forever etched on their minds. He smiled, *Oh, heck, I forgot all about that.*

Rick awoke with something crawling across his lips. He thought it was a small rat, but no, it was a big cockroach. He swept the thing away and jumped out of his rack. Rick's bare feet were cracking small creatures on the floor. Steve had been awakened as well, and he yelled, "Get up! Get up! Get up!"

The eight Marines billeted in the SEAhut started screaming when the overhead lights flew on. The entire hootch was crawling with giant cockroaches. These huge bugs were on the floor, on the cots, on the walls, on the ceilings. They were jumping on and crawling on the guys. The Marines were smacking them with their jungle boots, stomping them with bare feet, flailing at them as they landed on their backs, faces, necks, and arms. It was sheer cockroach pandemonium. The cockroaches kept scurrying from place to place trying to avoid the violent wrath of some very pissed-off Marines. The Marines kept going at them, not letting up. Snap, crackle, and pop they went as they were hit, spewing their innards all over everything. It seemed like every surface was covered black with these revolting, malevolent bugs. The fight went on for nearly an hour.

The Marines naturally won this battle, but the aftermath was nauseating and foul. Fetid guts of thousands of cockroaches were splattered everywhere, huge gobs of the reeking stuff. After catching their breaths and calming down, one of the guys dragged in a hose and they washed down everything and swept the gunk out both ends of the hut. No one went back to sleep.

Those things were about three inches long, thick, and dark colored. Maybe they were palmetto bugs which look like cockroaches. Who knows? Whatever they were, they swarmed that night and only that night. Whether they were mating, migrating, or searching for food, they picked the wrong hootch to invade. There was a lot of ardent and imaginative language that night.

Rick laughed out loud.

Tuan muttered, "Go to sleep."

CHAPTER SEVENTY-FOUR

The ambassador, several attachés, and the FBI agent who interviewed Rick about the disappearance of Steve a few months ago, sat at the same conference table in the American Embassy in Hanoi where Rick had given his report. They were waiting for a couple of high-level representatives from the Vietnamese government to arrive.

"Do any of you have a clue as to what this is about?" asked the Ambassador.

"Well, sir, we think it has something to do with some trouble with some rebels down south near Khe Sanh."

"So what? For years we've known all about them hunting down rebels. What has it got to do with us? It's an intra-Vietnam problem and none of our business."

The FBI agent stammered, "Well, uh, sir, uh. Well, we have reason to believe that an American Marine is operating with the rebels, and they have recently killed a couple of dozen Vietnamese commandos and had managed to wound a bunch more. We also have reason to believe that this man is now in Phnom Penh, heading for Thailand."

"Good God! This can't be true." The ambassador was incredulous. "We've dealt with drug smugglers and some prostitution busts when Americans were involved. But this is the most serious of breaches and it can egregiously affect international relations. If this is authentic, we'll need all pressure applied to find and bring this guy to justice.

"Promise them we'll cooperate. Go ahead and supply any open intelligence we can gather, just as long as we don't reveal any sensitive sources. Make them believe we're on their side. You know the dance, gentlemen."

They did indeed know the dance. It had been going on since relations were normalized back in 1995 by President Bill Clinton. No one took seriously any information or statistic that came from a communist country, and Vietnam was no exception. The World Health Organization takes a dim view of health statistics emanating from communist countries. As does the FBI for their crime statistics. The International Monetary Fund and the World Bank continue to be very suspicious of massive corruption and resource disappearances. Billions in investments and billions in aid had vanished over the past decades. But commerce and access to cheap labor were imperative to U.S. interests. Accordingly, everyone at the embassy does the dance. Add that Vietnam is essentially anti-China, and the tempo rises.

The ambassador stood to leave, "Dammit, I don't need this on my record. Prepare a report as soon as they leave and get it to me ASAP. And send the public relations rep into my office right now."

The ambassador walked out.

Ten minutes later, in walked Lt. General Nguyen Phiet who was the Under-Secretary for Military Affairs, and Maj. Gen. Pham, commander of all commando forces in Vietnam. Neither looked happy.

The military attaché' began, "Welcome to the U.S. Embassy gentlemen. How may we be of service?"

Lt. Gen. Nguyen began, "I'll get right to the point. We have reason to believe that a citizen of your country is assisting rebels in Quang Tri Province. They have killed 23 of Maj. Gen. Pham's commandos. We need your help to find the American and to help us eradicate the rebels."

"Of course, General. You will have our full and complete cooperation. Let's lay out all the facts and get to work."

The dance had begun.

CHAPTER SEVENTY-FIVE

At about three in the morning, Tuan's cousin and a Hmong guide arrived. Tuan and Rick were ready, and they followed the indefatigable tribal guide quickly into the forest. Tuan's exhausted cousin remained at the store and went to bed.

Turning southwest into a dark, narrow valley, the trio marched down a trail nearly invisible to all but a tribesman's eye. The manner in which people adapted to seemingly inhospitable topography, climate, and remoteness had always intrigued Rick. When he was little, his father had moved the family from San Diego on California's west coast to Elmont in New York's Long Island on the east coast. His dad, always the adventurous type often took back roads, the roads less traveled. They had passed through such places as Mesa Verde where the cliff-dwelling Anasazi once lived, and through the Ozarks to see real hillbillies. And here he was in the wilderness border-region jungles of Vietnam, Laos, and Cambodia. *Why,* he thought, *would anyone choose to live here?*

Seven hours later, at about noon, they arrived at a Hmong village. The guide said to stay, and he disappeared into a hut. A moment later, an old man exited the hut and greeted the visitors. Tuan translated, "This man is the chief. His name is Pao Lang. You can call him Lang. He says he is honored by your presence." With that, the old man invited them into the hut.

Before any talk, lunch was served by two of the chief's topless daughters. Rick knew this was a cultural nuance, not sexual in any way, but it was still quite distracting. The lovely Hmong girls brought in 12 dishes of various foods in several trips. Rick tried desperately to avoid looking directly at the girls' obvious assets. Thankfully, they left the men alone to eat.

213

When the meal was finished, the men moved to the porch and sat in a circle facing each other. Tuan translated. "Chief says you must have important reason to travel so far to this humble village."

"Mr. Lang, I thank you for the food you have most graciously provided. And I thank you for allowing us to impose upon you in this, your beautiful home."

"You will always be welcomed here, Mr. Rick. Now tell me why you have come."

"Mr. Lang, it is true we have ventured far to come to this place. I understand you have found a White man. Can you tell us the circumstances?"

"Ah yes, that. My son and two of our tribesmen were foraging deep in the jungle, as they are now. Near the mountain you call Hill 875, they smelled a death odor. You must understand that every once in a while, we will lose a tribe member to the spirits. They leave the village, go into the jungle, and never return. It is a sad price we must pay as mountain people. The jungle gives us sustenance, gives us our homes. But sometimes the jungle spirit takes one or two of us for its own needs. It is okay.

"So, my son and the others go to the source of the smell to see if it was one of our own, or if it was a large animal. It was neither. It was a White man with hair the color of straw. They were confused. Where did he come from? How did he get here? It seemed like he was dropped from the sky. By the time they found him, the man was mostly bones, scattered around a bamboo stalk. The animals and insects had eaten most of him. I am sorry. Such a fate comes quickly here.

"I do not know if it is your friend. But my son and the others buried what was left of the man. They brought to me a ring and some small papers that were found with the remains. Would you like to see the items?"

Rick nodded, unable to speak.

The chief brought out a folded and tied piece of tattered, red Hawaiian-pattern cloth. Rick knew the truth even before Lang unfolded the material. He handed the items to Rick.

The papers were in a thin leather wallet. Rick looked through it and found that the photo and the documents were all but destroyed by water, blood, and mold. Then he picked up the gold wedding ring. Even though Sharon was dead, Steve had refused to take it off, saying, "Just because she's gone, doesn't mean I'm no longer married to her."

If Rick had any lingering doubt that the dead man was Steve, the ring dashed all hope. He read the inscription. It said simply, *Sharon Loves Steve.*

It was a silly, endearing engraving on the ring that a young Sharon had given to Steve on their wedding day. She did it in response to the engraved engagement ring that Steve had given to her a year before they were married.

Shortly after their discharges from the Marine Corps, Rick was there at the jewelry store when Steve bought the engagement ring for Sharon. Steve had ordered it engraved with the words, *Steve Loves Sharon.* Rick exclaimed, "Dude! What, are you in the eighth grade? That's so immature."

But Steve was adamant, "Don't you get it, Rick? This says it all. Nothing else matters."

Rick leaned against the jewelry counter and shook his head, "Dude, you're so lame."

Rick sat cross-legged on the chief's porch, holding Steve's ring. "I get it now, Steve," he said out loud to the ring, "It was simple and beautiful. And it expressed it all."

Rick bowed his head and cried for a few minutes. He couldn't help himself. Tuan and Lang sat silently and waited.

When Rick recovered, he removed his solid gold, Marine Corps ring and gave it to the chief in exchange for the thin, modest wedding band of his best friend.

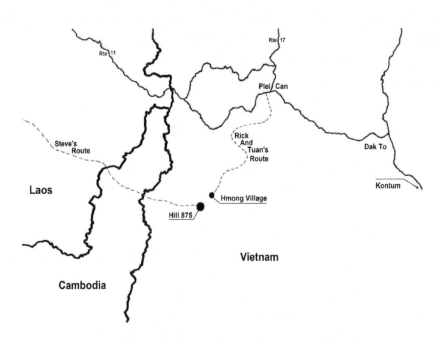

**Confluence: Laos, Vietnam, and Cambodia; and
Rick & Tuan's route to the Hmong village**

CHAPTER SEVENTY-SIX

It was two in the morning the following day when Rick and Tuan got back to the safe house in A Loui.

Tuan passed out on a futon.

Rick could not sleep.

Rick sat in the darkness contemplating just what kind of man he was. He had finally convinced his best friend, after many years of trying, to come to Vietnam on a tour. And because of it, his best friend was now dead. His other friend, Tuan, had acted above and beyond what any friend would be expected to do. Rick looked back on the last two months. Tuan had been there for him from day one. And Rick had nearly gotten him killed. Tuan lost four of his men because of Rick. And now here he was, totally dependent on Tuan. Rick knew his loyal Vietnamese friend would not let him down. It hit him hard that Tuan had shown true friendship, but he had not been the friend that Tuan had been.

Then Rick remembered the last thing he had said to his best friend. He had called Steve a wise ass. He wished he could take it back. Those two words would be the last Rick would ever utter to his best friend.

Rick could never, as Tuan had so strongly stated, go home. *What good would going home do? How many years are left for me to live anyway? Am I supposed to become dumpy and sedentary? Do I move into a senior community, play bridge with the other old farts, get my prostate removed, eat early-bird specials, and gripe about crabgrass? Is that how it ends? Lying in a nursing home crapping in my adult diaper? Waiting for dementia and Alzheimer's to set in? No! This changes now!*

Rick woke up Tuan. "I agree, I'm one of you now."

Tuan replied groggily, "I already knew that."

217

With Tuan back to sleep and snoring, Rick set new goals for his life. He knew Tuan needed him and he knew Tuan had saved his life. The mission to find Steve was over. His mission now would be to help his new best friend regain the lost Vietnam of his ancestors. He would become a true friend to Tuan, and to do it, he would revert to his military ways.

A sudden calmness came over Rick. His life was now simple. The military after all, was an easy life. All major decisions are made for you. You had one job and were expected to do it well. All extraneous and mundane choices do not exist. The mission is all that matters. Focus on the mission.

Rick was wearing Steve's wedding band.

CHAPTER SEVENTY-SEVEN

Trong felt miserable. He was now without authority and without forced respect and without kowtowing from people around him. He was constantly nauseous from the pain, and the pain was nearly unbearable. Kim had severed his urethra and the doctors could not repair the damage. Consequently, Trong had to have a permanent plastic tube sticking out of his abdomen to drain urine into a bag strapped to his leg. Fungus was growing around the belly tube drain port. The tube slowly leaked urine and he always smelled of piss.

Another police officer had taken over his duties and the local citizens breathed a sigh of relief that the tyrant Trong was no longer in a position to hurt them. They believed he had made a deal with the Phou Nhoi demons and now he was paying the price for his evil doings.

The only bitterness Trong felt was that he did not kill what he deemed his 'worthless wife' long ago. He blamed everyone else for his current predicament. Trong had tried to have his replacement killed, but he was met with laughter and was dismissed by those who used to do his dirty work.

One day when he could not stand the pain and humiliation any longer, Trong boarded the local bus on its way to Dong Ha on Route 9. After only seven kilometers, when they approached the Hairpin Bridge, he had the driver stop and let him out. Standing on the road, Trong watched the bus disappear around the sharp curve where the bridge crossed high over a tight, raging river gorge.

Trong hobbled out to the middle of the bridge and peered down over the side. He pulled off the urine bag and yanked out the tube connected to the drain port in his abdomen. He threw them into the roadway. Piss squirted out of the hole in his belly.

219

He started laughing, saying out loud, "Well, you don't see that every day."

He then climbed the barrier. He held onto the guard rail with one hand while leaning out over the torrent far below him. Trong paused for a minute trying to think of a prayer, and to whom to pray. Thinking of none, he shrugged, and let go.

Trong hit the rocks feet first, shattering all the bones in his legs, before being swept downstream by the violent force of the water. He wondered why he was not dead. He tumbled downriver and over a spillway. He was slammed between two large rocks and his right arm snapped in two, the ulna and radius bones splintering through muscle and skin. Intense pain surged through his broken body. Trong screamed and his lungs filled with water. He passed out. The rapids eventually flushed him into a wide lake. His body floated to tranquil waters in the bright sunlight, and then slowly sank.

The mountains appeared anchored to themselves like juxtaposed portraits reflecting mirrorlike on the calm lake. All was serene until a slight ripple disturbed the water's surface. It was the only indication that Trong's soul had been plucked down to Hell.

CHAPTER SEVENTY-EIGHT

At midnight, two days after returning from the trip to Plei Can, Tuan and Rick sat talking in the safe house. They could have tried driving to Hue on the only road from A Loui through the mountains, the old Route 549. But the driver of the Land Rover reported there were multiple roadblocks searching for the rebels. The mountain road to Hue would not be an option. Tuan figured the road back north and then onto Route 9 going east would also be a bad idea. Too many police and too much army in that area.

Tuan had not heard from the three rebels who had departed for Hue four days ago, nor did he expect to. They were making their way back to Hue by the safest way possible, through 34 kilometers, about 21 miles, of some of Vietnam's harshest mountain terrain. They would be lucky to make it across in 12 days, then another day or two on foot to get to a safe house.

"Mr. Tuan, what's your plan?"

"OK, Mr. Rick. At 3:00am, Land Rover come behind house. We load up you under rag bundles. Put cleaning supplies in cardboard boxes in back. Same-same last time. I ride shotgun. Easy to do, but long ride. We go south on Highway 14 maybe four hours. We arrive Huyen Dong Giang town. Stop at safe house. We rest and eat. Later we change to pig truck. You ride in middle of pig cages. We cover your cage top with tarp. Tarp keep you not get pooped on. It stink ride but safe."

"A pig truck? Are you kidding me?"

"Land Rover no good to go Da Nang. Cleaning supplies come from Da Nang. Not go to Da Nang. Police wonder why and stop Land Rover. We take pig truck. Never mind. Police not stop pig truck. Big stupid."

"Aww, Tuan. How about a log truck or a sand truck?"

"Not have those. Have only pig truck."

"OK, so we're in Huyen Dong Giang and we load up on the pig truck. Then what? We go to Da Nang?"

"We go close Da Nang. We go east on Highway 14G for maybe three hours more. New road, but narrow. We pass through Happy Valley north side of Charlie Ridge. Then we go through Leech Valley."

"Oh, this is getting better by the minute. I'll be in a truck carrying a couple hundred pigs, of which I will be one, going through Leech Valley. What other surprises do you have for me?"

Tuan had a big smile on his face, "That worst of it. We stop at slaughterhouse in Tuy Loan west side Da Nang, give pigs. You wash there because you stink. I bring new clothes for you. We get picked up in old car. We go to Hoa Bac in Elephant Valley to safe house. We stay one night. Next day go Hue in rush hours."

"I'm starting to think maybe we should hump the 21 miles through the mountains to Hue instead."

"Ha! You too old, Mr. Rick. I have to carry you whole way. No, we go my plan. Never mind."

"And you're too old to carry me. I guess we go by car and pig truck."

Rick laid back to rest before the drive. He was starting to feel old. The intense physicality of being a warrior was taking its toll. He was no longer the young Marine full of grit that he was in 1969. The only grit he feels now is in his joints. He thinks maybe his body is starting to break down. He knew he had no way out of this, and he knew his days were numbered.

He had three choices. One, he could give himself up. He would then be tortured for information about the rebels and later executed. Or worse, after the torture, he'd rot in a Vietnamese prison, sick, broken, and infirmed until he died. Two, he could keep running with the rebels and get more of them killed, because they would always be looking out for the old man. Or three, he could go out in a blaze of glory helping to rid Vietnam of its many tyrants.

He picked the latter. But he would not go easily. Rick was determined to fight until the end, and to be facing the enemy when he dies. He closed his eyes for a couple of hours sleep.

Through The Gates of Hell

CHAPTER SEVENTY-NINE

At 3:00am, the Land Rover pulled up to the back door. They quickly loaded Rick into the back seat and covered him with a sheet. Tuan gave him a couple of water bottles, and a loaded handgun. With the bundles of rags piled on him and the boxes of cleaning supplies loaded in the back, they headed south again on Highway 14.

The sun had just risen when they crossed the A Vuong River and arrived at Huyen Dong Giang town. At the junction with Highway 14G, they turned east and within a mile, Rick could smell the pig farm. He groaned. He much preferred the lemon and pine scent of the Land Rover.

The driver guided the car into a barn and the doors slid closed behind them. The guys exited the car and walked into a large hut behind the barn. Breakfast was ready for them. Coffee, baguettes, spring rolls, hardboiled eggs, and of course, pork. Despite the stink of pig all around, Rick found himself hungry and he enjoyed the meal.

"We rest here until 2:00pm. Then go Tuy Loan give pigs. Then go safe house Elephant Valley."

Rick woke after five hours of sleep on a futon. Tuan was already up making sure the pig truck gambit would work. All was in order.

"OK Mr. Rick, you ready for luxury ride?"

"What's so luxury about riding in the middle of a bunch of smelly pigs?"

"It luxury because when get to Tuy Loan, you don't get slaughtered like pigs." Tuan starts laughing hysterically again.

"Well, I can't argue with that. I guess it's all a matter of one's perspective."

224

The pig truck carries three tiers of cages, 15 cages per tier, three cages wide, five cages long, five pigs to a cage, for a total of 225 pigs.

Rick came out of the hut and stopped dead in his tracks, "Tuan! These aren't pigs. They're hogs."

"Hogs, pigs, same-same."

"No, hogs are much, much bigger."

"That good, Mr. Rick. Hide you better. Never mind."

Rick shakes his head, "OK, how do I fit in with these devine creatures of the swine species?"

"First layer 15 cages, OK, never mind. Second layer we put six cages in front two rows. Put you in cage by self. See? Luxury. No pigs share with you. You big shot on truck. They put cages left side you and right side you. Then six cages behind you. Put tarp on top your cage so no pig poop in deluxe hotel room. Then top layer, 15 more cages. You nice and cozy. Good, yes?"

"Terrific, Mr. Tuan, just terrific. Maybe you will share my deluxe hotel room on this glamorous pig truck ride?"

"No can. I ride shotgun, tell driver where go. Maybe next time." Tuan laughs again.

The cages containing five hogs each were lifted one by one using a crane device. After 45 minutes all were loaded and lashed down.

With Rick safely ensconced in the middle of his swine sanctuary, he settled in, leaning back on the bars of his cramped, low cage. As the truck lurched forward, the hogs squealed, and Rick felt something hot and wet soak his shirt. One of the frightened hogs had let go a stream of urine on Rick's back. "Dammit, Tuan! I'll get you for this!"

The rest of the ride was uneventful. The hogs calmed down, but poop and pee continued unfettered for the rest of the ride. Rick sat the whole way with his knees drawn up to his chest, dead-centered in his cage, avoiding any additional urine streams. After three hours of torturous road, they pulled into the slaughterhouse in Tuy Loan.

Securely within the compound, Tuan comes to the side of the cages, "Mr. Rick, you OK?"

"Just fine Mr. Tuan. I've made a lot of friends. I think I'll stay here for the night thank you. I hate to give up such a nice, deluxe hotel room."

"Ha, Mr. Rick, you funny. We have you out in 20 minutes. Maybe 20 hours." Again, Tuan starts laughing.

The slaughterhouse crew started the unloading of the cages using a forklift. Rick sat silently, waiting his turn. When his cage was on the ground, he crawled out and surveyed the tarp covering. Six large poops from the five hogs in the cage above him were splattered on the tarp. "See Mr. Rick? I take good care of you."

"Once again, Mr. Tuan, it's all a matter of perspective. Where can I wash and change?"

"Follow me. You stink big time. You stink pig time." Tuan went into hysterics.

Rick shook his head, "You sure do know how to entertain yourself, Mr. Tuan."

CHAPTER EIGHTY

After Rick washed and changed, he and Tuan got into the same old Honda taxi that had brought them to Khe Sanh a little over two months before. As they traveled east in the dark, Rick could see the glow of the city of Da Nang on the horizon. They turned north on Highway 14B and cut left onto the new Highway AH1, Asian Highway One. At Route 601, they headed west into Elephant Valley for about ten miles along the south side of the Cu De River to the Hoa Bac safe house.

Tuan opened the house with a key, and he, Rick, and the Chinese driver, Chung, settled in for the night.

They waited until late the following afternoon to depart. It was still daylight, so Rick was stashed under a blanket, lying cramped on the back seat. On top of him were several large, funeral flower arrangements. In Vietnam, funeral arrays were considered very bad luck unless they were for one's own family. This deep-seated superstition would deter the police from searching the car if they were stopped.

They backtracked along the river to Highway One, blended in with the northbound rush-hour traffic, and followed the road into the tunnel under the Hai Van mountains. From there, the trip to Hue took a little under three hours. Chung was careful to maintain the speed limit and he drove prudently to avoid attracting the attention of the authorities.

They pulled up to a safe house deep within a dark neighborhood near the western wall inside the Citadel. Tuan and Rick entered the house, and Chung drove away. Inside were two rebels who greeted Tuan warmly. He introduced Rick to the two men and told them of Rick's heroics in the battle with the commandos and how he is now one of them. The two men remarked that they had received a burner cell call from the other three survivors. They had told them about the American, that he could be trusted. The three men were making good time traversing the mountains from A Loui and they should arrive in about a week if all went well.

The rebels informed Tuan that his wife was secure in another safe house a few kilometers west, but that his own house was being watched by police.

Tuan told them that his house is of no consequence. He said they must begin to plan their next operation. But for now, he needed to see his wife.

"Mr. Rick, I must go to my wife. She is in another safe house not far from here. You stay this house. I shall return on the second night from tonight with your money."

"Mr. Tuan, it is now our money. I have little need for it anymore. Keep the money where it will be safe and spend it as needed for our Cause."

Tuan was humbled. There must be $50,000 U.S. dollars left. It was a fortune. He said, "Mr. Rick, I think you may have been sent to us by Buddha himself." He brought his hands to a prayer position, fingertips touching his lips, and bowed to Rick.

Rick did the same in return. He smiled and said, "I'm one of you now, remember?"

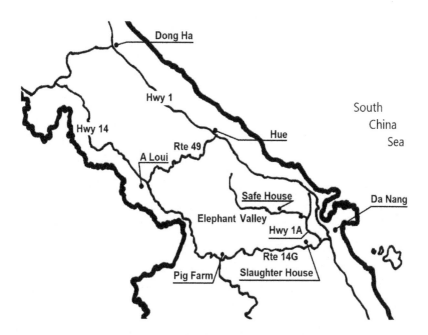

The convoluted trip from A Loui to Hue

CHAPTER EIGHTY-ONE

Two nights later, Tuan was back at the safe house with Rick and the two rebels. The first words out of his mouth were, "I think next target be commando base at Vinh."

Rick got a chill down his spine. He recalled meeting Russian police officers in some kind of exchange training at the NYPD. A Soviet police officer had served at Vinh during the Vietnam War. He said his job was to train the North Vietnamese to fire Soviet anti-air artillery. He refused to say if he personally fired the guns at U.S. warplanes. The Cold War was still going on and Rick did not want to put himself in jeopardy if he confronted the man. But Rick was sure the Russian did more than train the enemy gunners.

Rick snapped out of his memory.

"What? What purpose would that serve, Mr. Tuan?"

"They all Northern commies. They attack us without mercy. Our attack will show we not afraid of them and we are strong, make them defend this time, not us always run away. It send big message."

"Mr. Tuan, the base holds a battalion of commandos with an extensive collection of weaponry at their disposal, including artillery and MIG's. Any attack is doomed to fail. We will lose many good men."

"Maybe attack not fail. I can have 90 rebel fighters quick-quick. Commandos lazy guarding base. No one attack base when not war. We catch by surprise."

"Yes, at first we could surprise them due to their lax security. No one takes seriously the guarding of a base in peacetime. But these soldiers are highly disciplined. They will recover quickly, and they will all join the fight. Their counterattack would drive us out of the base into the town. We would be too far from the mountains. They would slaughter us in the streets. It would be hopeless for us. What can 90 rebels do against 600 commandos? What we would gain in prestige from this desperate attack, we would lose by provoking the commandos to redouble their efforts to ruthlessly seek out and destroy any and all resistance. It is also possible, probable, that every one of us would die a painful death, leaving no one alive to carry on the Cause."

"OK. But you must admit, Mr. Rick, it would be glorious."

"Yes, Mr. Tuan, it would be glorious. But also big stupid. Do you have any other ideas?"

"Yes. Big shot dignitaries be at festival Emperor Tu Duc's tomb 19 July. Plenty, as you say, high-value targets."

"I've been to the tombs of Tu Duc. Wasn't he a bad emperor in the 19th Century? Didn't he enslave thousands of local people to build the massive 'Summer Palace' that later would be his tomb? Why have a festival to him?"

"Ha, Mr. Rick, you know good history. Yes, Tu Duc bad man. He puppet of French conquerors. Many want dig up body and throw away, but family clever. They have king buried someplace in palace grounds nobody know. They cut heads off gravediggers, so they no tell where. Even now, nobody know where find body. But not festival to Tu Duc. Festival he dead. Now tomb Summer Palace, belong people. Anybody go. Now we say King. Not say Emperor. Never mind."

"So, how do we use the festival to further our Cause?"

"You say another word I think very good, 'hard-core' commies. Many old timer hard-core commies come from Hanoi give speeches, tell all how good commie life. People must clap hands, pretend happy with commie words. I think we kill hard-core commies. Then young soft-core commies get power. Life get little bit better. Soon later kill soft-core commies. Get old

Vietnam back. Get freedom. Get democracy. Good for all Vietnamese peoples, even Northerners.

"In Phou Nhoi, we be hunted. Now we be hunters. Better much, I think."

"Now that sounds like a plan, Mr. Tuan. We have only a few weeks to organize the attack. Let's get to work."

CHAPTER EIGHTY-TWO

For an entire week, Tuan and Rick labored over the attack scenario. How many dignitaries and which were to be targets, numbers and strengths of security forces, ingress and egress, attack coordination and contingencies, individual rebels and their duties, weak-link redundancies, escape and evasion, and plausible denials were all considered and refined multiple times.

Rick was in his element. Planning an attack instead of a defense was an energizing fixation. Marines were shock troops. They were first in, first to fight. Placing Marines in defensive positions was alien to them. They were not trained to defend. They were trained to be hunters, not prey.

The back door of the safe house opened and in walked the three rebels from the Phou Nhoi battle. They had been dropped off by Chung who had, coincidentally, picked them up near the Tu Duc Tombs, just a 20-minute drive away. Happy greetings were shared. The three men were exhausted, thin, and hungry. Tuan cooked them a meal as they sat at the table nodding off. After eating, the three men bedded down and did not awake until the following afternoon. It would take nearly a week of rest and food until they were back in fighting shape. But Tuan decided to keep these men out of the Tu Duc mission. Tuan always took good care of his men, and he knew they had been through a lot in the mountains. Besides, he had enough operatives to do the job.

One of Tuan's contacts was the head manager of cleanliness and maintenance at the tombs. He knew every hinge, every piece of wiring, every loose rock in every stone wall, every trap door through every attic, and every narrow, secret tunnel under every building. Other resistance fighters worked as tourist bus drivers or dragon boat pilots. Still others worked in souvenir booths outside the tomb wall near the main entrance. Some pretended to be beggars, dressed in rags with scraggly beards and dirty hair.

On 12 July, Tuan called a briefing of all operatives who would take part in the attack. Speaking in Vietnamese, he began, "In one week we will deal a deadly blow to the communist regime. Many hard-core commies will be at this year's Tu Duc festival. Unfortunately, the President and Prime Minister will not attend. Of the 10 or 12 high-level government mucky-mucks, we have the Minister of National Defense, the Minister of Public Security, the Deputy Prime Minister, and the Chief of the Vietnamese Fatherland Front, the VFF, as primary targets. Of these, our most important target is the Chief of VFF. As you know, the VFF is made up of rabidly pro-commie government factions, and therefore it holds all the power behind the scenes. They make the Nazi SS look like schoolgirls. The Chief of VFF must be taken out at all costs.

"I have an inside man at tombs, we call him 'tomb-man.' No real names. Tomb-man has given us a diagram of the tunnels under the Hoa Khiem Royal Temple and the Minh Khiem Royal Theater. The speaking platform will be at the top of the steps leading up to the temple. The dignitary reception area will be set up in the Royal Theater, where they will be hosted by Hue government commie propagandists. The largest gathering of dignitaries at one time will be inside the Royal Theater where they will socialize and be fed, waiting for their turns to speak. This is when we will detonate the explosives hidden under the floor. The theater is a small, sturdy building of large timbers made from ironwood which should contain the blast to the occupants within, resulting in as little collateral damage as possible. If any dignitaries escape the explosion, they will be quickly dispatched with knives to their throats as soon as they come out of the smoke and confusion. Those of you who are dispatchers will then disperse and blend into the pandemonium that will surely follow the blast and the shootings.

"This will take place as the Chief of VFF is speaking. He must be taken out dramatically, in public, in front of the crowd as he is talking. Mr. Rick is a trained sniper. He will shoot the VFF Chief. As he falls, the Royal Theater will erupt in a fireball.

"Now, there will probably be at least one other dignitary alongside the VFF chief who will run to the one and only public exit. Doing so will make sense to him since it will be where his car will be waiting. That 50-meter run between the temple and the exit is where Mr. Rick's specialty will be critical. He will surgically pick off the man as he flees. He will be careful to not purposely injure any innocents. If, for some reason, Mr. Rick misses, our operatives in the souvenir booths will cut down the dignitary as he exits the tombs."

They turned and looked at Rick, who had not understood any of Tuan's rapid-fire, Vietnamese words, "Yep. What he said."

They all laughed.

Tuan continued, "Mr. Rick will be directly opposite the speaker's platform, hiding outside the wall in brush on the high hill overlooking the lagoon and the Xung Khiem Pleasure Pavilion. He keeps referring to the hill as 'the grassy knoll' but I don't understand what that means. He says many things that don't make sense. Anyway, he will be positioned there with a sniper rifle. I will be his spotter and will reveal to him which persons on the platform are the enemy. He will rid the world of the VFF chief first, then the theater explodes, and then he takes down targets of opportunity as they present themselves.

"The night before the festival, Mr. Rick and I will travel in darkness. He will prepare our sniper nest and I will go with tomb-man and set the explosives to be triggered electronically by me with a code from my cell phone. On the morning of the festival, you men will arrive at the festival like any other tourists and take your positions.

"We will have four knife-wielding dispatchers stationed near the theater as it explodes to slay any escapees, who will be disoriented, deafened, and possibly wounded. They will be easy to deal with. Two men will be at their souvenir booths ready to kill any enemy who make it to the exit. Four of you men will be our beggars. I want you to 'accidentally' trip people running away to slow down the stampedes and to cause confusion as to which way to run. Mr. Rick and I will overnight in the woods outside the tombs and be in place at sunrise. That's it. Any questions?"

The rebels looked back and forth at each other. No one spoke up. "There being no questions, we will disperse now and meet here again on the eve of the attack."

After the rebels were gone, Tuan reached under the table and brought out the sniper rifle that had been strapped there, along with two ten-round stripper clips. Rick looked incredulous at the old SKS. He thought he would receive a much better rifle.

Tuan looked at Rick's face. "It good gun."

"Rifle," replied Rick.

CHAPTER EIGHTY-THREE

During the next five days, Rick disassembled the rifle several times and cleaned and oiled it more times than he cared to count. He preferred a Remington 700 bolt action sniper rifle chambered for competition-grade .300 Winchester Magnums.

But he would have to make do with this old semi-automatic, Soviet-era SKS. All its components were stamped with a '1' meaning it was sniper-grade, but that would have been sniper-grade more than 50 years ago. All-in-all though, it was in great shape, its barrel lining still perfectly chromed. The internal ten-round box magazine had to be fed with stripper clips, but that was okay, too. He did not think he would get off ten shots without being spotted.

Rick was not worried about not having a tweaked-out 1,000-meter true sniper rifle. His range from hill to podium was only about 150 meters, about 165 yards. His only worry was he would not have the opportunity to fire the weapon until it was showtime. He would have liked to have fired at least 200 rounds to familiarize himself with the weapon's idiosyncrasies. But they could not afford the risk of someone seeing him or reporting the sound of the rifle in practice sessions. He did practice dry firing to accustom himself to the trigger pull and break, and to gain some muscle memory. He would have to have faith in his Marine Corps training, and faith in the Soviet manufacturer of the rifle. The first came easy, the second not so much.

Rick even cleaned the rounds. He picked up each 7.62mm bullet dozens of times trying to gauge the weight of each. When he was satisfied that he had six of the exact same weight, he loaded those first; the next four nearest the key weight went in next. He would carry the spare clip of ten just in case.

Tuan was busy sorting eight one-and-a-quarter-pound blocks of C-4 plastic explosive and playing with the detonation triggering devices. Every time Tuan would send a code from his cell phone, the relay in the device would click its solenoid, sending a short stream of electrical spark into the air making Rick jump. "Dammit, Tuan! Be careful with those things. You'll set off the C-4. No more safe house. No more Mr. Tuan. No more me. Oh, bloody hell, I'll move the explosives into the closet myself. You make me nervous."

"No worry, Mr. Rick. C-4 need blasting cap to explode. Need electric spark to make blasting cap blow first, then C-4 explode big time. Blasting caps in kitchen pantry. Never mind."

"I know Mr. Tuan, but it still makes me nervous."

After Rick was done stowing the plastic explosive, Tuan said, "Mr. Rick, watch this."

Tuan had all eight trigger devices in a circle on the table. He keyed a code into his cell and then touched 'send.' All the devices shot a short bolt of electricity into the air simultaneously. Tuan grinned. "See? Each bomb get own device with own blasting cap. Same-same code for all." Tuan smiled brightly.

"You never cease to amaze me, Mr. Tuan."

"I know."

"You know what else, Mr. Tuan? The best plans are the simple ones. And this plan is as simple as they come. We are using only one rifle, essentially one bomb as eight wired together, a few knives, and maybe two handguns if needed by the souvenir vendors. Only you and I are involved in the main attack. The other ten will appear to be frightened tourists and vendors. Mr. Chung will come for us after things calm down. And from what your tomb-man has told us, so far there has been only one patrol outside the tomb walls and after that, all security was confined to inside the grounds. Big stupid."

CHAPTER EIGHTY-FOUR

The last briefing was called on the eve of the attack. The rebels who would be involved in the attack had arrived, and the plan was reviewed once again. It was indeed simple and should be effective. All of them were confident and were on the same page.

After the operatives departed, Tuan and Rick gathered their handguns and ammo and wrapped the SKS in a blanket. They then wrapped the blanketed rifle with long branches until the package looked like a bundle of kindling, a common site in Vietnam. The duo donned pajamalike black clothes and rattan conical hats. Carrying their hidden weaponry, they left the safe house at 10:00pm for the six-kilometer hike to the tombs. They eased out of the Toan Chinh Tay, the west gate, and across the moat bridge that surrounds the Citadel. Waiting for a long lull in the late night, sparse traffic, they dashed across Highway One and over the railroad tracks.

They were now in the dark, western suburbs of Hue City. Tuan led the way quickly southwest through a labyrinth of motorbike and cart trails that ran helter-skelter amidst humble houses hidden by high hedges. Every once in a while, Rick would spy the glow of a color TV, but for the most part, the suburbs seemed fast asleep. After about two kilometers, Tuan turned into an arched hedge and tapped lightly at a window. The side door opened slightly, and a woman waved them in. "Mr. Rick, this is my wife, Thuy."

Rick smiled and bowed slightly, "It is a great pleasure to meet you, Ms. Thuy."

Tuan interpreted for his wife. She smiled, bowed, and left the room.

"Sit, Mr. Rick. We rest while Thuy prepares food. She will feed us."

Thuy was a small-boned woman of about 50 years, but she was fit and had the firm, toned muscles of a person used to working hard. Her face was attractive and had a particular expression of intelligence about it. Rick soon smelled delicious aromas coming from the next room.

Within 30 minutes, Thuy had called the men to come into the kitchen to eat. The food was amazingly good. Both had second helpings.

When they finished their tea, Tuan said, "Time to go, Mr. Rick. We must be at Tu Duc long before sun. Big day today."

Rick thanked her and smiled, rubbing his stomach. Thuy giggled. He waited outside while Tuan and Thuy said their intimate goodbyes.

They walked south and soon came to the Perfume River, about a kilometer east of the Thien Mu Monastery. It was from that monastery in 1963 that Monk Tich Quang Duc left the temple, drove to Saigon, and burned himself to death in protest of the government's treatment of Buddhist people. There is a seven-tiered pagoda, built in 1601, at the monastery's entrance. The monk's sacrifice had always been an inspiration to Tuan. It taught him the embodiment of total commitment to a Cause.

At the river's edge, a long, slender rice boat was waiting for them, and they were quickly being rowed across the river. Exiting the boat on the south side of the river, Tuan and Rick wasted no time moving south at a rapid pace, past a cement factory, and keeping to the rice paddy dikes and back roads.

They arrived at 2:30am at the Tu Duc west wall, behind the main compound. The tomb grounds were brightly lit, workers were busy making last-minute preparations for the morning's festivities. Using his burner phone, Tuan dialed tomb-man who met them and guided them through a hidden gap at the base of the wall.

240

Through The Gates of Hell

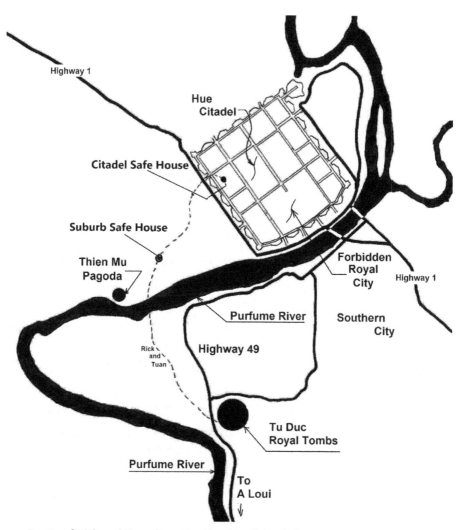

Route of Rick and Tuan from the Hue Citadel safe house to Tu Duc Tombs

241

While Tuan waited, tomb-man led Rick through the pine forest on the tomb's 30-acre grounds and out yet another hidden hole low in the northeast wall. They followed the outside wall south until they were atop a hill that overlooked the wall and the small man-made lagoon. Rick was looking directly at the main temple plaza and the platform where the dignitaries would speak the next day.

As tomb-man continued on his way, Rick went right to work setting-in his shooting perch in an overgrown and highly concealed section of the hill. He enhanced the lair with more camouflage than necessary, but Rick had been well-trained at Marine Corps Base Quantico's 10-week Scout-Sniper Course. He was not a sniper in Vietnam. He learned the trade when the NYPD had sent him to the course as a member of the Tactical Patrol Force. It was great working with, and learning from, active-duty Marines again. They were extremely professional and took everything so seriously.

By the time he was finished and satisfied with the sniper nest, Tuan and tomb-man were under the Royal Theater and were laying-in the last blocks of C-4 and inserting a blasting cap into each one. Tuan decided to run wires between all the blocks as a precaution. The wiring was a redundancy in case any of the electronic detonators failed to work. Wiring all eight blasting caps in parallel would ensure that all the C-4 detonated even with only one electrical firing device working.

When Tuan was satisfied with his handiwork, tomb-man led him through the forest the same way as he did Rick, being sure to keep to the shadows. Squeezing through the wall they walked up to the hill. When they got to the top, they could not find Rick. They wondered what had happened to him. From directly in front of them, they heard Rick say, "Bang, bang. You're both dead."

242

They both looked directly at Rick, but they could not see him, even in the refracted light coming from the temple work area. Rick pushed the rifle muzzle through the camouflage, and they finally knew where Rick was. Tomb-man was impressed. Tuan told Rick to stop showing off.

CHAPTER EIGHTY- FIVE

The sun rose slowly, breaking through a cool, foggy morning. There were no clouds. It would be a bright sunny day, which was a good thing because Rick was facing west toward the dignitary platform, the sun at his back. If the dignitaries and the police looked toward the sound of his shots, the mid-morning sun would shine directly into their eyes. It would make the sniping safer and more lucrative.

Rick and Tuan had taken turns power-napping in their cozy, camouflaged hideout. Now refreshed from their sleep, they chewed dried meat and drank water flavored with powdered Gatorade that Rick had brought from the U.S.

At 8:15, a patrol of PAVN soldiers, the People's Army of Vietnam, who were uninterested in patrolling, passed by their lair within a few yards. But Rick had prepared his hideaway well and they were unseen, even in sunlight. The bored soldiers wandered on their way. Rick and Tuan eased their pistol safeties back on, happy they didn't have their mission compromised before it began.

At 10:00am, right on time, the festival began. Punctuality was not a forte of the Vietnamese people, but when the totalitarian government ordered you to be at a certain place at a certain time, you were there. The celebration was kicked off with propaganda speeches.

Rick eased his rifle into position. Tomb-man made himself scarce. The 'beggars' moved into place. The dispatchers took their posts near the Royal Theater and hunkered down, knives at the ready.

Much to Tuan's delight, the first three dignitary speakers remained on the platform while the Vietnam Fatherland Front chief was giving his speech. They wanted to be seen with the man who was the power behind the power.

Lying side-by-side with Rick, Tuan pointed out the communist tyrants, making sure Rick knew each target. He said, "Mr. Rick, we are ready to begin. Shoot the VFF chief first. Then take out the others. You can shoot now."

Tuan keyed the code into his cell phone, waiting to tap 'send' when Rick eliminated the VFF chief.

Rick pulled the stock firmly into his shoulder. He sighted down the iron sights, lining up the rear notch sight with the hooded post sight at the muzzle. He squeezed the trigger to just before its break, timed his breathing, and pulled gently back. The bullet, aimed at the VFF chief's forehead, blasted through the man's neck and spine at the same moment Rick felt the recoil. Rick thought, *ding*, and he registered the shot five inches low. He moved his aim to the man next to the chief, the Minister of National Defense, who had just turned to the sound of the chief's snap and gurgle. The sights were on the man's hairline. The hit tore the minister's lower jaw from his face, spraying blood and teeth on the people sitting behind him.

Ding. OK, so the SKS shoots five inches low. No time to adjust the sights.

Boom! The Royal Theater's walls seemed to bulge for a split second, and then blasted outward, the heavy roof dropping onto those inside. No one escaped the theater. The knife men faked alarm and joined the frightened tourists.

By now the screaming crowd was either hugging the ground or was running in every direction, some even jumped into the lagoon. It was sheer panic. The beggars fell in front of the persons first reaching the exit gate.

As expected, the two remaining targets started running in unison for the exit to get to their cars. But they found their way blocked by crowds of people who had fallen over each other trying to get out. The Deputy Prime Minister turned and ran back toward the platform. As he tried to leap up two steps at a time, the man smashed face first into the marble stairs, the back of his head blasted away.

Ding.

Rick's nickname during the war was Dinger. The guys started calling him that because he rarely missed his targets, even under extreme pressure. The made-up name was based on the 'ding' noise that BB guns made when hitting the metal targets moving back and forth in carnival gaming booths. Rick was thinking of that as he cut down the communist dignitaries, one by one. In his mind he repeated "ding" every time a commie dropped, mortally wounded. He was remembering back when he was a kid and he got to shoot in the traveling carnivals when they came to town. But he would win no kewpie doll this time.

Policemen had their pistols out looking for a place to shoot, some were knocked down by fleeing clusters of tourists. Soldiers who had been milling around the souvenir vendors pushed their way into the complex, hampered by the panicked crowd and took up positions from which to fight.

Finally, the Minister of Public Safety grabbed two young women and held them tightly to his body, using them as shields. He moved toward the now cleared exit still holding the girls who were screaming and crying.

"You can do it, Mr. Rick. Concentrate."

The soldiers started shooting blindly into the trees all around the complex, although they saw nothing. The police joined in the shooting.

Rick lined up his sights two inches above the Minister of Public Safety's head and followed his movements. When the minister stopped moving for a moment, Rick's bullet punched a hole right between the man's eyes.

Ding, and done.

A soldier who had been shading his eyes, looking east, saw Rick's final muzzle flash and screamed, "There! On the hill! They are shooting from there!"

With all targets eliminated, Rick and Tuan had already backed out of their lair and started down the hill in the opposite direction from the tombs. Several policemen scaled the wall and gave chase.

If anyone had been attentive, they would have felt the tremor in the ground as it sucked down 12 dark souls into the Void. But in the chaos, no one was paying attention.

CHAPTER EIGHTY-SIX

Rick and Tuan were on the move. To the police they were the only obvious persons to pursue. If there were any others, the police and security forces could not identify them in the hundreds of people running in every direction. For now, these two would have to suffice. All their efforts would be spent to capture the rebels or to kill them.

Rick and Tuan ran east down the hill, dodging a hail of bullets from the security cops. But their police revolvers were highly inaccurate at such a distance. Only a lucky shot would hit the rebel duo. After 100 yards, they were at the bottom of the hill in a tree line where rice paddies began. Soldiers reached the police atop the hill. They opened fire with their rifles, but Rick and Tuan were hidden by the trees and underbrush. They turned north running along paddy dikes for 150 yards. Circling back around to the west-southwest, they made their way back to the hidden opening in the wall they had used before. They squeezed through the stones, reentering the Tu Duc complex. They made their way in the thick, pine forest to a hiding spot near where tomb-man had preset a high-sided cart filled with straw. Before long they saw tomb-man meandered along the dirt path and they slipped into the cart and covered themselves with the straw. Tomb-man wheeled the cart to the back of the 'Pleasure Pavilion' and walked away. The duo eased out of the cart and Tuan led Rick into a trap door that opened into a tight crawlspace under the pavilion.

Meanwhile 60 PAVN soldiers and dozens of policemen were searching for them outside the walls in the tree lines by the rice paddies. Rick and Tuan were once again hiding, unseen, not really in plain sight, but where no one would suspect.

While the police and soldiers were milling around the attack sites, the tomb-man was moving between them trying to clean up as best he could. He had a notebook, and with fake tears in his eyes, he also took measurements to make repairs. No one bothered with the sad, old man.

In the darkness of the crawlspace, Rick whispered, "Why do they call this the Pleasure Pavilion?"

"This building looks over lagoon. Very pretty. Very peaceful. Here King Tu Duc would write poetry, surrounded by dozens concubines."

"Ah, it does sound quite pleasurable. Dozens of concubines," joked Rick.

"He have maybe 150 concubines, but I think pavilion collapse with that many ladies. So he keep half harem at Forbidden City palace Hue. He never have child. He get smallpox when little, break his baby nuts. No make little fishes. Still, I think he have good time."

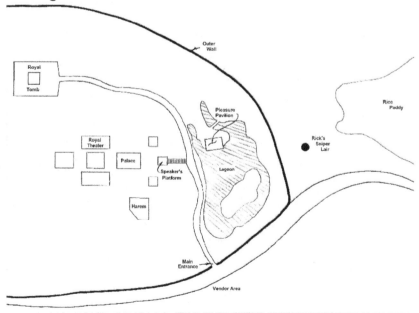

The attack at Tu Duc Tombs

CHAPTER EIGHTY-SEVEN

Word of the attack reached Hanoi before noon. The President and Prime Minister called in the deputy ministers of the agencies whose leaders had been killed. The President appointed them acting chiefs for the time being. Security was tripled around the Presidential Palace and the Parliament Building. The subservient government offices saw security double. All politicians were looking over their shoulders, each afraid they would be next.

In a conference call to General Pham in Vinh, the President ordered him to send all available commandos to Hue to find the perpetrators. Pham promised to have them on the road and moving toward Hue that very night. The President gave Pham official carte blanche to do whatever was necessary to destroy the rebels.

The President ordered a ten-billion-dong reward, about $435,000 U.S. dollars, to anyone who provided information to bring down the criminals responsible.

In addition, all government offices were ordered closed for one week for safety reasons.

With the meeting over, politicians and Hanoi government workers went into hiding.

In Vinh, Gen. Pham had already ordered the assembly of 400 commandos with full battle gear. He was nearly drooling with excitement. He would get his revenge on the American and maybe even kill a bunch of rebels. Pham never thought he would have such power. Because of the president's edict, he was even stronger than the chief of the Ministry of National Defense.

Pham was busy ordering trucks to amass at his base to transport his men to Hue. One of his calls was to Lt. Minh, who had made the first organized search alongside Rick and whose

250

men had found the drag marks and one of Steve's hiking shoes months before.

Pham told Minh his orders were from the President through him. Minh believed Pham. No one would be so stupid as to claim such authority if it were not true. Minh said he could arrive in Vinh with four trucks from his Vandergrift base and another eight trucks from his headquarters in Cam Lo. He would be in Vinh by 9:00pm.

In Hue, a company of PAVN troops were combing the hillsides around the Tu Duc tomb complex, searching for Rick and Tuan. All off-duty and vacationing police were called in and given sectors of the city to investigate.

Lt. Minh sat in the front passenger seat of his army van, leading his 12-truck convoy through the Vinh commando base main gate at 8:30pm. He had them refuel at the diesel pits and then directed them to pull into spaces beside eight other trucks that were already assembled. Four-hundred commandos, who had been standing by, clambered aboard, 20 to a truck.

At precisely 10:00pm all 20 trucks, with Pham in the lead in a covered jeep and Minh bringing up the rear in his van, left the base and headed south toward Hue.

That night before he left for the evening, tomb-man dropped a bag of food and water close to the trapdoor at the back of the Pleasure Pavilion.

CHAPTER EIGHTY-EIGHT

The day after the attack, police and investigators were still coming and going at the tombs. With the Summer Palace closed, the souvenir vendors had shuttered and secured their booths and had gone home. A construction crew arrived to remove as much antiquity as possible from the destroyed Royal Theater. They would eventually rebuild the bombed-out 19th-Century structure. Ever the dutiful employee, tomb-man moved about with his notebook taking measurements to repair, or making lists to replace, what little he could. The goal was to reopen the complex, less the theater, within a week.

Pham had arrived at the tombs with his convoy at six in the morning. He had made the 350-kilometer run, about 220 miles, from Vinh to Hue in record time. His men patrolled wider and wider search patterns, looking for clues to the rebel duo's whereabouts. They found nothing other than the sniper lair, which revealed no useful information. The hidden holes in the palace walls were left undiscovered.

Rick and Tuan were quite comfortable under the Pleasure Pavilion. It had been pre-stocked with two woven bamboo mats, bottles of water, and even two pillows. They were able to catch up on their sleep, one staying awake in case the other started snoring, which may have given away their location. They had one problem. They seemed to have invaded what may have been the world's largest breeding ground for the daddy-long-legs species of arachnid. The spiders were a constant annoyance, but at least they were a non-biting variety. One plus was that there were no mosquitos in the crawlspace because they were a favorite food of the ravenous spiders. Rick noted to Tuan, "Count your blessings where you find them."

Rick and Tuan remained in the crawlspace for the rest of the daylight hours. It was still too dangerous to come out of hiding in the bright of day. They could only relieve themselves outside under the cover of darkness. They had to hold it in during the daylight hours, a small price to pay to avoid discovery.

At one point, Tuan's burner phone had vibrated. An operative left a quick message saying that hundreds of commandos had arrived and were spreading out in the Tu Duc hills. Tuan related the message to Rick who replied, "We must have really pissed them off, Mr. Tuan. The commando base is far away from here."

"Yes, but they know PAVN is no match for our rebel force. So they send commandos. They should have learned lesson at Phou Nhoi. They should have stayed home."

Late that afternoon, Pham was sure the rebels had exfiltrated and were no longer in the area. He pulled the bulk of his commandos back to regroup in Hue. As a precaution though, he left a dozen listening posts all around the hillsides that night, two men to a post.

At about midnight, Rick and Tuan cautiously emerged from the pavilion crawlspace. It was deathly quiet, as one might expect of a tomb. The cleanup crews, the police, and the investigators had left when it began to get dark. Tuan told Rick to leave the SKS under the pavilion on a bamboo mat. They took only their handguns and ammo. Tomb-man, when it was safe to do so, would retrieve the rifle and deliver it to other rebels for future use in the Cause.

Rick and Tuan slowly and quietly made their way to the secret hole in the compound northeast wall and squeezed through to the outside. The night was pitch dark with only a few stars peeking through the warm haze. Tuan knew the area well. He had grown up here. They walked south along narrow animal trails. Tuan heard soft talking and he stopped and crouched down. Rick mirrored his movements. Not ten yards in front of them were two commandos conversing quietly. Rick and Tuan had not been paying close attention. Had the soldiers not been talking, they would have walked right up to the commandos. Tuan signaled Rick to move back the way they had come. When sufficiently distant, Tuan whispered, "Listening post. These two big stupid. Never should talk on post. We circle, keep going."

"We're not going to kill them?"

"No Mr. Rick, they not threat. Kill only if necessary. They see us, we kill. No see, no die. They not enemy right now. Hardcore commie always enemy. Commandos they young. Finish military, go home. Never mind."

"Well, let's be more careful. They would happily kill us. And I'm sure there isn't only one LP out here."

Tuan nodded and made a quick burner call. They then started down an alternate trail, being much more vigilant.

Responding to Tuan's call, Chung picked them up at the side of a forest clearing about a kilometer south of the Tu Duc tombs. Instead of driving them back to Hue, on Tuan's orders Chung drove them to the safe house in A Loui.

Along the way, Chung told Tuan, who interpreted for Rick, that the government was furious with the attack on their leaders. The army, the commandos, the national police, and the local police were shaking down known and suspected criminals for intelligence. He said they were being very rough.

In addition, the government had promised a reward of ten-billion-dong for information leading to the capture of the perpetrators of the attack during the Tu Duc Tombs festival.

"What do you think about that, Mr. Tuan? Did we go too far at Tu Duc?"

254

"No, I expect this from government. But after next attack, same-same kind attack, government react more gentle. They be afraid for own safety. They begin agree changes in freedoms. They coward. They corrupt. They want save own skin. We did good for Cause, my friend. This just beginning."

They arrived in A Loui at 3:30am, washed up, and went to sleep on futons. It was an intense two days for Rick and Tuan. As Rick dozed off, he realized that he will not survive for long in his newfound life. For some reason, he finds solace in this fact. He eases into a comfortable, dreamless sleep.

Chung stayed up the rest of the night playing video games on his cellphone. He was too excited to sleep.

CHAPTER EIGHTY-NINE

It was too dangerous for Tuan and Rick to go back to the citadel. The place was still in chaos. Chung waited until after lunch and then returned to Hue by himself.

Meanwhile, a lot had taken place since the attack two days prior. The U.S. Embassy had sent the FBI agent to Hue when they heard the American was still in Vietnam and not in Cambodia as they previously believed. Once again, he was ambiguously ordered to pretend to cooperate. And so, the agent began to dance. But the ambassador still wanted all information the FBI man could gather about the American Marine.

General Pham was also there. He had arrived in Hue at 6:00am yesterday, the day after the attack. Pham had already ordered the PAVN troops out of the Tu Duc countryside and had replaced them with his elite commandos. He then deemed the rebels long gone and had withdrawn his troops, as well. The commandos were relaxing in university housing and were enjoying Hue. The students were on summer break.

At 6:30pm, General Pham and the FBI Special Agent were in a meeting with the National Police Chief, Hue Branch. They were discussing strategy for locating the rebels and the American when an aide barged into the room with an unknown man. Roused from his concentration, the angry Police Chief admonished the aide, "We are in a meeting! How dare you enter without being directed."

"I am sorry, chief. I thought this important. This man is Mr. Chung. He is here to claim the reward. He will need an interpreter fluent in Chinese Mandarin."

All hearts skipped a beat when they looked, in excited anticipation, at Chung. The chief told his aide, "Bring an assortment of refreshments for us and for our honored guest.

And make sure they are high-quality indulgences. After all, our guest, Mr. Chung, is soon to be a very rich man and he is to be afforded every respect."

This made Chung smile and he relaxed a little.

A college professor fluent in Mandarin was brought in. For three hours the men grilled Chung for information. He told them everything he knew. He told them about picking up the American at the airport in Da Nang and bringing him to Khe Sanh. He told them about the safe houses in A Loui, in Hue, and in Elephant Valley. He told them about the pig slaughterhouse in Tuy Loan. He told them about the three Phou Nhoi rebels who had crossed the mountains in the west. When Chung had given the address of the safe house in A Loui and that he had brought Tuan and the American there early that morning, General Pham left the room. That was all the information he needed.

Pham had the already-fueled trucks loaded with commandos in record time. The convoy stopped briefly at the tombs to pick up his night LP troops who had come in to rest there earlier in the day. With the convoy fully loaded by 8:30pm, it started a high-speed run on the winding mountain roadway toward A Loui. Once again, Pham was in the lead in his jeep. Minh was at the back of the column, in his van.

Right from the start Lt. Minh believed Gen. Pham was in too much of a hurry. The heavy trucks were old Russian models, their suspension designed for tremendous loads and a slow, steady momentum. Not a Le Mans road race.

As soon as Pham's jeep crossed the Perfume River and headed west on Route 49, the old wartime Route 549, he had his driver accelerate at an alarming rate. Over the radio, he insisted the trucks keep up. When you are a low-ranking truck driver and a general orders you to go fast, you go fast. The drivers pressed down on their gas pedals.

It was a perilous and stupid thing for a general to do. Minh radioed Pham, "General, I know this road. It is very dangerous with many switchbacks and poorly graded areas. There are few guardrails and many drop-offs. It is almost dark and there are no streetlights on such a remote road as this. I implore you. We need to slow down."

"Dammit Minh! You are a coward. My orders are the voice of the President himself. You will obey or you will return to Hue and lock yourself in a prison cell and I'll deal with you when I get back. What is your answer?"

"Speeding up, sir."

At about an hour into the drive, the first two trucks in the convoy, while trying to keep up with Pham's jeep, careened over the cliff on a hairpin turn. The drivers could not see the sharp turn until it was too late. The first truck made a futile attempt to brake, and the following truck smashed into its rear sending them both over the edge. All the side rails and the 40 commandos were flung into the air from their bench seats in the back of the open truck beds. Thankfully, the other trucks were able to stop in time. Minh came running up to the head of the convoy and started ordering the commandos off the trucks to try to rescue any survivors. As the men were climbing down from the trucks, General Pham returned from a half mile ahead. "Minh! What the hell are you doing?"

"General, we've lost two trucks and 40 commandos and two drivers and two assistant drivers. They went over the cliff because they could not both see and maintain the speed you set. We need to see if any are left alive."

"Minh, get back to your van. The convoy will continue."

"But sir. The men."

"They are unimportant. We carry on with the mission."

"But General, 44 men are at the bottom of the cliff. Some may still be alive. We must try to help them."

Pham drew his pistol. "Get back to your van, lieutenant. Or I swear, I'll blow your head off."

Minh hesitated, "Yes, sir. But just so you know, the road gets much worse from this point on. Please consider my plea. If you keep us going so recklessly fast, you may get to A Loui with no trucks and with no commandos."

General Pham got back into his jeep. Minh's words sunk in. Somewhat. Pham reduced his speed, but it was still not as slow as Minh would deem safe. The convoy moved on.

As Minh, in the last vehicle in the column, passed the place where the trucks went off the cliff, he said a short prayer for the lost men. Then he cursed Pham.

CHAPTER NINETY

At 9:45 that night, Tuan picked up his burner phone and answered, "Yes?"

"There is a large convoy of commandos rushing toward A Loui on 49. ETA is one hour. I'm not sure if you are compromised. One of the men spotted Chung's taxi in the National Police Headquarters parking lot. He was probably arrested and may have been tortured for information. I advise you leave the safe house and go somewhere else, immediately. I'll call back when I get more information."

Rick read Tuan's face as he listened to the caller. Rick got up and began collecting handguns and ammo, some packages of dried meat, and his bush knife.

Tuan hung up, nodded at Rick, "Could be very bad."

Tuan hastily packed his gear. He reached into a tall kitchen cabinet and opened a false panel. He pulled out two well-maintained, short-barreled AK-47's with side-folding stocks and four bandoliers of fully loaded 30-round magazines. "We go now. Not wait. Commandos coming."

"Where to?"

"Laos."

Suddenly sirens sounded throughout the town. Tuan looked across the street. Policemen were pouring out of their headquarters running toward the cleaning store.

"Quickly, go out back!"

They ran into the darkened neighborhood, easing along hedgerows. They stayed in the shadows if any light poured from illuminated windows or doorways. After a half hour of careful maneuvering, they were at the westernmost edge of the town facing wide rows of dried rice paddies interspersed with a series of low rolling hillocks, tree lines, and tiny hamlets with dirt roads everywhere. It would make undetected escape very difficult. The mountain foothills were an hour's hike away. There was activity everywhere. Off to the right Tuan spied a collapsed, rotting barn. "This way, Mr. Rick."

They scrambled under the wreckage, pushing out termite-ridden boards to hide their tracks. They hunkered down waiting to see if the police had followed.

An hour and a half had passed. The sirens had died out. There was no more commotion in the town. When they thought all danger had passed and they were contemplating emerging and moving westward, they felt the reverberation of heavy trucks and heard diesel engines. Many diesel engines. "That be commandos. Come for visit."

"Sounds like many more commandos than we had to deal with at Phou Nhoi. Our plight just got a whole lot more complicated, Mr. Tuan."

The trucks roared into A Loui and parked down several side streets. A truck ground to a halt not 100 meters from where Tuan and Rick lay under the rubble. The commandos jumped down from the trucks and spread out into a perimeter around their vehicle.

"The world just got much smaller, too, Mr. Tuan. I guess we stay here tonight."

"Good idea, Mr. Rick. You never cease to amaze me."

"Ya know, Mr. Tuan, you're getting to be a real wise ass."

Tuan smiled and nodded agreeingly.

CHAPTER NINETY-ONE

At first light, General Pham called a briefing of his company and platoon commanders. Overnight, he had already begun to envelop the A Loui area with his remaining 360 commandos. He spread his platoons in a wide arc. To the west, eight kilometers away in the foothills, 200 commandos were blocking access to the mountainous border with Laos. To the south two kilometers away, and all along the north side of the A Sap River to the new Tuy Dien hydroelectric dam, Pham had spread out 120 of his men. To the north, eight kilometers away, the 150 commando reinforcements he had ordered from his Vinh base last night had already arrived and were finishing their preparations just south of Tiger Mountain. He would leave the National Police to seal off Highway 14 through the town of A Loui. He kept 40 of his finest commandos close at hand. He tasked them with searching all obvious hiding places in the town. They started on line, in pairs, along the road and stepped off into the side streets searching every home, every building, every haystack.

Once all his units were in place and ready in the countryside, Pham set into motion what he called Operation Big Squeeze. His fielded commandos began the slow and careful, meter-by-meter march toward A Loui leaving no stone unturned. Despite the hardships facing his men in terms of heat, terrain, and other difficulties, the commandos were ready to mete out some payback. Not so much for the killing of the politicians, but for their embarrassment at the failure to capture the rebels at Phou Nhoi nor at Tu Duc. And they needed to avenge their dead. The prospect of retaliation is a strong, motivating emotion.

Late last night the police had raided the cleaning supply store across from their headquarters but had found no one. The police then helped themselves to cases of soaps, cleansing chemicals, cleaning tools and equipment, as well as furniture, food, and all the sundry possessions typical of any house. From his commandeered command office in the local National Police Headquarters Building, Pham watched them, disgusted. It was a waste of precious time by poorly disciplined and corrupt local police. Focus was needed on the mission and these clowns were a distraction.

Meanwhile, the National Police in Hue had raided and razed the safe houses in Hue and Hoa Bac, finding nothing of consequence. The owners of the slaughterhouse in Tuy Loan had been murdered by special police and their business confiscated by the government. Two days later, the same fate awaited the pig farm owners near Huyen Dong Giang. The driver of the pig truck was jailed and awaited imminent torture and execution. They found the Land Rover in Hue, but its owner had it registered under a false name. He would go on to wreak havoc against the communists in the years to come.

By midday, Pham's troops had yet to uncover anything of value. They had partitioned two kilometers of ground, tightening their grip on A Loui. Their resolve still strong, they continued on their mission.

CHAPTER NINETY-TWO

Back in Hue, Chung had spent the night in the guard's quarters behind the police command center. Now he was in the chief's office demanding his reward money and Chung was getting obstinate. The chief was getting annoyed, "Mr. Chung, I have told you several times now, the money is coming from Hanoi, and you will have to wait a few days. I advise you to go home. We will call you when the money is ready."

"Come on! They can transfer the money to my account with a few keystrokes. And I can't go home. The rebels may have figured out it was me who betrayed them. I need protection from you, or they will kill me. Do your job!"

"I see your conundrum, Mr. Chung. I will have my most trusted officers take you to a safe place after dark and I will push to have the money transferred quickly. After all, you have been most helpful."

"Well, that's better. Sorry for being so tough, Chief, but fair is fair."

"I quite understand. You may wait in the headquarters café. Order anything you want. It will be free to you. I will send my men when it is dark and safe enough for you to travel undetected by the rebels."

When Chung left, the chief called his men into the office and gave them their orders.

At 9:00pm, two of the chief's 'trusted' officers escorted Chung to a darkened-window SUV and drove away to the east.

At 9:45pm they arrived at a dimly lit compound on a desolate stretch of beach on the South China Sea. Entering a nondescript building they had Chung sit at a table sticky with dried blood. "What the hell is this?" Chung demanded.

He was answered with a hard slap across the face.

264

"Shut up! You will speak only when asked a question."

"I don't understand this."

Another hard slap. Chung then understood.

"Answer this, why did you not come forward when you first helped the rebels?"

"I, I don't know. I didn't think I was doing anything wrong. I was just making money as a taxi man."

Another slap. "Liar! You knew you were collaborating with the rebels. You know they want to overthrow the government. The money they gave you was far in excess what any taxi man would receive."

"Please. I am a lowly Chinese man who escaped China. Like you, I hate China. I can be of great help to you. Please, I don't want the money. You take it for the police."

"You are a Chinese spy. We found no record of a visa for you, no passport. You are in our country illegally. You are a spy! Why do you not need an interpreter now? You speak as well as a Vietnamese. What else are you hiding?"

"Nothing! I swear it!"

Now punches were rained down on Chung and he fell to the floor. They lifted him back on the chair. "Admit you are a spy! Admit you want to overthrow our government!"

Chung's nose and lips were bleeding badly. One of his ears was torn. "Please, no more. You are hurting me. I swear I am not a spy. I love Vietnam."

"What about your command of our language?"

"I was apprehensive. I thought I would be laughed at because of my accent."

The interrogators relented. "You swear you are definitely not a spy?"

"Yes, yes! I swear it. I love Vietnam."

"You understand why we needed to be rough. We needed to be sure."

"Yes, I understand. It was necessary. You are good at your job. Thank you for believing me."

"Very well. We have no running water here. Let us go out to the surf and get you cleaned up."

Chung and the two men exited the back door and walked to the water's edge. Chung waded in and splashed water on his face. The seawater stung a little, but he knew it was the best thing for his cuts. Besides, it was a very warm, late-July night and the water felt good on his sweat-soaked body.

Suddenly, strong hands gripped the back of his neck and pushed him underwater. He felt knees press into his back. Chung knew they were killing him, and he knew his struggling would do him no good. He had miscalculated. Commies were commies no matter where he went. He realized too late that the only people he could trust were the rebels, and he had betrayed them. Chung relaxed and let fate take him.

A few days later, Chung's body would wash up on one of the Cham Islands farther south. His death would be deemed 'accidental drowning.' His body would never be claimed. All of Chung's relatives were far away in China and they would never know what became of him.

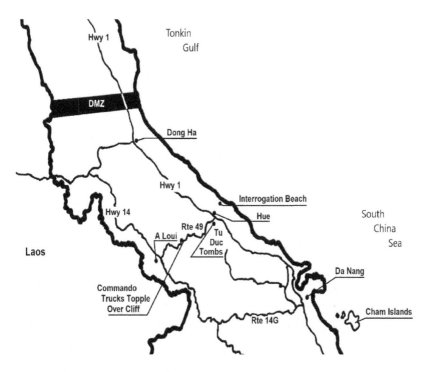

Commando convoy; Chung's demise

CHAPTER NINETY-THREE

The day after the convoy had arrived, the town of A Loui was abuzz with activity. Police vehicles roamed the streets. Their loudspeakers announcing that the commandos were there to protect the citizens from two extremely dangerous criminals, one a Viet rebel, the other an American. The police also announced over and over, the ten-billion-dong reward for anyone's direct help in apprehending the duo.

Even with this possibility of becoming very rich with very little effort, the local citizens of A Loui were wary of official promises. Out there in the border regions, they had been ill-treated, exploited, and brutalized by the police for too long. They did not trust the government.

From their hiding place, Tuan heard the loudspeaker blast announcements and translated for Rick. They assumed the prospect of a big payday was strong on the minds of the locals, making even movement in the dark tenuous at best. People would be alert to anything out of the ordinary. Perhaps, if Tuan and Rick understood the local's attitude toward the police, things may have turned out better in the end.

Late in the afternoon, two commandos came poking around the collapsed barn. Peering into the rubble the younger of the commandos jerked his head back and stumbled to the ground, scooting backwards on his butt. It took him a shocked few seconds but he pointed and said to his partner, "They, they are there."

The partner peered into the same place as his cohort. He died instantly. Having no choice, Rick and Tuan burst from the debris, shot the still-shocked commando, and took off running across the dried rice paddy. They disappeared into the dense tree line and heard yelling behind them from the other side of the paddy. They were being pursued.

Rick announced, "This is bad, Tuan, really bad. Which way do we go?"

Tuan looked around, thought for a second, then said, "Only way is up."

They slung their rifles, made sure their equipment and provisions were well-secured to their bodies, and started climbing the tallest tree in the vicinity. They ascended to the highest, heaviest branches and hunkered down in the thickest concealment possible.

They heard shouts and very quickly commandos and trucks descended on the area. The platoon leader bellowed orders and his men spread out like a bunch of angry ants and swarmed over the nearby hillocks and paddies, searching for Tuan and the American.

Rick had never slept in a tree before, and he did not intend to sleep that night. But he had learned that he should always tie himself onto a limb in case he dozed off. It would keep him from falling to the ground. Rick thought to himself, *Thank you Marine Corps instructors.*

Night fell, and Tuan whispered to Rick, "We can not move in day. They see us. We can not move at night. We not see no thing. We can not stay in tree. We have only little food. Also, can not fly."

"Thanks for pointing out the obvious. Do you have a plan, Mr. Tuan?"

"We move very early morning. When army not full awake. Very little sun. Better if rain, but no rain now until two month more. We go only short way toward mountains. Then climb tree. Wait again. We move before very dark. Again go very short way toward mountains. Then climb tree again. Do maybe four days, two moves each day. That eight moves. Get to mountains and jungle. Then easy to Laos. We know jungle better than commando. Maybe go to Hmong people. Make new plan then."

"It will be very dangerous, my friend. We will run out of food for sure. Four days, tops. After that, we'll be too weak to do anything. But I see no other way. Your plan is the only plan."

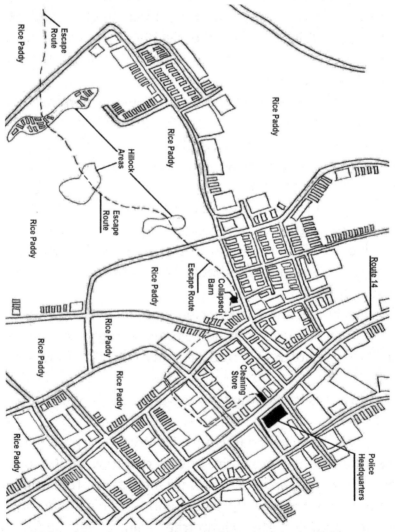

Rick and Tuan's attempted escape from the A Loui safe house

CHAPTER NINETY-FOUR

Pham sat in the dark at his desk, pondering what to do. Yesterday, the envelopment had stopped at about three kilometers in when the sun went down. He had two dead commandos, killed by the rebel and the American. *Or,* he thought, *was it them? They had tricked us before with diversions and we chased after them like hungry dogs chasing a rabbit. They must have laughed at us. No! Not this time!*

Rather than calling in his spread-out troops, consolidating them, and making a fully concentrated effort in the area where the commandos were shot, he ordered the men to continue their previously assigned mission in the Big Squeeze.

Pham doubted the culprits had gone back into town. There were too many police and commandos working the area. He believed the locals would be searching, too, motivated by the reward money. Pham figured the rebels would have no choice but to move west, would need to move west. They could not go south. His men had moved as far north as the southern edge of town and had dug in along an east-west line blocking anything going south.

By the end of the day, General Pham's men coming down from the north would be in position to block all movement in their direction.

Yes, west was the only logical direction for the rebels. The bulk of Pham's men were still searching in the western mountains, moving slowly east. *There was no escape for the killers. Let us hope we are chasing the Viet and the American.*

The 40 commandos, now 38, the best of the best, that Pham had kept in town, would be tasked at sunrise with redoubling their efforts to find those responsible for killing the two men here and the 23 up in Phou Nhoi.

An hour before dawn, Rick and Tuan untied themselves from their tree-borne haven high above the ground. They started down, carefully and silently. On the ground once again, they stood still and just listened. Satisfied there was no movement or worrying sounds, they walked slowly, crouched, westward until they reached the next series of dried rice paddies. There they low-crawled alongside the dikes, snaking over one perpendicular dike after another until they reached the next hillock. This one was higher than the last, as they would all be the closer they came to the actual mountain foothills, and with it the jungle that would mean survival.

The horizon to the east was barely starting to brighten. As they moved into the thick hillock foliage, they heard the murmurings of soldiers awakening. They realized they had walked into a bivouac area. They had no idea how many commandos were there. Rick and Tuan looked up searching for a tall tree to climb. All of them were too short and thin there near the edge of the rice paddy.

They backed into some brush, Rick whispered, "We have to make a break for it. We just start running west. The commandos will be confused until they get a good look at us. The darkness will give us the element of surprise. If one of us falls, the other keeps going. The Cause is too important for both of us to die trying to save the other."

Rick knew he was the slower of the two and of lesser importance to the Cause. He would do all he could to make sure Tuan escaped.

They both unslung their short-barreled AK's and set the selector switches to full-automatic fire. Rick counted, "One, two, three, move!"

They both took off running through the bivouac area. Half the commandos were still dozing. Some were sitting up rubbing the sleep from their faces. Rick ran square into a commando taking a piss and knocked the man to the ground. He kept running. The man shouted, Này, coi chừng! *"Hey, watch it!"* The shout caught the attention of one of the men who was standing last watch on the west side of the hillock. He turned, seeing a tall American running at him. He raised his rifle. Tuan put a short burst of AK rounds into the man's side, killing him instantly.

Now all the commandos were awake and reaching for their weapons. Rick and Tuan hit the next series of dried rice paddies running hard, leaping across perpendicular dikes like they were running the hurdles. As they reached the next hillock, enemy rounds were hitting all around them. This gave Rick comfort that there were no commandos bivouacking on this hill. The commandos would not fire in the direction of their own men.

Melting into the brush, Rick and Tuan hunkered down for a moment. "You OK, Mr. Tuan?"

"Yes. That fun, Mr. Rick. But we go now chop-chop. Here come army."

Rick grabbed Tuan's arm. "Wait, Tuan. Let's slow them down a little bit."

Rick opened up with a few bursts from his AK. Tuan followed his lead. The commandos hit the dirt, covering their heads, some hunkering down behind a dike.

"OK, Mr. Tuan. Now we go."

They took off running again, crossing the hillock, the next paddies, and onto the next hill, which was much wider than the others. They ran through what Rick thought was an abandoned hamlet. "Where are all the villagers?"

Tuan said, "They hiding. Must have hear shooting. Never mind. Keep moving."

Rick and Tuan were running light, compared to the commandos who were laden down with heavier gear. They were

273

making better time, spreading the distance between them and their pursuers.

This cycle continued as Rick and Tuan changed their direction several times, west, southwest, northwest, trying to shake the commandos.

Rick's lungs felt like they were near bursting when they reached another seemingly abandoned hamlet. Rick and Tuan had been evading for over a half hour and they both were exhausted. They believed they had finally escaped the commandos. Passing through the hamlet, they stood together on the outer dike of a huge, final paddy that remained between them and where the foothills began.

Rick said, between gulps of air, "I hate mountains – but right now – they are the – most beautiful things – I've ever seen."

Tuan smiled and nodded at Rick. Then he tensed up, sensing something strange, "This not good place. We go now."

Rick trusted Tuan's instincts, "I'm with you."

But then Rick feels himself being pushed back over the dike into a ditch. He hit the ground and rolled instinctively protecting his rifle. He looked back and saw Tuan's body being riddled with bullets from six commando rifles hidden in the tree line on the other side of the field. Tuan's head exploded, a commando full-metal-jacketed round smashed through his front teeth, expanded to twice its size, and burst into Tuan's brain at supersonic velocity. The blast took off the back of his head. The blue sky above Rick turned a misty pink.

"Oh my God! No! Tuan, not you. I'm sorry." For a few moments, Rick sat staring at what was left of his loyal friend, "I'm sorry, Tuan. I'm so sorry."

In the Vietnam War, it was first revealed to Rick just how delicate the human body is. It is no match for white hot, jagged steel, nor for lead punching through flesh at supersonic speeds.

Rick had been just a kid, as most of Marines were. Before war, he never knew what color brains were. Before war, he had never heard the sound of a sucking chest-wound. Before war, he did not know about traumatic amputations, that arms and legs, and sometimes heads, could be instantly ripped from a body. And before war, he did not know that he could vomit from the stench of burning flesh.

Rick was intimately aware of how people come apart with horrifying ease. There is only a thin layer of skin and muscle, and pitifully fragile bone, holding in the intestines, liver, lungs, kidneys, bladder, heart. Those things, or pieces of them, appear alien covered in dirt as they lie on the ground or on the inside of vehicles or aircraft where they have been blasted from their connections to a once living person. It is obscene.

Rick was always astonished at how very quickly a robust person can become a corpse.

And now they had killed Tuan. Shaking off his shock, Rick started burning with hate. He realized he was in the middle of a classic hammer and anvil tactic. Rick and Tuan had been driven by the hammer of the pursuing commandos directly into elite forces, acting as the anvil, who were dug into the next tree line and waiting to gun them down.

Rick ran low and parallel to the dike, keeping it between him and the dug-in troops on the other side of the paddy. He then turned and ran back into the village between the huts. He flanked the five oncoming 'hammers' who, in their haste, did not notice him. He shot two of them in the head and shouted, "How do you like it, you sons-a-bitches?"

The three remaining commandos hit the deck and returned fire in Rick's direction. But Rick had already left the flank and had run behind them. He emptied the rest of the magazine into the trio, killing all three men.

He snapped his last 30-round magazine into the rifle.

"Now for the rest of you bastards." He crawled up to the dead commandos and took one of their bandoliers of fully loaded AK magazines and draped it over his neck and shoulder and crawled to cover.

CHAPTER NINETY-FIVE

Rick could hear the dug-in troops calling to their comrades. Hearing nothing in return, the six "anvil" troops cautiously exposed themselves in the dry paddy. They started walking toward Tuan's body to have a look at their handiwork.

From his hiding spot, Rick had a clear view of them. He waited until they were halfway across the wide-open paddy, wishing he had grenades. Rick switched the rifle to semi-automatic mode. He would take them one at a time.

Rick sighted in on the commando farthest away, which wasn't all that far, maybe 50 yards. The man fell flat on his back, blood gushing from his chest.

"Ding," whispered Rick out loud.

The others spun around looking at their comrade sprawled on the ground. The next bullet went through a commando's neck.

Ding.

The remaining four men began to run in all directions.

Ding.

Ding.

Ding.

Ding.

In less than 15 seconds, those four commandos were lying in the paddy like the first two, unmoving.

Rick walked over to Tuan's body. "Well Mr. Tuan, I guess you were right. Someone betrayed you, after all. Now you are dead. Now I have no friends, nowhere to turn, nowhere to go. But I have avenged your death, my friend. I have killed the bastards who have killed you."

From the middle of the paddy, he heard a loud groan. Rick looked up, "One more, Mr. Tuan. Watch this."

He walked out to the middle of the paddy, to the man who was still barely alive. For a few seconds he watched the man squirm in the dirt. Rick raised his rifle and squeezed the trigger slightly. Then he hesitated a moment. He eased off with his finger and the trigger returned to its neutral position. Rick realized he could not do it. He could not murder this young commando who was no longer a threat. It wasn't something in his mind, for he still burned with hate. Something in his heart had stopped him. He thought of his friend, Steve, when he had talked about being unable to shoot the wounded Marine who was making those horrible goat noises. Rick thought, *Hey Steve, we're not so different you and me.*

At that moment two large trucks pulled up, one at each end of the rice paddy. Rick stood there as ten commandos jumped off each truck and walked towards him from opposite ends, all with their rifles aimed at Rick. Still holding his rifle at the ready, Rick looked slowly around, contemplating his options. *None,* he thought. Rick slowly flipped the selector back to full-automatic fire. It was an instinctive reflex, his mind sending the survival command to his thumb to match the threat.

The 20 commandos stopped ten yards from him, each with a 30-round magazine loaded in their AK-47's. Each rifle was capable of firing 10 rounds per second. A barking voice from behind the commandos shouted an order and the soldiers formed an arc, all facing Rick, all with their rifles trained on him, all with abject malice on their faces.

The man with the barking voice came forward, "Well Mr. Carrofermo, I am impressed with your military prowess. The Marine Corps taught you well. What is it they call you? Ah, yes, they call you people jarheads. Is ridiculous name, it insults you.

"Let me introduce myself, I am Major General Pham, the supreme commander of these men."

"Your man here is badly hurt, General. Don't you think you should get him to medical care?"

"His life is insignificant, Mr. Jarhead, as is yours. You killed many of my men. It is my pleasure that I will now take you into custody and bring you to Vietnamese justice."

"I've seen your government's version of justice. I want no part of it."

"Mr. Jarhead, I grow impatient with you. In the name of the Socialist Republic of Vietnam, I order you to lay down your weapon and surrender! You will comply or I will have my men kill you."

"Maybe you're right, General Pham." Rick bent down to lay his rifle on the ground. "Then again, maybe you're wrong."

Rick fired his remaining rounds on full-automatic into General Pham's chest.

It cost Rick his life.

All 20 commandos opened fire at once and stopped only when their rifles were empty. In less than ten seconds, Rick had been hit with 600 bullets, his body was shredded into small pieces of torn flesh and splintered bone.

He never felt a thing.

Pham, on the other hand, felt the Hand of Hell pull him down to eternal anguish.

CHAPTER NINETY-SIX

Tuan reached down and helped Rick to his feet, "Come with me, Mr. Rick. I found your friend."

As he started to follow, Rick looked back and saw in the bloody mess what used to be him. All he could say was, "Damn!"

They stepped over the paddy dike and walked through the village into a small clearing. And there was Steve, grinning at him, "Took you long enough, el Capitano."

"Wise ass."

"Look who else is here."

Rick turned and saw that Steve had with him 17 Marines from their unit who had died in the war. They came up to Rick, all smiles, man-hugging him and patting him on the back. They still wore the trappings of warriors, but their weapons were long ago discarded, unneeded.

Steve said, "There was a demon here watching you when you were going to kill that wounded commando."

"I wanted to. I was so angry at what they had done to Tuan. But something stopped me." Rick looked into his friend's eyes, "It was you, wasn't it?"

"I really pissed off the demon."

Rick chuckled, "I'm sure you did, Marine. I'm sure you did. What now?"

"I guess we – I really don't know."

One of the long dead Marines said, "We've been waiting for you, Rick. We will all go to the other side now. This place is just sort of a limbo. We're all anxious to see what lies ahead."

Steve jumped in, "Well, let's not waste time. We're together again. Let's go."

The Marine said, "I'm sorry, Steve, but you're not going with us."

"What? Why? What did I do wrong? We're all Marines. We're all dead."

"All we know is there's a different place for you. We don't know how we know it. We just do. We knew Rick was coming, and when he did, we could go to the better place."

The other Marines were nodding in agreement.

Tuan walked over, "Mr. Rick, I must leave you now. I came to say goodbye."

"Where will you go, my friend?"

"I go Phou Nhoi, get Tiger and the others. They waiting for me. You go with Marines. Not know where you go but know it good. Never mind."

"Yes, I'll go with these men. It feels right. You were a great man and a great friend, Mr. Tuan. Thank you for everything. God Bless you."

And with that, Tuan was gone.

Behind Steve, way back at the edge of a dirt road, Rick saw Sharon. She was standing still, looking at them, waiting. "Steve, turn around."

Steve was stunned. Happy tears formed in his eyes. Sharon smiled. They ran to each other and embraced for a long time, saying nothing. Nothing needed to be said.

After a few minutes, Rick sauntered up, "Hey Steve, I hate to break up this little love fest, but I have something for you."

He handed Steve the wedding band, "I was going to keep it, but it has a sappy engraving on it."

~ ~ ~

ACKNOWLEDGEMENTS

The task of writing may be a solitary, lonely endeavor, but it is not accomplished alone. The seeking of encouragement and advice, and the need for egotistical uplifting comes into play long before an author even nears publication. Without input, output would be poor put.

So why did I get such obnoxious remarks and scoffing? Gee whiz! Folks were brutal. But ego-bruising is sometimes a good thing. It forces an author to reevaluate, to introspect, to "Oh yeah? Well, I'll show you!"

Thanks to the following people, the original clumsy story is but a mere shadow of the finished product. Therefore, I wish to express my gratitude to:

Sgt. J.K. Balcom, Vietnam veteran (2nd Battalion, 7th Marine Regiment, 1st Marine Division) and scholar of all things 'Vietnam' who provided insightful and thoughtful suggestions.

Mr. Michael Chiusano, a reader of my early attempts who didn't let me get away with anything, and who told me that I better add a lot more dialogue. He also read my final manuscript, made many concluding recommendations, and gave me an 'atta-boy.'

Renowned author, **Ms. Karen Gravelle**, who warned me about *info-dump,* to not introduce characters with their backgrounds, skills, and flaws too early, explaining that one does not know everything about a person until weeks, months, or even years after meeting them. Sage advice. She selflessly mentored me throughout the creation of this story.

Mr. Ronald W. Hoffman, (1st Battalion, 13th Marine Regiment, 3rd Marine Division) Vietnam veteran and author of the highly acclaimed true story, *To Hear Silence.* Ron labored tirelessly to recraft my primitive attempt at map making.

Ms. Malia Jarrett, the loveliest of daughters, who encouraged me to keep writing when I wanted to quit the project, several times. It's amazing what daughters can get their Daddy's to do.

Mr. Dave Macedonia, Vietnam veteran (1st Battalion, 501st Regiment, 101st Airborne Division) who was one of my earliest critics and made it easier to find my way.

Ms. Ginny Mileto, who read the novel-in-progress many times and pointed out inconsistencies, as well as *I-don't-get-it* (a lot) from a non-military person's perspective, all of which made the novel better and more accessible to people of all backgrounds.

Dr. Vincent Mileto, OBGYN, Ret. who corrected my initial details about internal female anatomy and abdominal structure. Evidently, I had it wrong.

Captain Gene Miller, Ret. (Los Angeles County Fire Department) and Vietnam veteran (Company A, 1st AmTracs, 3rd Marine Division) who taught me the dynamics of wildfires, and how the flames progress uphill with gentle winds driving them. This provided an authentic reality to one of the more disturbing chapters in this book.

Mr. John Strunk, Vietnam veteran (Kilo Company, 3rd Battalion, 5th Marine Regiment, 1st Marine Division) who sent to me what he called 'flyspecks' of the nearly finished manuscript. These minor changes helped to bring a professionalism to the book. Overlooking the minor things can lead to collapse. John authored the gripping non-fiction, Vietnam War memoir entitled, *We Walked Across Their Graves.*

Ms. Jessica Tookey, artist, who went above and beyond my flawed book-cover concepts and created the book's leitmotif with her stunning artwork and hidden phantasmagorias.

Mr. Steve "Whit" Whitiker, creative writing instructor, who taught me the meaning of *nuance* in fiction writing, and that readers do not need every detail explained. His advice tightened the story and helped to eliminate the superfluous. Few folks appreciate a 'wordy' novel; get to the point already!

GLOSSARY

I have included the following lexicon of some uncommon words you will find in this novel. By no means is this list exhaustive.

For a reference work containing over 2,500 Vietnam-era words, lingo, slang, and phrases, see my non-fiction book: *VIETNAM War SPEAK: The Distinctive Language of The Vietnam Era.* It is available on Amazon, eBay, or directly from me.

~~~

106mm Recoilless Rifle: Breach-loaded, single-shot, rocket-launcher

.45 Automatic: Colt .45 caliber standard-issue handgun

.50 cal: See M2

.51 cal: A 12.7mm communist heavy machinegun

70mm HEAT Missile: 2.75" wide High Explosive Anti-Tank, fin-stabilized, armor-piercing rocket

Agent Orange: The most powerful of the dioxin-laced defoliants sprayed on vegetation in Vietnam to deny enemy cover. It causes 11 types of cancer, as well as many other debilitating diseases.

Airborne: Soldiers who are parachute jump-qualified; paratroopers

AK or AK-47: Alexi Kalashnikov (AK) standard Soviet infantry/service rifle, replaced the SKS

Ammo: Ammunition

Ao Dai: Traditional Vietnamese dress (high-collar silk blouse, pajama-like pants, long two-panel skirt)

ARVN: Army of the Republic of (South) Vietnam; sometimes a single SVN soldier

ASAP: As Soon As Possible

Automatic Fire: Constant, uninterrupted projectiles exiting a weapon as long as the trigger is engaged

Azimuth: Horizontal line gauged clockwise in 1° increments of a 360° circle from North on a compass

B40: Soviet anti-tank, rocket-propelled, shoulder-fired, 70mm warhead, 40mm grenade rocket launcher

Baguette: A narrow loaf of bread inspired by the French

Bandolier: Sash-like belt with a series of pockets worn across the chest for holding ammo clips or magazines

Bird: Slang for Helicopter

Bivouac: Temporary camp without tents or cover

Body Bag: Zippered, heavy-duty, plastic sack for dead, combat casualties

Boonie Hat: Soft, full-brimmed, cotton poplin, or rip-stop fabric, military hat with crown vents and a thin chin strap

Bracket: Placement of artillery rounds around a target, adjust for accuracy from those impacts, and then fire on the target

Bru: One of 54 tribes of Montagnard (mountain people) for in Vietnam, Laos, and Cambodia

Bulkhead: Navy lingo for wall

Bunker: A mostly underground, reinforced, fighting post or protective refuge from artillery, rockets, and mortars

C-4: A soft malleable, clay-like, plasticized high-yield chemical explosive

CAP: See Combined Action Platoon

Carte Blanche: Absolute authority to act as one decides best

Chaplain: A religious clergyman assigned to a branch of military service

Chicom: Chinese Communist; usually a hand grenade, but can be anything made in Red China

Chop-chop: Quickly

Chow: Food

Citadel: A walled city fortress

Claymore: Above-ground, 60° fan-shaped, directional, anti-personnel mine w/700 ⅛" steel balls, and a 55-yard kill range

CO: Commanding Officer

Co: Several meanings dependent on inflection, but in this novel it means Mountain

Cobra: Bell Aerospace AH-1; tandem-seat, single-turbine, helicopter gunship

Cockpit: A separate seating space in a helicopter for the pilot and co-pilot

Code Of Conduct: List of six specific rules for U.S servicemen to follow if they are taken prisoner

Collateral Damage: Unintentional killing of civilians or destruction of non-enemy property

Column: When individuals or elements are placed one behind the other

Combined Action Platoon: Marine unit living within a Vietnamese village to train and improve local life

Commando: Lightly-armed, highly-trained, elite soldier, specializing in hit-and-run raids

Commie: A person believing in and following the communist way of life; see Communism

Communism: Theory favoring all property and means of production be collective with no social or economic classes

Concertina: Coiled razor wire used as a perimeter obstacle

Contour Lines: Map lines that depict equal points of height above sea level

Convoy: A group of vehicles (or ships) proceeding together usually escorted by armed troops and/or helicopters

Corpsman: Navy enlisted-grade medical man serving in a Marine unit

Covering Fire: Usually rifle and/or machinegun shooting that makes it difficult for the enemy to fire at maneuvering troops

Crew Chief: The crewmember, usually enlisted grade, who maintains and assures the flyability of an aircraft

Cruise Book: Similar to a high-school yearbook, and covering a period of naval deployment or other tour-of-duty

Defense Attaché: A military person with diplomatic immunity serving abroad in an embassy

DMZ: De-Militarized Zone; "neutral" area separating North Vietnam from South Vietnam

Don Ho: A Hawaiian-American singer and entertainer popular in the second-half of the 20th Century

Dong: The basic Vietnamese monetary unit; at the writing of this novel the exchange rate was 23,000 Dong to 1 US dollar

Double-Time: At twice the pace of a normal march, similar to a trot

Dragon Boat: A small, colorful tourist boat with a dragon's head at the bow

E & E: See Escape & Evasion

Easter Offensive: Failed 1972 NVA conventional warfare invasion of SVN utilizing 25 divisions and 700 tanks

Evacuation Hospital: An emergency medical center or ship, mobile or fixed, that has surgical capabilities

Escape & Evasion: A pre-determined or spur-of-the-moment, survival route to avoid capture or death; aka E&E

Exfiltrate: The exit from an area of operation; usually clandestine

Firebase: Artillery/mortar unit(s) usually on elevated terrain and secured by infantry; aka FB

Fire Support Base: Usually a temporary base for artillery/mortars to bombard the enemy in an operation; aka FSB

Firefight: A violent exchange in which small-arms weaponry is utilized between opposing elements

Flank: The movement of troops to confront the side elements of the enemy forcing him divide his forces and focus

Flanks: The extreme right or left side of the main group of troops

Fleshette: Small, steel dart fired in a cluster from a shotgun, rocket, artillery or tank round

FO: See Forward Observer

Forward Observer: Person trained in the calling in of artillery and all other forms of heavy fire upon enemy targets

FSB: See Fire Support Base

Grenade: A short-range hand- or rifle- or launcher-projected, gas, smoke, or explosive weapon

Gunnery Sergeant: Enlisted-grade E-7, Marine Corps staff non-commissioned officer

Gunship: A heavily-weaponed attack helicopter or other aircraft that can deliver substantial firepower on a target

Hamburger Hill: Name given to a May 1969 10-time assault by the 101st Airborne up Hill 937 to uproot the NVA

Hamlet: A small village

Harbor Site: Special Forces/Recon/SEAL hunker-down area, with heavily-vegetated concealment

HEAT: High Explosive Anti-Tank; a fin-stabilized armor-piercing projectile

Hill: Any rising elevation above sea level marked in meters on a map

Hmong: One of 54 tribes of Montagnard (mountain people) for in Vietnam, Laos, and Cambodia

Hootch: Shelter or residence, usually a SEAhut; a simple, rural Vietnamese home

Hot: Under fire by the enemy

Howitzer: A cannon, either self-propelled or towed, that is capable of high or low angle firing

Huey: Affectionate nickname for the Bell UH-1 *Iroquois* series of helicopters, and the iconic image of the Vietnam War

In-Country: In Vietnam

Incoming: Loud, verbal warning that enemy artillery, mortar, or rocket fire is, or is about to, impact your position

Interdiction: The act of stopping or disrupting enemy movements and/or supplies of a looming enemy force

Internal Affairs: Law enforcement agency of a police force that investigates police misconduct

Ironwood: A tree producing very hard and dense timber

John Wayne-ing: The act of pushing through pain and fear of death like that Hollywood hero would

Khmer Rouge: Cambodian communist troops

Kilometer: A unit of metric system measurement equaling 1,000 meters; approximately 62/100 of a mile

Kodak Moment: A photo opportunity

Landing Craft, Utility: Shallow-draft boat designed specifically to transfer troops and equipment from sea to shore

Landing Zone: Any place a helicopter can land

LCU: See Landing Craft, Utility

Listening Post: Nighttime hole or hide for 2 or 3 troops located outside their unit's perimeter to act as an early warning

LP: See Listening Post

LZ: See Landing Zone

M2: Browning .50 caliber, heavy machinegun; 550-rounds per minute

M-14: Springfield .30 caliber, 7.62mm, standard U.S infantry semi-automatic battle rifle which replaced the M-1 Garand

M-16: Colt Manufacturing .223 caliber, 5.56mm, standard U.S infantry automatic assault rifle which replaced the M-14

Ma Deuce: See M2

Machinegun: Automatic-feeding rifle, capable of rapid nonstop-firing as long as the trigger is held pressed

Magazine: Spring-loaded cannister that holds and feeds ammunition into a weapon

Mama-san: Bastardized Japanese word meaning honorable mother; and older Vietnamese woman

Mandarin: The official and foremost language of Chinese dialects

Medal Of Honor: The highest military award offered by the United States for auspicious bravery in combat

Medevac: Medical Evacuation from the battlefield by helicopter

Meter: A metric system measurement equaling 39.37 inches

Mi-8: Russian twin-turbine, 5-blade, medium helicopter

MIG: Mikoyan-Gurevich (MiG) Soviet fighter-bomber, jet-aircraft, subsonic MIG 17; supersonic MIG 19 and 21

MMAF: Marble Mountain Air Facility

Mobile Surgical Hospital: A field hospital with its own transportation means and surgical capabilities

Monastery: Usually a complex of temples and building that house and teach religious monks

Monolith: A geological, single upright mountainous rock formation

Monsoon: Wet, prevailing seasonal wind bringing prolonged rains

Montagnards: French term meaning *People of the Mountain*

Mortar: A base-plated, muzzle-loaded, tubed, high-angle firing, short-range, crew-served gun

Muzzle Flash: The high-pressure, high-temperature flash following a projectile from the forward end of a gun or rifle

Muzzle: The forwardmost end of a gun or rifle

Nationalist: One who vigorously supports their own nation, regardless of the interests or exclusion of other nations

NCIS: Naval Crime Investigative Service; in this novel, it refers to the popular TV program

Newbie: Anyone who is fresh into the war or to a unit

Nui: Vietnamese word meaning mountain

NVA: North Vietnamese Army; also lingo for a single communist North Vietnamese soldier

Observation Post: Daytime hole or hide for 2 or 3 troops located outside their unit's perimeter to act as an early warning

OP: See Observation Post

Operative: A person operating in a clandestine manner to obtain information or to take part in subversive activities

Outpost: A small military position some distance from a much larger military force

Padre: Affectionate term for a military chaplain; literally *Father*

Pagoda: A Buddhist temple or place of worship

Parris Island: U.S. Marine Corps boot camp for recruits whose home of record is east of the Mississippi River

PAVN: People's Army of (North) Vietnam

Perimeter: A position's, or base's, outer boundary

Platoon: A military unit consisting of 26-55 fighters; 3 to 4 squads, plus a lieutenant or a captain as the commander

Point: The forwardmost man leading a column of infantrymen

Posthumous: After death

PRC-25: Portable Radio, Communications; standard field radio

Probing Action: An attack to determine if a position is weak and can be exploited or broken through or overrun

R & R: Rest and Recreation; a 5- or 7-day, once-per-tour vacation to one of 10 countries; also a 3-day in-country break

Rations: A share of food

Razor Grass: Sharp-bladed, concertina-edged grass that would cut through uniforms and tear skin

Razorback: A long, sharp peaked mountain to the northwest of The Rockpile

Reeducation Camps: Brutal prison camps where torture and abuse were used to indoctrinate the communist way of thinking

Rest and Recreation: See R & R

Revetment: A three-sided earth or built-up barrier used as blast protection, usually for parked aircraft

Rice Boat: A narrow, low-freeboard watercraft, rowed or powered, used on rivers and canals to transport goods, usually rice

Rockpile, The: A famous monolith on the northside of Route 9 about halfway between Dong Ha and the Laotian border

Round: An artillery or mortar or naval gun munition or bullet, whether assembled or its projectile

RPG: Rocket-Propelled Grenade

RVN: Republic of (South) Vietnam

Saddle Up: A term meaning to put on one's combat gear and be ready to move out

Same-same: Equal to; much alike

SEAhut: Southeast Asia Hut; plywood and tin, one-story housing for rear-area troops

Semi-Automatic: General reference to any gun or rifle that will fire once with each trigger pull without reloading

Shrapnel: Fragmented pieces of a bomb, shell, rocket, or other munition that are violently expelled as it detonates

Silver Star: The third highest award offered by the United States for valor in combat

Six: Lingo for the last man in a column; directionally, six-o'clock on a watch

SKS: Soviet .30 caliber, 7.62mm, semi-automatic, 10-round, 1,000-meter range, infantry rifle; precursor to the AK-47

Song: Vietnamese word for river

Special Forces: Soldiers cross-trained in combat arms, counterinsurgency, language, airborne, LRRP, and covert actions

Special Weapons And Tactics: See SWAT

Squad: A military unit consisting of 8-14 fighters; 3 to 4 fire teams, plus a corporal or a sergeant as the commander

Stripper Clip: A device that holds ammunition cartridges in line to facilitate easy loading into a magazine

Support Fire: Any bombardment, but usually from artillery or aircraft, that assists a unit in an attack

Survivor Guilt: The emotion of shame for having lived when others died

SVN: South Vietnam

SWAT: Special Weapons And Tactics. Police task force trained in close-quarters combat, sniping, explosive entry, high-risk arrests, and hostage rescue.

Sweep: A placement of soldiers abreast of each other and move through an area

Tactical Patrol Force: See TPF

Tail-End-Charlie: The last man in a column of infantrymen on a combat mission; aka Six

Tet: 5-day Vietnamese Lunar New Year celebration; but generally a reference to the infamous 1968 communist offensive

Tet Offensive: The 1968 NVA & VC coordinated attack on 100 SVN cities and towns during the declared ceasefire

The Wall: The Vietnam Veterans Memorial in Washington, DC

Tonkin Gulf: A body of water that starts, more of less, at the DMZ and runs north along North Vietnam to China

TPF: A mid-60's NYPD unit tasked with suppressing the heroin epidemic and its associated violence in the inner city

Tunnel Rat: Soldiers, usually of small stature, sent down into tunnels to search for supplies and to kill the enemy

UH-1E: Bell Iroquois series Bell UH-1 *Iroquois* "E" variant helicopter; the iconic image of the Vietnam War

UNESCO: United Nations Educational Scientific & Cultural Organization; promotes peace through various programs

UXO: Unexploded ordinance

VC: See Viet Cong

Viet Cong: Vietnamese Communists; indigenous South Vietnamese who believed in and fought for totalitarianism

Wire: Barbed or concertina wire variants strung around a perimeter

A Brainteaser Challenge

The artist (Jessica Tookey) has cunningly inserted a number of images and illusions onto the front & back cover artwork. Most were intentional, but some appeared on their own, including a nasty little unintentional demon that's freakin' me out. Just like in the jungle, evil lurks in the darkest of places. There are a total of 20 phantasmagorias (some are easy to find; some are elusive). See if you can locate them all:

- Eyes
- Eyes
- Eyes
- Eyes
- Face
- Helicopter
- Shadow figure
- Shadowy face/skull
- Shadowy face/skull
- Shadowy face/skull
- Soldier
- Soldier
- Soldier
- Soldier
- Steve's crucified body
- Two shadowy figures
- Unintentional demon
- Unintentional demon face
- Unintentional walking figure
- Wedding ring

To request an answer key, email the author at:

www.lzflashback@yahoo.com

About the Cover Artist

Jessica is blessed with an endless well of creativity to amaze, enlighten, and inspire. Whether through her art, her teaching, or her life guidance she delivers peace, love, and light to lives all over the world. Her journey has taught her to be a way-shower, helping others find their way out of darkness.

Jessica burst on to the art scene in Boise, Idaho in 2015, a year after her daughter graduated from high school. An award-winning artist and teacher, she decided that travel was also needed in her life. In 2019, she sold everything and bought a Toy Hauler. The garage space is her art studio (and a room for her three cats). She has lived with her cats, and love of her life, in nearly all of the lower 48 U.S. states. They have no plans of stopping anytime soon.

Whether left-handed, right-handed, or both hands at the same time (watch this on YouTube) she creates the perfect art for her clients' homes, offices, or gifts. Her desire is to infuse spaces with the love that this existence on this earth provides and show everyone that it is possible to follow your dreams and live a life you love. Make the decision and you can live your passion, too.

If you would like Jessica to design artwork for you, or if you would like to book an exhibition or instructional sessions, please peruse her website at:

http://www.JessicaTookey.com/
Email: Jessica@JessicaTookey.com

About the Author

William W. Stilwagen served in Vietnam in the United States Marine Corps. In 1969, he was a field radio operator on the DMZ with HQ Battery, 12th Marine Regiment, 3rd Marine Division based at the Rockpile and Dong Ha. In 1970, he flew as a machine gunner with HMM-364 (Purple Fox Squadron) out of the Marble Mountain Air Facility. He holds eleven military decorations, including the Air Medal for heroic action, the Purple Heart for shrapnel wounds, as well as the Combat Action Ribbon and the Vietnamese Cross of Gallantry. He is authorized to wear the coveted Combat Aircrew Insignia and the Rifle Expert Badge.

In 1970, he was presented with the Conspicuous Service Cross by then Governor of New York and future U.S. Vice President, Nelson A. Rockefeller.

To name just a few of his post-war activities: he has served as the Executive Director of the $1,400,000 Suffolk County Vietnam Veterans Memorial Commission; has been active in veterans affairs on the local, state, and national levels; provided over 300 seminars internationally on the realities and the legacy of the Vietnam War; and was Chairman of the Town of Brookhaven Anti-Bias Task Force. In 1990 and 1992 he worked with Soviet Afghanistan veterans in their homelands on techniques to effectively deal with their PTSD and suicide issues.

In 1994, some of his accomplishments were read into the Congressional Record by then U.S. Representative George J.

Hochbrueckner. Also in 1994, he graduated from the SUNY Stony Brook Honors College, Magna Cum Laude, with degrees in Social Sciences and American History.

He is a founder and current president of the non-profit tour company, *Vietnam Battlefield Tours, Inc.* His first love, for which he is highly qualified, is returning to Vietnam as a bush guide for his brother warriors, which he has done 68 times in the last 26 years.

Bill is the author of the lexicon: *VIETNAM War SPEAK: The Distinctive Language of The Vietnam Era.*

This, his first novel, will also be his last. Bill has been diagnosed with Stage-4 metastatic prostate cancer with bone, lymph node, and lung metastases, courtesy of Agent Orange.

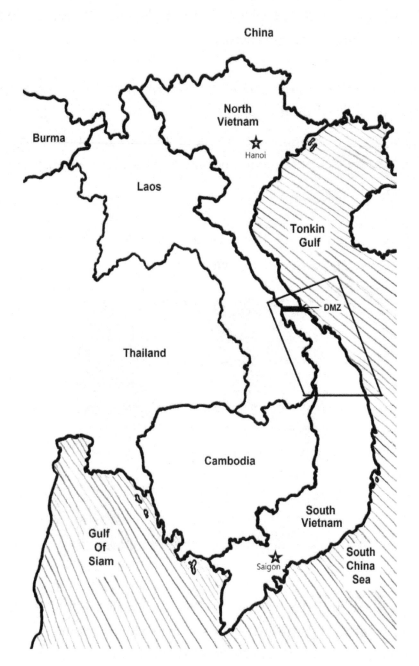

Southeast Asia; Area of Detail

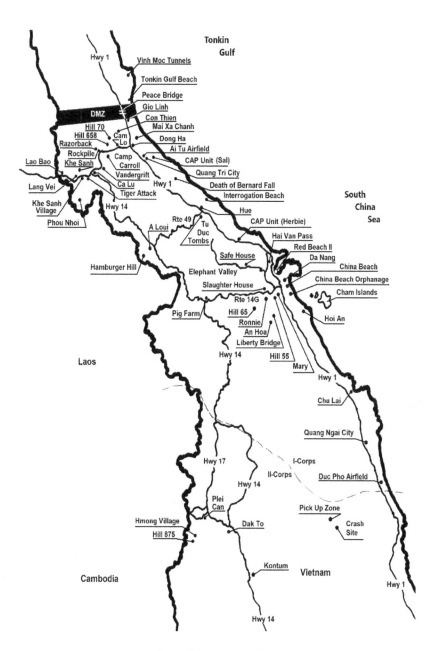

Area of Detail locations

Made in the USA
Las Vegas, NV
04 May 2023

71574413R00174